ICEAPELAGO

(**Iceapelago** / *n. (pl.* **-os** or **-oes**) 1. A group of islands surrounded by ice. 2. A frozen land mass with many islands. Gk **pelagos** sea (orig.= island of Ireland post the collapse of the Gulf Stream)

ICEAPELAGO

La Palma, Canary Islands
The Greenland Ice Sheet
Irish Continental Shelf

Three Stories:
One Conclusion

Dr Peter Brennan

For Clive, Rory, Martin, and Caitlin

Contents

Prologue: Arctic Foxes 9

CHAPTER 1 12
La Palma • *Augusta, Georgia* • *Glencairn*

CHAPTER 2 53
Faro de Fuencaliente • *Summit Station* • *Galway Harbour*

CHAPTER 3 102
Instituto Volcanológico de Canarias • *The River Corrib* • *RV* Celtic Explorer

CHAPTER 4 141
Roque de los Muchachos • *Hotel Icefjord, Ilulissat* • Holland 2

CHAPTER 5 172
La Cumbrecita • *Sites ZX* • *PLU*

CHAPTER 6 220
Reventon • *Twin Otter* • *Eriador Seamount*

CHAPTER 7 239
Observatorio Roque de los Muchachos • *Qooqqup Kuua River* • *The Gulf Stream*

CHAPTER 8   263
Pico Bejenado • Black Bush • Merrion Street

CHAPTER 9   294
Barlovento • Cobh • Tasiilaq

Epilogue   324

Prologue: Arctic Foxes

THE ARCTIC FOX, AN endangered species, is a hardy animal that survives in a frigid treeless environment. The tundra is not an easy place to live. It is barren, rocky and without much vegetation.

The Arctic foxes' pelts are the warmest of any animal found in the Arctic. Enduring temperatures as low as minus seventy degrees Celsius, the fur provides them with a consistent body temperature. In winter, they have a deep pure white fur coat that allows them blend into the tundra's ubiquitous snow and ice. As it was late summer their coats were a mix of brown and grey. Patches of white fur hung from their delicate bodies like dreadlocks.

Arctic foxes have furry soles and compact bodies to minimise the surface area exposed to the cold ground and air. Like a cat, the fox's tail aids their balance as well as providing a warm covering in cold weather. They usually live in burrows and they tunnel into the snow if conditions get bad.

The last of their litter had died of starvation several moon cycles ago as red foxes and grey wolves competed with them for a sharply declining supply of food. The waterfowl and other seabirds – usually easy prey – had flown south as temperatures plummeted to record low extremes. As the ice thickened into deep crusts the small invertebrates such as worms and snails also disappeared.

Their trek south-east from Vindelfjällen in northern Sweden, where the skulk had lived for generations, had taken several months and had been a journey of necessity, one of survival. While some episodes of good hunting, usually for fish around shallow ice pools, had kept them alive, the crossing over the last flat-ice surface had been the most difficult.

Deliberately, very deliberately, the male probed what remained of a gull's nest with his right paw. His mate sniffed the bitter cold air and observed him with a keen sense of anticipation as they had not eaten for many days. The nest was barren like so many others in the area.

Arctic foxes are so highly strung that an unexpected loud voice can cause them to die of fright. They have acute hearing with wide, front-facing ears that allow them to locate the precise position of their prey beneath the snow. Startled by a black crow, the male made a sharp *kak-kak-kak-kak-kak*, a sound more like a bird than a member of the canine family.

A strong northerly wind drove light snow flurries that settled on the frozen rocky ground. The covering was more than half a metre deep, on a thin base of granite, slate and loose stones. If current conditions prevailed for much longer, their time was limited on this inhospitable island, unless they found winter shelter and a source of food.

They would have to decide soon where they would set up an underground den for winter. The initial exploration of this rocky outcrop suggested that a sandier location was needed.

They paused, huddled together and observed their surroundings from the base of the small quarry that provided some measure of relief from the fierce blizzard, which was building up on the eastern horizon.

The sun was beginning to set over the dome of Killiney Hill in the southern suburbs of Dublin, on the east coast of Ireland. As the temperature slowly dropped they studied the outline of what remained of Dublin Bay with their piercing blue eyes. In the mid-distance, twin towers and isolated and abandoned high-rise office blocks were surrounded by a desert-like, rubble-strewn moonscape of flotsam melded into a fusion of frozen ice mud.

Like the humans that shared this space, they would have to adapt to survive.

The male decided they should walk across the ice to a snowy island hilltop in the distance that the humans called Howth.

This was part of Ireland's new landscape, its Iceapelago.

CHAPTER 1

La Palma

'COME IN, COME IN please.'

Twin brothers Ros and Simon Rodriquez entered the spacious office of Luis Laffino, the Professor of the Geophysics Department at the University of Cádiz. He got straight to the point as soon as they sat down.

'You have been successful in your applications for summer work at the Pico de la Nieve research centre on La Palma. *Felicidades muchachos*. To be honest with you, it wasn't a difficult decision given your academic results and your knowledge of the island.'

'But I thought that the research centre had been abandoned due to budget cuts?' said Simon. 'The last I heard the roof was leaking, equipment had been moved into storage and the broadband was disconnected.'

'Well, eh, that was the case,' said Professor Laffino, 'but we got sponsorship at the last minute from the Instituto Geográfico Nacional. The faculty decided that giving you the opportunity of conducting experiments around the Caldera de Taburiente would help you both complete your doctoral studies. The Caldera has huge potential from the perspective of volcanic research. You two know the island's geology and volcanic history more than most and certainly better than I do.

'Professor, we're delighted to accept your generous offer,' said Ros, keeping eye contact with Simon.

'Were any other student candidates successful?' said Simon.

'Yes, Maria and Claudine Marin-Rabella have also been assigned to La Palma but to the smaller research station near the Caldera de Teneguia on the south of the island. Do you know them?'

'Simon may know Maria,' said Ros with a knowing smile. Simon blushed red.

The Professor moved to conclude the meeting.

'I'll ask the manager of the research centre at the Instituto to talk to you about the practicalities and logistics – and your stipend of course. You might discuss your project plan with him.'

'Thank you, Professor. We won't disappoint you,' said Ros.

'I know.' He smiled in a grandfatherly way.

The boys walked across the campus back to their rooms.

'Maria will be on the island?' said Ros.

'I guess so. But she hasn't yet been told,' said Simon.

'I hope you can manage your love life remotely. It's a long way from Pico de la Nieve to the south of the island,' said Ros.

'We'll easily manage on two hundred euro a week,' said Simon, trying to change the subject.

'That's for sure. Shopping options are a bit limited where we are going,' said Ros.

'We've learned an awful lot at the Professor's lectures but reading about volcanoes from a textbook is one thing: walking the calderas of volcanoes and doing real hands-on research is what I want to do,' said Simon.

'Me too, brother,' said Ros. 'While there hasn't been any volcanic eruptions on the island for over eighty years, the dormant volcanoes do need to be monitored.'

'Professor Laffino is right, the Caldera de Taburiente and its National Park are a perfect natural laboratory,' said Ros.

'Yeah, and Barcelona is a perfect football club,' teased Simon.

'Now that's unfair, brother. Barça is the best. Just look at their track record since …' said Ros.

'… Johan Cruyff was appointed manager. I think I've heard that line before.'

The twins were fascinated by the geology of Isla de la Palma, on the western edge of the Canaries Archipelago off the coast of Africa. It was one of the highest volcanic islands in the world, situated directly over a dormant magma plume – an upwelling of abnormally hot rock. Only a fraction of the volcanic island was visible above ground. As with icebergs, most of the base of the island was underwater – to a depth of almost four kilometres on the western flank. Submarine volcanic activity had played a major part in shaping the island's jagged and mountainous landscape. The Caldera de Taburiente, an extinct shield volcano that was formed by three large overlapping volcanoes, dominated the centre and northern side of the island. In geological terms Isla De La Palma was young: a mere infant.

It may have looked tranquil from sea level, but the twenty-kilometre-long ridge of the Old Summit (Cumbre Vieja) that ran along a north-south axis through the centre of the island had history. Covering some two-thirds of La Palma, the volcanoes along Cumbre Vieja had erupted on seven occasions over the past six centuries. La Palma was situated far from the edges of the tectonic plates that run into the mid-Atlantic (and further north to Iceland). However, the Canaries was an active zone. A sizeable submarine earthquake – 5.6 on the Richter scale – had been recorded between Tenerife and Gran Canaria in May 1989.

Scientists started to take a keen interest in Cumbre Vieja in the 1980s as emerging geological evidence suggested there was a medium level of risk that, during a future eruption, a catastrophic collapse of the western side of the island could result in upwards of five-hundred square kilometres of rock – a volume the size of several football stadia – falling into the sea. The resulting tsunami would be likely to cause devastation over a large area of the eastern Atlantic seaboard of the United States, with twenty-five-metre-high waves hitting Florida some nine hours after the event.

The huge landslide deposits off the shores of La Palma, and other Canary Islands, provided evidence that dramatic landslides of such a scale had happened in the distant past. Local geologists rebutted this scenario on the grounds that there was no evidence to substantiate such a claim. They produced contrary data to contest the 'western flank collapse' theory. They argued that the island is the least seismically active of the Canary Archipelago and decades of records maintained by the Instituto Geográfico Nacional attested to this fact.

Given the risk profile of Cumbre Vieja, in 1997 a European funded research centre was set up on Pico de la Nieve, at the edge of the Caldera de Taburiente, with support from the Smithsonian Institute in Washington. The research was part of a wider global endeavour to assess the historical impacts of collapses of island volcanoes and the effects that volcanic eruption phases had on landslides. The aim was to build up a model of volcano activity on a par with what had been done for the Hawaiian Islands, another identified hot spot.

Before the Rodriquez brothers travelled to La Palma, the erstwhile operations manager of the research centre, a grim academic who rarely moved far from his books, gave them minimal instructions with a degree of disinterest that he didn't hide. His enthusiasm for the activities of the Pico de la Nieve research centre was commensurate to its funding, which was at a record low.

It seemed clear that they were going to be left largely to their own devices during their four-month assignment. Being unsupervised was one of the main reasons why this summer job was so attractive.

The brothers travelled to the Pico de la Nieve research centre a week after the end of the final semester.

The research centre had the capacity to house ten resident scientists across two buildings. The complex also included two laboratories, work benches, a small living room and a kitchen. Over the years, poor maintenance, combined with high annual rainfall levels and cold harsh winter temperatures, had led to the deterioration of the fabric of the buildings. They spent the first few days carrying out essential repairs, reconnecting the broadband and making the centre habitable.

As a compensation of sorts for its lack of creature comforts, the site commanded stunning views of the island's National Park, some thousand metres below. Access to the stony outcrop where the research centre was located was by footpath, an hour's trek through the pines and broom from the main road that ran the length of the Caldera.

The routine of volcanic observation demanded patience and a strong self-discipline and that was why the Rodriquez brothers had been chosen to man this remote research centre.

They were not identical twins in terms of looks but had an identical sense of purpose. They were reliable, diligent and most importantly supportive of each other in their shared love of science. Their inherent inquisitiveness had drawn them to the behaviour of volcanoes and their well-honed research skills meant they were well qualified to help predict the one remaining geophysical mystery that had defied generations of scientists.

They had a deep love of life: *carpe diem* was the mantra that had been drilled into them by their Jesuit teachers. They were gregarious, relaxed and appreciated the optimum work–life balance without being too dogmatic about it.

Over the following weeks they installed nearly twenty remote sulphur dioxide gas detectors around the base of the National Park and beside the known vents around the Caldera de Taburiente. After water vapour, sulphur dioxide is the most abundant gas found at the surfaces of volcanic activity. They monitored how much of the gas arrived at the surface with their improved test devices, which could detect the slightest readings and transmit the data to the monitors at the Pico de la Nieve research centre. This meant that there was no need for a physical inspection once the devices were installed. These devices were prototypes – adaptations of old models – that the brothers had designed and built during their studies in university. As a consequence, they were eager to put them to the test in a live environment and, more importantly, to see if their inventions could perform to the technical specifications that were set.

In addition, over a period of ten years, many somewhat out-of-date seismic detectors had been placed close to the volcanic peaks of the Caldera de Taburiente by previous groups of summer students. They were located close to known areas of seismic activity. These too had to be monitored on a regular basis.

In installing the gas detectors, the brothers took full advantage of the hiking trail called GR (Grand Route) 131, the island's renowned 72kilometre long walking trail, which starts at the Faro de Fuencaliente lighthouse on the south coast and rises 3,600 metres to the crest of Somada Alta on the western side of the Caldera de Taburiente. While only four kilometres directly opposite the Pico de la Nieve research centre as the crow flies, it was a half-day's walk to Somada Alta over zigzag mountain paths with views that gave even those with no vertigo cause to reflect. At certain points there was a sheer drop of almost 1,000 metres. To the south and along the eastern edge of the Caldera the mountain range extended some twenty kilometres to Pico Bejenado. The terrain, while offering some of the best mountain scenery in Europe, was rugged and steep. An ideal location for mountain goats and ambitious young scientists.

On most days the Rodriquez bothers were above the cloud cover. From the Atlantic, thin white clouds raced up the front of the cliff face of the Caldera and spun off the rim falling as drizzling rain. As a consequence, it was cold and often wet. And when it rained at altitude, being out in the open was only for the brave. Even if the very brave (and foolish) wore their designer rain gear they got saturated. In contrast, the temperature at sea level was over thirty degrees Celsius in the summer; it was less than half that at altitude on a good day. It was also extremely windy at that height. Walking anywhere near the unprotected rim of the Caldera was both stupid and dangerous.

In short, the weather was totally unpredictable. As a result, it was necessary for the brothers to have clothing and equipment that worked best in rapidly changing conditions, from gale force winds in bright sunshine to calm in a total downpour of cold rain.

The daily chores were to take the readings, log them, analyse the data and pass on the material to the smaller research station near the Caldera de Teneguia. Here sisters Maria and Claudine Marin-Rabella did similar work in monitoring the inactive volcanoes of Cumbre Vieja located to the south of the island. They had the added responsibility of coordinating readings from other volcanic research centres on the nearby islands of La Gomera and El Hierro. The girls were in first and second year at the same University. They too were keen scientists.

Maria, the younger of the two by a year, had started to date Simon a few weeks before they were all assigned to work on La Palma.

Simon didn't think of himself as attractive to girls. While he liked walking, he shunned more athletic sports so was somewhat heavier than Ros. His uniqueness was his outgoing personality. He could talk to anyone and he did – all the time. When Maria appeared at one of his tutorials, he was struck dumb for a change. This took him by surprise. By the time the second tutorial was scheduled they were holding hands, both smitten. No need for Tinder or other dating apps: lots of coffees and *torta* in the cafes of Cadiz in between lectures did the business. They were love birds by any reckoning.

Maria was different. The fact that she was the most attractive woman on the campus went over Simon's head. He didn't see her beauty but only her personality. When they discovered they had been selected to work on La Palma they felt this was serendipitous. Or at least it was until they found out the location of the two research centres was so far apart they might as well be living on different planets. Given their respective locations, the two teams of siblings had no expectations of meeting up on a regular basis while they undertook their summer duties. At least they could talk daily using Zoom Conference software. Most importantly, for Simon and Maria, they could see each other.

Claudine was a scientist, pure and simple. She based everything – religion, music, love and politics – on her perception of the latest available evidence. She never took things at face value. Everything had to be debated to a standstill. She took no interest in suitors and had no time for boys – or girls for that matter. She was most comfortable in jeans and jumpers talking to her scientific peers. Her vocation was volcanoes. She got her kicks from analysing data sets and writing predictive behavioural algorithms of lava flows. She was in her element on La Palma.

When it became clear that Maria had taken a serious shine to Simon, she didn't offer motherly advice – or indeed sisterly advice. Once she found out that Maria's love interest was a fellow scientist, Claudine only wanted to talk about his academic papers on volcanoes. She had no interest in such mundane issues as his personal interests or character.

While Ros and Simon had to make do with very rudimentary accommodation, the sisters Marin-Rabella were staying with their aunt and uncle in their villa on the outskirts of Los Canarios, the most southerly inhabited town on the island, just a thirty-minute walk from their work base.

'What were the readings?' said Ros as he moved closer to the bench to get his coffee. He looked at the array of monitors in front of him. They were quite dated but were sufficient for the tasks at hand. Until midday his cafetière was in constant use. The regular consumption of strong coffee was very much part of his personal routine. His chipped Barcelona FC mug, with a faded image of Lionel Messi, was his pride and joy: a constant reminder of his love of *fútbol*, the beautiful game. Unlike Ros, Simon was a football agnostic and teased his brother about his unashamed fanaticism for Spain's most famous club at every possible opportunity. It was good natured repartee.

After all, as they only had each other for company a bit of leg pulling passed the time.

'Same as yesterday. In fact, the same as all of the yesterdays for quite some time,' replied Simon.

'OK then, I'll send the daily report to Claudine,' said Ros.

'Let me have a look first,' replied Simon.

What they were looking for was any change in the flow of sulphur dioxide that might indicate an early sign of volcanic activity. Unlike older devices, the detectors they had designed at university were capable of picking up the smallest micro-millilitre changes in the emissions of this deadly gas. Their work on their doctoral theses on volcanology, specifically on sulphur dioxide measurements, had ingrained in them a deep awareness of the importance of probing every small piece of evidence, even if the monitoring device registered a barely noticeable change to the data.

The large A3 printouts from the various sites showed what at first sight appeared to be a flat line. No sulphur gas meant no volcanic activity.

'Look at this, Ros. See the readings from the northern side of the Caldera de Taburiente near Roque de los Muchachos? Two detectors in close proximity show a barely perceptible reading, it hardly registers, while all the others show no sign of activity. The spike lasted less than ten seconds. These measurements are quite recent and were recorded a few hours ago.'

'Let me see,' said Ros. He stared at the expanse of coloured data points to make sense of what looked likely to be an anomaly, and a very small one at that. He was aware that sudden changes in gas composition, even small readings, often presage a change in potential volcanic activity. And yes, there was a pinprick of a reading. Not only that, but the first reading was followed almost immediately with a reading from the second device located about nine hundred metres away. This suggested the two were connected. 'Maybe the detectors are faulty, or the solar energy panels we installed have packed in. We might as well go and inspect the devices as not much else is going to happen here today.'

'I agree,' said Simon.' I'll transmit the data to Claudine and tell her and Maria that we're going walkabout.'

Simon logged in. The sisters were at their workstations. Claudine was in her customary jeans with unkempt hair but Maria, since the video option on Zoom was used daily, was dressed elegantly in a smart skirt and blouse, with her hair groomed attractively. By this stage, Ros and Claudine had worked out the pair were a serious item and allowed them some space when they were on air.

'Hi Maria,' said Simon. His face went deep red.

'Hi Simon,' said Maria. She smiled at her boyfriend and blew him a kiss.

'I like your hair. Do you often wear a bow?' said Simon.

'Only when I'm meeting someone special,' said Maria.

'Would I fall into that category?' asked Simon sheepishly.

'Maybe,' said Maria with a broad smile.

'You'll be wearing your hair in a bow for a long time to come,' said Simon.

'Maybe,' said Maria as she laughed.

'Anyway, just to give you a heads up,' said Simon, 'our prototype devices have recorded their first reading. We are going to physically inspect the devices. We'll keep you briefed on our return. Talk soon. *Besos*.'

More kisses were blown.

It was back to business for the Rodriquez brothers.

'Let's get the gear,' said Ros.

'I'll brew up the coffee and pack some food and water. Don't forget to bring your new camera,' said Simon.

It was a good three-hour walk to the sulphur dioxide detectors at the Roque de los Muchachos. Despite being at an altitude of over 2,000 metres, it was already relatively warm. As midday was four hours away, the brothers knew they had to take all the necessary safety measures. They were well used to wearing protection suits and hard hats in the midday sun and having oxygen masks and protective clothes and equipment in their backpacks. They got ready and were provisioned for the short journey in no time at all.

The outdoors was where they were most at ease. They had spent many summers walking through the mountains and valleys of La Palma. The extent to which their army-standard hiking boots moulded to their stockinged feet was testament to this. They knew the terrain and trails as well as any professional guide. It was both rocky and unstable under the scree, loose stones and impacted dark ash residue, so they were always prudent and un-hurried as they made their way along the well-trodden footpaths on and off the GR131.

The mountain walking demanded that more attention was paid to the two or three metres in front of you than to the wider surroundings. A slip or a trip along gritty and often slippery slopes had to be avoided at all costs. There were sheer falls of over 1,000 metres just a metre off parts of the winding trail to the Roque de los Muchachos. That's why hiking along this trail wasn't allowed in high winds.

'I'm surprised there are so many tourists up here,' said Ros, as he spotted a large walking group of twenty or so that were moving slowly in a long line ahead of them. Their air-conditioned coach was parked a short distance away. As they approached, the hikers could be heard chatting away in a relaxed manner while soaking in the sun and the scenery. The group leader, who was wearing a red and yellow head scarf, was clearly visible at the front and the same coloured scarf was worn by his colleague who took up position at the back of the group. They had all been supplied with a standard issue tall walking stick: a critical piece of equipment given the nature of the terrain.

'Germans, I guess,' said Ros. 'You can spot them straight away as they have the latest gear and equipment.'

'There are far more walking groups in the mountains nowadays. When we started to spend our summers here the place was almost deserted.' observed Simon.

While most tourists sought out beaches, bars and bodegas, the more discerning hiker had different priorities. The tourist authorities in La Palma had invested heavily in way-finding signage and detailed maps. People hardly ever got lost on La Palma's 900 kilometres of trails. The GR 131 trail was by far the most popular on the island, despite its challenges. It took fit and experienced climbers at least three days to complete.

Simon leaned on his walking poles and took in the vast arena of scenery. This beats a desk job any day, he mused to himself.

As it was late August, the sky was almost cloudless, and the air was crystal clear. A steady light breeze kept the temperature below ten degrees Celsius. The Caldera de Taburiente was visible in all its glory as far as the eye could see. The edge of the massive volcanic crater rose to heights of almost 2,400 metres with many peaks towering even higher. The almost sheer cliff faces were beautiful but also potentially lethal for anyone who wasn't cautious. The terrain was defined by rocky outcrops, ridges, spurs, lava mounds (called 'roques') and open areas bordered by thin lines of Canary pine trees with their characteristic branches. The bare rocks along the rim of the Caldera were natural works of art shaped by centuries, perhaps millennia, of wind and rain.

In contrast, the vegetation at the base of the National Park was lush, comprising shrubs, bushes and thickets of all hues, interspersed among a dense array of forest plantations. On the lower parts of the rock walls, changes in colour indicated different materials. The escarpments were a violet-grey colour. The 308 species, subspecies and varieties of plant located in the National Park displayed every combination of colour. The dominant pine trees added a canopy of greens.

The only blot on this otherwise pure natural landscape was the array of six enormous telescopes and radio dishes constructed adjacent to Roque de los Muchachos as part of the International Astrophysical Observatory. Opened in 1985, this observatory took full advantage of the island's clear night skies. Called the ORM (Observatorio Roque de los Muchachos), it was the best location for optical and infrared astronomy in the Northern Hemisphere and, as a consequence, it hosted the world's largest single-aperture optical telescope.

Unlike the Pico de la Nieve research centre, the facilities for its multinational team of scientists were state of the art. The ORM had four-star hotel facilities. It had a kitchen and a chef, a recreation area, a gym and spa, and individual bedrooms with all mod cons. And the roof didn't leak. In sharp contrast, the brothers Rodriquez cooked over an open stove, slept in a Portakabin, and had the stars for companionship in the evenings. The two research centres operated as completely separate entities while both sharing the glory that was the Caldera de Taburiente.

'Perhaps trekking up volcanoes is the latest way of getting fit?' said Simon.

'That or they want to see the island before the next Big Bang,' replied Ros.

'Let's hope we're not here to see the action,' said Simon.

'As we'll be the first to spot any sign of volcanic or seismic activity, we may witness just that,' said Ros.

When they arrived where the spectrometer was installed, on the northern side of Roque de los Muchachos some thirty metres to the right of the walking trail, Ros paused before he examined the device. Unlike the old standard instruments that were designed to measure the amount of sulphur dioxide in a passing air mass, the new TOMS (Total Ozone Mapping Spectrometer) kit that the brothers had taken so much time to install could provide data in units of milli-atmosphere centimetres. The readings could be detected by the NASA Goddard Space Flight Centre – provided, of course, that a relay feed had been set up, which it hadn't.

'I really hope we're not going to get data indicating volcanic activity,' said Ros.

'Don't be so pessimistic,' said Simon.

'I'm being realistic,' replied Ros.

'The data we saw recorded a small, barely perceptible reading,' said Simon. 'Just a spike in sulphur emissions. This is not normal as this old vent hasn't recorded a flow since the older monitor was installed decades ago.'

'What does that mean?'

'I don't know to be honest. Let's double check the instrument,' responded Simon with little confidence.

Ros bent over the vent and extracted the spectrometer from its casing. It was functioning normally. The solar batteries were fully charged. He opened up the screen and sure enough saw a reading showing a minute amount of sulphur dioxide over a period of two minutes, before it stopped for no obvious reason.

'Simon, the spectrometer is in good order. We must accept the readings.'

'Is this the only site where a flow was recorded?' said Simon.

'No, the other spectrometer is located on the far side of the ridge to the right of the roque,' replied Ros.

'Why don't we check it out?'

'OK,' said Ros.

Once they had replaced the instrument back in its casing, the brothers set off the short distance to the next monitoring site.

Augusta, Georgia

The azaleas were in full bloom. Shade tolerant, they grow best near or under trees. A wet and short winter and the early arrival of spring had them in pristine condition.

These bright pink-coloured bushes were a signature feature at the Masters, one of the 'majors' golf events, played every year in early April in Augusta, an otherwise nondescript town in the State of Georgia in the USA. The event, the equivalent of the World Cup of golf, was top of the 'must visit' list for fans of the sport.

'He's in trouble,' said Lars Brun, talking to himself.

He was seated on the packed stand directly opposite the par three, 147-yard, signature twelfth green that was part of 'Amen Corner', the name given to a set of the most difficult holes on the course. He had a perfect view of the golfer and his caddie, who was eagerly prodding a large clump of azaleas with the shaft of a golf club. As an amateur golfer, he appreciated there is nothing more embarrassing than hitting a shot off target that disappears into the foliage well wide of the intended target. It must be so much worse in full view of a packed gallery and live on television.

Augusta's azaleas were thick and wiry and the final resting place of many a lost ball. Lars could only sympathise with the acclaimed Spanish player who, at least at this stage, was the tournament leader.

Lars fitted in with the crowd. Like nearly everyone else he wore regulation clothes befitting an avid golf spectator: the compulsory 'Masters' golf cap, grey stripped knee socks worn above his expensive all-weather leather golf shoes (also grey), designer shades made by an established fashion house, a bright pink golf shirt and deep-blue shorts. It wasn't his usual attire but like the chameleon lizard he blended in seamlessly with his fellow fans.

'I've the solution,' said a fellow spectator, who had sat beside him a few minutes earlier, clutching a large plastic beer glass in one hand and a sandwich of some description in the other.

They may have been strangers but, like everyone else in the stand, their mutual focus was on the now frustrated golfer who was returning to the tee to re-take his shot. His loud, ill-tempered muttering could be he heard clearly in the bleachers.

'A better swing would be the best way to sort out his problem,' opined Lars.

'He rushed his shot and sliced the ball out of control to the left. He's under pressure, obviously.'

'Perhaps.'

They fell silent as the anguished golfer played another ball, a two-shot penalty, that he executed with skill landing it on the green. The crowded gallery applauded politely as he walked off the tee knowing he had lost his place at the top of the leader board.

'If he had used my golf ball he wouldn't be in such trouble,' said the man beside Lars.

'I beg your pardon?' said Lars.

'I've designed a prototype hard core golf ball that has an in-built tracker device. With my technology anyone can find the location of their ball, even in the deepest azaleas of Augusta. It's so efficient and successful that the companies who manufacture golf balls are lobbying the world's golfing bodies to have my ball banned. It would be dreadful, would it not, if us amateur golfers didn't have to buy so many of their expensive products.'

Lars' attention switched effortlessly from golf to work in a split second.

'I'm Sean Pitcher by the way.'

'Lars Brun. By your accent, I guess you're not American.'

'God no! I'm Irish. And you?'

'Norwegian.'

'The support of this great game knows no boundaries,' said Sean.

Sean, in sharp contrast to Lars, wore grubby ill-fitting, well-worn, multicoloured trainers, short purple socks, knee-length denim shorts with pockets everywhere and a long sleeve maroon sports shirt with 'Supermacs' printed in a prominent position on the front and a crest with the word 'Gaillimh' underneath over the heart. The outfit was completed with a traditional tweed cap that did little to hide his flowing locks of curly red hair. He would have mixed inconspicuously with football fans but looked out of place in the hallowed fairways of Augusta. With his untrimmed red beard, one could have spotted him at fifty paces. He certainly stood out from the crowd.

'It's quite simple really,' said Sean. 'We embed a chip with an individual identity into the hard core of the ball. It behaves like a transponder by sending out a low frequency signal that can be picked up by a phone App within a range of around one hundred metres. What the golf ball manufacturers don't like is that the performance of the ball is not affected in any way. Here's a sample.'

Digging deep into his trousers' pocket, he produced what for all intents was a normal golf ball, but one without a manufacturer's logo. Instead it had a large green shamrock printed on the surface.

Lars took the golf ball in his hand. He rubbed it gently. The feel and look of the ball were no different to what he usually played with.

'Does the chip not get damaged with the impact of the golf club?' asked Lars.

'Ah, that's another innovation,' said Sean. 'I've encased the chip in a durable thin-layered plastic cover that cushions the blow and does not affect the transponder.'

'Fascinating, truly fascinating,' said Lars. 'I may have another use for this golf ball of yours.'

'Tell me more.'

'I'm a climate scientist, when I'm not playing golf and attending golf events,' said Lars. 'I lead a research group that's doing work on the Greenland Ice Sheet and surrounding glaciers.'

'Interesting what us golfers get up to in our spare time! Seriously though, what type of research?'

'We're trying to measure the extent of the ice melt across the Greenland Ice Sheet. It's increasing at a great rate, but in a largely random manner. We want to be able to predict the pace, flow and direction of the meltwater with a much higher degree of accuracy.'

'How can my golf ball help?'

Sean sensed that he was about to get a business pitch right in the middle of the final stages of the world's most prestigious golf event. He was conflicted. Watch the golf as he had planned, or listen to the Norwegian who was clearly agitated and excited?

'I've monitored the progress of the Greenland ice melt using various electronic devices and satellite images, but have never managed to track the flow rate and direction of the ice as it descends some three thousand metres from the apex of the ice sheet down multiple invisible crevasses into the Greenland Sea close to the North Atlantic to the East and to Baffin Bay to the West. Satellite tracking can assist us up to one hundred metres below the surface. But at lower depths we can't get a reliable signal.'

They fell silent as the Spanish golfer finished his putt for a double bogey. He scowled and frowned as he was no longer the tournament leader. A lip reader who could speak Spanish would have detected a few profanities directed at the poor caddie who was obviously to blame for his player's mishap.

Sean decided that listening was the best option, not that he had any choice.

'Could your invention be adapted to serve as a detector of the flow of the meltwater beneath the Greenland Ice Sheet?'

Sean smiled.

'I think I may be able to help. In life, everything is possible. Nothing is impossible. We Irish are born optimists. Perhaps we might meet up after the golf for a beer and a bite?'

'I know just the place,' said Lars. 'I'll book a table at the French Market Grille. It's a bit out of town. They do the best bowl of Jambalaya in these parts. Let's meet at eight o'clock.'

'Fine by me,' said Sean.

They abandoned their conversation as quickly as it had begun just as the next three ball moved onto the adjacent tee box amid loud roars from the partisan crowd chanting support for their American heroes. Europeans and others were second-rate golf citizens in Augusta.

The restaurant was packed to capacity. As arranged they met at the bar and got their table with a minimum of delay. A four-piece bar band was playing with great gusto. The lead singer was obviously a fan of Neil Diamond. The noise of the music drowned out conversation from adjacent tables.

'What will you have Sean?'

'A bottle of Coors Light will do.'

A waiter took the order.

Sean observed that Lars was staring at his shirt and not for the first time. 'You seem interested in my clothes, so I should explain. It the official jersey of the Galway Gaelic football team.'

'I don't understand,' replied Lars.

'My county plays in an annual Gaelic football championship against the other thirty-one counties in Ireland. Everyone, and I mean everyone, supports the team and the best way to show your colours is to wear the colours. Maroon means Galway. I've three jerseys, by the way. This is my evening one.'

'You're a football fan?' asked Lars.

'A Gaelic football fan, yes, and a proud one at that.'

'I can see you have a lot of energy,' said Lars.

'And I'm innovative and a bit of an entrepreneur at the same time.'

'Obviously, and a confident one as well, I suspect,' said Lars with a smile.

After they ordered their meal, they spent the next while engaged in small talk. Lars talked about his golf handicap, his family, Norway (of course) and his satisfaction that the Spanish golfer won the Masters despite his poor score at the twelfth hole. Sean also talked about his family background and his start-up business.

Sean sensed that the serious business of the evening was approaching. However, the revellers singing the chorus of 'Sweet Caroline' rendered proper conversation impossible.

Lars spoke as the band took a break. His tone was serious – a bit too serious for Sean's liking.

'Let me put my cards on the table, Sean. We barely know each other, yet I'm certain you can help me solve a puzzle that I've struggled with for the best part of a decade.'

Lars emptied his bottle of Coors Light with a sense of purpose.

'As I said earlier, I've been doing climate change research in Greenland since I left college. It's a fascinating area for a scientist, but also quite frustrating as getting reliable evidence is a big problem.'

'Please explain,' said Sean helpfully.

'I've two theories that, if proven correct, could alter the way everyone – even the American president – think of the impacts of climate change.'

To Sean's surprise, Lars pulled out a large map of Greenland from his coat pocket. It filled the table when he unfolded it.

'Last year, during the summer months, there were ten earthquakes at the locations in the centre of Greenland

marked here with an 'X'. Many were above a three magnitude on the Richter scale. These incidents have little
to do with tectonic plate movements, as Greenland is
stable compared to its island neighbour Iceland. What
appears to have happened is that once the glaciers move
this generates seismic waves. Some of them are the size
of Manhattan and a ten-metre jolt can happen within
ten minutes. This is not a new phenomenon. Researchers
have recorded such incidents over the past decade. What is
different now is that the tremors are more frequent, more
severe and concentrated at three known locations that are
at the base and sides of the ice sheet. Most importantly,
the tremors usually happen towards the end of the summer
melt season.'

'I don't remember seeing any press reports about this,'
said Sean.

'That's the problem. Because they are not tectonic
movements of the earth's plates and no visible damage
is caused, nobody died, these incidents have been swept
under the proverbial scientific carpet.'

'You need a carpet beater. Someone to shake off the
dust,' said Sean, trying to be sympathetic.

'That's one way of putting it,' replied Lars.

Lars knew he had to be careful how he explained the
consequences of his research proposition to Sean.

'My theory is that the melting ice across the centre
of the Greenland Ice Sheet is carving out deep caverns
just below the surface. The speed of the meltwater as it
descends down ravines causes further erosion of the deep
ice formations. As the meltwater flows down inside the
glacier, it hollows out internal rivers and lakes of melted

ice deep within the glacier. These lakes – some big, some small – are collapsing on top of one another. That's the root cause of the tremors as millions of tonnes of water are displaced with each incident. The secondary effect is that there are now enormous hidden caverns across the length and breadth of the Greenland Ice Sheet. Unseen by us, the Greenland Ice Sheet has already lost a significant amount of its volume.'

'I can see why you're a bit agitated,' said Sean.

'After five years of record high temperatures at the top of the glacier, an unprecedented volume of meltwater is drilling out much of the central parts of the Greenland Ice Sheet. If seismic events caused the collapse of the top sections of the ice sheet, or at the glaciers that are the front of the ice sheet at sea level, this will be a tipping point. A point beyond which only one conclusion is possible: the destruction of the Greenland Ice Sheet that was expected to take a thousand years to happen could occur within decades.'

'That sounds a bit dramatic, Lars.'

'It is,' said Lars. 'Once a tipping point is reached there is no going back.'

'Scary,' said Sean.

'I need the evidence to convince the governments of the countries around the North Atlantic, not just to invest in my research, but to pay more attention to what is happening. Tinkering at the edges and denying the science – the current policy of the Americans – is unsustainable, and wrong.'

'Where do I fit in?' said Sean still unclear as to what the sales pitch was.

'We lack any evidence about the extent to which meltwater is hollowing out the innards of the Greenland Ice Sheet. We need to find out where surface meltwater goes once it descends into the bowels of the ice sheet. And we also need to know how and where the meltwater flows and its exit points and, critically, the speed – the flow rate – of the meltwater.'

'So? How can I assist?' probed Sean, wishing Lars would get to the point.

'I need to know if you can manufacture a device, a golf ball, that can be tracked as it moves down the ice rivers that descend inside the ice sheet. Ideally, I need a device that will show me the direction and speed of descent of the summer ice-melt from multiple locations across the top of the Greenland Ice Sheet as the meltwater progresses to the Greenland and Baffin Seas, and onwards to the North Atlantic. Can you do that?'

'Lars, my golf ball is a hardcore ball that was designed to be hit at significant speed by a golf club. What you are looking for is a softcore ball that can float.'

'Exactly. Can you do that?'

Lars' eagerness was beginning to show. He was, as Sean suspected, a man in a hurry.

'No reason why not. The technology I've developed for the outer surface would allow us to lighten the golf ball while not compromising its hardcore exterior. The shape, sturdiness and the density of the ball is not an issue to be honest.'

'Two more beers please,' said Lars to the waiter. He needed a drink.

'What interests me most is the idea of developing a tracking function whereby a satellite could monitor the golf balls deep within the Greenland Ice Sheet,' said Sean. 'That, to my mind, is a technology fix that my engineers should be able to sort out. They love a challenge.'

'How soon could you develop a prototype?'

'What timescale do you have in mind?'

'Ten weeks from today. I need to have these devices at my research base at the Summit Station ready to deploy no later than the third week in August.'

'That's a tall order Lars, regardless of the logistics.'

'It may well be, but I can't afford to let another summer season pass without this vital research being completed. While we can expand the programme next year, I need as many golf balls as possible this year. If this experiment works, we can ramp up the scale of the operation. But, as you have probably gathered by now, I'm desperate to make a start. Can you produce a thousand of these ice golf balls by any chance?'

'I'll do my best Lars. By the way, what's the Summit Station?'

'It's a research facility located at the top of the Greenland Ice Sheet at 3,000 metres above sea level.'

Lars eyes lit up with excitement. Sean clearly understood what he needed. Lars was thankful that serendipity had brought them together earlier in the day. Sean Pitcher was a man he needed to build a relationship with as a priority.

'You have skin in the game Sean,' said Lars. 'I will explain in more detail later, but the data your golf ball devices will generate could have a profound effect on predicting weather forecasts in Ireland.'

'What's the connection?'

'Our data, which has yet to be published, points to the Greenland meltwater pouring at record volumes into the North Atlantic. This pure water is mixing with the saline waters of the Gulf Stream.'

'That gives us our temperate climate. That's what I was told at school.'

'Yes, the Gulf Stream gives Ireland and Western Europe much warmer summers than would otherwise be the case given your latitude.'

Sean was discovering slowly but surely that Lars had a tendency to be long-winded.

'We've evidence that the sub-surface dynamics that drive the Gulf Stream from the Caribbean towards north-west Europe have already stopped at many locations. Should the ice melt continue at its current pace, and perhaps intensify if seismic activity caused parts of the Greenland Ice Sheet to collapse, then unprecedented volumes of non-saline water would flow into the North Atlantic. When this happens – and it is only a matter of time – the benign effects of the Gulf Stream will slow down and eventually stop.'

'You are kidding me?'

'I'm afraid not,' said Lars. 'Something similar happened some twelve thousand years ago, not a long time in geological terms. There is evidence that the glaciers of Central Canada melted and burst into the North Atlantic through the Gulf of Saint Lawrence. Over time, a mere few decades, the Gulf Stream stopped. The Ice Age arrived with sea ice coverage as far south as northern Spain.'

'You're not suggesting something similar will happen?'

'There is no evidence to substantiate such a calamity. What we know is that freshwater ice-melt, is lighter than salty water which means that it floats on the surface of the ocean and in so doing disturbs the normal sinking of dense, cold saltwater to the ocean floor.'

Sean nodded but looked like he didn't fully grasp the nuances, so Lars kept going with his explanation.

'Your golf balls will help us determine the velocity of the meltwater and track its progress within the Greenland Ice Sheet. The volume of ice-melt that passed through the Gulf of Saint Lawrence all those years ago was, conservatively, not even a third of what the Greenland Ice Sheet could off-load into the North Atlantic.'

Lars looked Sean straight in the eye.

'When that happens, you'll need more than full thermals all year round. The prospect of such a cataclysmic change in the Gulf Stream's influence over the weather will have profound effects on the economies and societies of the countries of north-west Europe.'

Sean rubbed his beard vigorously. What have I gotten myself into? Far too late for such questions, he thought to himself. All this talk about climate chaos is perhaps real.

'Another round of beers please.'

The waiter duly obliged. Judging by their sad demeanour, he sensed these customers wouldn't be going anywhere soon.

Glencairn

The gardens of Glencairn House were full to capacity on the occasion of the garden party to celebrate the King's official birthday. The Wicklow grey granite exterior, rolling lawns, rose beds and imposing porticos provided the ideal setting. Judging by the buzz of good-natured chatter and laughter, everyone was enjoying the balmy summer's evening. Marquees were set up on the fringes of the main garden where generous amounts of sponsors' alcohol and food were available. Serving staff mingled effortlessly among the guests. A six-piece army band played a selection of military airs at a short distance from the main crowd that comprised a who's who of Dublin's political, social and business elites, with a fair share of journalists as well. The official residence of the British Ambassador to Ireland since the 1950s was being put to good use, yet again.

Billy van Os observed the scene while standing aback from the window in the Japanese room located on the first floor of the building. The room was dominated by a tapestry representing the rising and the setting of the sun and a portrait of the King. As the resident Defence Attaché, or 'spy' to the layman, he liked to stay out of sight. He could see but could not be seen. After all, his profession was one of the oldest and required discretion.

This was his second posting to Ireland, the first being during the height of the 'Troubles', the thirty-year conflict that had impacted both Northern Ireland and the

South. His hands-on style in one notorious operation in Dublin, where he was technically supposed to be an observer, required that he was extracted out of the jurisdiction at short notice with his American CIA counterpart. That was a long time ago, a distant memory for some. His involvement in a bombing and that of his American colleague were dead-ended by the police on both sides of the Irish Sea. The operation was all but forgotten, despite the traditional enquiry into the fatalities that came to no conclusions. Given his track record, he really didn't want to be back in Ireland despite the many intervening years. But, as this was his last posting before his imminent retirement, he had no choice in the matter. Sure, nobody would remember him after such a long period. Old spies never die, they just fade away.

He had a different mission this evening. On checking the guest list, he discovered his target had accepted the Ambassador's invitation as he had known he would. The profile on file suggested his target was a bit of a bon viveur. He observed patiently and tried to spot him among the mass of people mingling below. He didn't have to wait too long. The Irish loved parties and were uncharacteristically punctual in attending one of the more sought-after invitations of the year.

Ireland's Chief Scientist cut quite a dash in a tailored Magee blazer, Saville Row tie, ironed chino trousers and black Barker shoes. He was talking in an animated manner to a government minister. He wasn't aware that his plans for the evening were about to be rudely interrupted.

Van Os summoned one of his staff. 'Please ask Professor Gilmore to join me.'

Shortly after, he saw his officer discreetly tap the Chief Scientist on the shoulder and whisper into his ear. The professor looked suitably surprised. He hesitated before he excused himself from the company and walked towards the main building.

Minutes later Professor Gerard Gilmore, or 'Gerdy' to his friends, was greeted by van Os.

'Sorry to disturb your evening Professor. My name is Billy van Os. I'm the Defence Attaché at the Embassy. Please take a seat.'

'Yes, I know who you are. The question is why am I here?'

Gilmore was used to asking, not answering questions.

'We need to talk about a matter of mutual interest that demands a certain degree of sensitivity.'

'Tell me more,' said Gilmore, with a hint of impatience. He had no idea what van Os was alluding to. He didn't like intrigue or innuendo. He preferred open and direct communications.

'Please let me explain,' said van Os. 'Last week Skynet Six, the UK's most recently launched military communications satellite, recorded readings of seismic activity from seabed sensors that are usually used to track and monitor Russian submarines in the Atlantic Ocean. The location of the seismic activity is along a 150-kilometre line abutting the western edge of the Rockall Plateau at the limits of the Irish Continental Shelf in the area of the Eriador Seamount.'

Gilmore knew this area, located north-west of Ireland, quite well as he had supervised several seabed mapping surveys of this region. The Eriador Seamount rose some

1,500 metres from the sea floor at the very edge of the Irish Continental Shelf. However, to date, this feature hadn't been comprehensively mapped.

'But there has been no recent history of seismic activity at this location to my knowledge. Has something changed?' Gilmore stated what he thought was the obvious. He was puzzled as to why British Intelligence wanted to share this information with him.

Van Os continued, 'There appears to be a pattern of recent sea floor volcanic activity stretching in a wide arc from Iceland to the Canaries. Isolated low-level seismic readings have been detected in areas where there was no known record of such activity. A British navy destroyer, HMS *Barnes*, and a government research vessel are on their way to investigate the northern end of the line. As Ireland has jurisdiction over the part of the continental shelf around Rockall, we want to propose a joint investigation effort. Hence my approach to you, as you're responsible for the deployment of resources in that neck of the woods, so to speak.'

He knows more than I do thought Gilmore. As it happened, the Irish Government's marine research vessel, the RV *Celtic Explorer*, was preparing for a scheduled four-week research programme. It would be ready to set sail in the general direction of Rockall within days.

Van Os, who had earlier briefed his senior contact in the Irish navy, was aware of this.

'What's your request?' said Gilmore.

'I understand you're planning a short scientific voyage to test the salinity levels of the columns of sub-sea water that power the Gulf Stream.'

'Yes,' said Gilmore. He found it hard to lie to anyone. He does know a lot thought Gilmore. Be careful he told himself. This guy is as slippery as an eel.

Van Os leaned forward in his chair.

'Best you continue with that research. No reason why both activities can't proceed simultaneously.'

'Both?'

'Here's the nub of it,' said van Os. 'We want you to take a three-person manned submersible and supporting technicians and sail to the locations where recent seismic activity has been recorded. I'm told that the RV *Celtic Explorer* has the capacity to house both a remotely operated vehicle and a manned submersible. Correct?'

'Well, yes, but it will be a bit of a squeeze.'

'We've borrowed a manned submersible that's designed to do the work required from our American friends. It lands in Shannon Airport the day after tomorrow. It will be quayside at the RV *Celtic Explorer* in Galway Harbour by the end of the week.'

'That's impressive. What's the rush?' said Gilmore in a surprised tone.

Van Os touched his goatee beard as he eyed a clearly engaged Chief Scientist.

'Professor, we've grave concerns, on the basis of the initial evidence to hand, that a partial collapse of the eastern side of the Irish Continental Shelf resulting from increasing volcanic activity could cause tsunamis that would hit the western coast of Ireland within sixty minutes and the whole of the British Isles within ninety minutes. A risk of this significance makes it a matter of national security. I need not tell you what would happen if a calamity of that magnitude occurred. Hence, all the cloak and dagger stuff. We need to find evidence as to whether the current levels of volcanic activity are likely to stabilise or increase in intensity. Either way we need eyes on the ground – or in this case, the seabed – and that's where you and your colleagues on the RV *Celtic Explorer* come in.'

Gilmore was quite taken aback. No wonder the British wanted the matter kept under wraps.

'I should add that you will be accompanied by an Irish naval vessel. I've already spoken to the Chief of the Defence Forces who has approved the mission. That means we'll be able to use secure communication lines to our geological-monitoring satellite assets and deploy additional resources if so required.'

'That seems to make sense,' conceded Gilmore.

'Once on location, we'll provide you and the manned submersible team with live encrypted feed from the Skynet Six satellite. Let me show you.'

Van Os opened his laptop and typed in his password code sequence. The screen lit up.

Gilmore could see in 3D format small but readable measurements of seismic activity indicated by a red mark tracer over a long longitudinal area, just as van Os had described. On another screen, the powerful infrared features of the satellite revealed outline features of the sea floor as if it were daylight. He could see sea-floor valleys and the steep slopes to the west of the Porcupine Bank, the area around the Rockall Plateau and the Rockall Bank and out as far as the Eriador Seamount. Gilmore wasn't aware that technology had advanced so far as to facilitate a real time view of the topography of the sea floor. He tried to hide his amazement.

'Can you zoom in to the Eriador Seamount, please?'

As van Os moved the cursor, the key features of the Eriador Seamount began to appear in more detail. What was initially a vague shape emerged from the depths as the satellite's lens focused. The sloped plains to the west of the Eriador Seamount were clearly visible as were the broad outlines of the rocky crags that formed the easterly part of this ancient volcanic structure that was some one hundred kilometres long in a north-south direction.

'It's like Google maps but with more definition,' said Gilmore. He was genuinely astonished at the level of detail provided.

Van Os smiled. He had landed his fish with the bait of the latest in infrared technology.

'Is there anything else I should know?' asked Gilmore.

'A few more points of detail. I will be assigning Jonathan Drew, a colleague from London HQ and an Irish citizen to be our Liaison Officer. Johnny, as he likes to be called, will be based on the Irish navy corvette that's being assigned to the project. If you need to contact me do so through Johnny. He is my eyes and ears on the mission and is acting on my direct authority. You might also let your people know that the Prime Minister will call your Taoiseach tomorrow afternoon to talk to him about our operational requirements and how best the two teams might collaborate and share whatever results emerge. Your own minister is being briefed as we speak. And finally, under no circumstances are you to let the captain, the crew of the RV *Celtic Explorer* and the Irish researchers on board know the true purpose of the voyage until you are ready to set sail. As they say: be economical with truth.'

'As you can appreciate, I will not be taking instructions from you Mr van Os. But it seems you have set up this operation in anticipation that we'll cooperate,' said Gilmore firmly.

'Exactly. And by the way we're calling this operation Project Eriador.'

'So be it. You will excuse me then.'

They shook hands politely as professionals do.

Gilmore got over the shock of such a direct and arguably aggressive approach quite quickly. He knew he had a job of great importance to attend to. He left the embassy by a side door and sat in his car to gather his thoughts. His first decision was that he had no option but to sail with the RV *Celtic Explorer*. His plans to take a few days off with his wife would have to be cancelled.

From his encrypted car phone he contacted his minister to express his concerns only to be instructed in polite but in no uncertain terms to do everything possible to facilitate Project Eriador. The minister told him that the project had the strong personal backing of the British Prime Minister and the Irish Government. Van Os knew how to pull the levers of access. Gilmore was reluctantly impressed.

The short drive to his office gave him a bit of time to think through the calls he had to make given the unambiguous instructions from his Minister. The first was to Julie Motherway, the Chief Executive of the Marine Institute, as she was directly responsible for the crew of the RV *Celtic Explorer* and the setting of the project briefs for all the ship's research voyages. She accepted that this unusual request would have to be accommodated, admitting that the minister's office had already been in contact to mark her card. She undertook to call the ship's captain but not to go into too much detail as Gilmore would brief him when he arrived aboard.

His second phone call was to Barry Carew, a close personal friend and fellow alumni of Trinity College's Science Department. They had known each other for the best part of forty years as their careers developed. Carew was head of the research team at the Office for Weather in the National Oceanic and Atmospheric Administration, based in Washington DC. NOAA specialised in predicting and analysing high impact weather events. Under Carew's careful supervision, NOAA controlled a series of low orbit GOES-17 Series geo-stationary satellites that generated real-time 3D images of severe weather patterns anywhere on the planet.

'I was expecting the call, Gerdy. I was told a few hours ago that the British were in a bit of bother about recent sea floor seismic readings along your side of the Irish Continental Shelf. They need access to our assets. We never say "No" to anyone we've a "special relationship" with.'

'Do you intend to travel?' asked Gilmore.

'I've already bought my ticket and expect to be in Shannon tomorrow evening.'

'That's quick off the blocks!'

'I would never refuse an official invitation to visit Ireland. Or in this case offshore Ireland,' said Carew.

Gilmore probed his friend. 'What are you hearing? Are the Brits over-reacting?'

'On the contrary. Our satellites have picked up remote instances of low-level seafloor seismic activity for several months. That's quite normal as you know. However, last week we got more than we bargained for. As a Russian nuclear submarine passed one of the seabed sonar detectors on the Maury Channel, to the west of the Eriador Seamount, a 2.8 Richter scale event was recorded. This was followed within days by severe aftershocks. The Brits, and indeed you guys, need to check out what is happening. The only way to do that's to dive to the locations where there has been seismic activity to check out the extent of the problem.'

'Hmm. I was worried you'd say something like that. What's the story with the manned submersible?' asked Gilmore.

'Luckily, we've just completed a complete re-fit of one of our state-of-the-art manned submersibles. It came out of the navy dockyard at Pensacola last week. I was about to assign it to support research off the Hawaii islands when I was alerted to the situation at the Irish Continental Shelf. So, instead of packaging and flying it to Honolulu, it is being prepared for a military airlift to Shannon Airport along with its operator and support technicians.'

'Who will crew it at such short notice?'

'I don't know exactly, but phone calls are being made to one of your universities to source an oceanographer and a specialist in volcanology. I'll know more in the morning. What is more important is a GOES-17 Series satellite has been assigned to me for the duration of Project Eriador. It has the capacity to produce colour enhanced infrared images as well as water vapour images. I wouldn't have gotten the green light on this if the powers that be in NOAA didn't believe the Brits.'

Gilmore was glad his lifelong friend was going to join him. They had a strong bond since their college days. They had shared beers, banter, books and even the occasional girlfriend. Carew was more than a good friend. He trusted him. And as Carew was taking personal responsibility for the deployment of his assets who was he to question the bona fides of the planned mission.

'The good news is that we can share a whiskey or two over the coming weeks. I'll stock up at the duty free.'

'Yes, a bottle or two of Bushmills Black Bush would be nice. Bon Voyage.'

CHAPTER 2

Faro de Fuencaliente

HIKERS OF ALL SKILL levels were attracted to the pear-shaped island of La Palma because the mountain trails were clearly sign-posted, well-worn and attractive to tourists who wanted to walk during the summer months at an altitude that meant the temperatures were more comfortable for hiking. The island's tourism office advertised a series of interlinked walking routes that criss-crossed the interior of the small island that was just twenty-eight kilometres across. Hardcore hikers of all nationalities and ages had multiple trails that tested their stamina and footing.

The Hotel Taburiente, located a few kilometres south of the island's capital Santa Cruz de la Palma, was abuzz with activity. Over a hundred people packed the reception area. The buffet breakfast of Spanish omelettes, freshly squeezed oranges, cheese, frittatas and fried meats of dubious origin was long forgotten. Meeting their guides and getting on the road (and up the mountains) was everyone's priority.

This was Damian's third day with this walking group. To avoid the rush, and so that he could be heard amidst the loud chatter, he had assembled them around a tourist desk away from the main entrance. He started his briefing.

'Our coach will take us from the hotel to the starting point at the Visitors' Centre of the Volcán San Antonio, near the village of Los Canarios.'

'Are we doing the volcano walk today?' Judith, one of the walking group, asked the obvious question.

She was tall and strong, evidence of her athletic lifestyle, and holder of many medals for orienteering in her native county of Wiltshire. She was the unofficial leader of the group from the Malmesbury Hiking Club, judging by the respect her friends gave her. They clearly valued her opinions.

'Yes, we are,' said Damian. 'We call this trail the *Ruta de los Volcanes*. This is the famous seven volcanoes walk and probably the best the island has to offer. While most hikers start in the north at the Caldera de Taburiente and walk thirty kilometres south, I've decided to do something a bit different as it will better test your skills and stamina. En route you'll see huge craters, lava tongues, volcanic desert conditions and banana plantations along the coast. It's a walk that rivals Tenerife's Las Cañadas or Lanzarote's Timanfaya. This should be the highlight of your holiday. Let me show you what to expect.'

The group of fourteen gathered around in a wide circle to see the map and the display of photos that were numbered and annotated with key signposts. Damian's 1:80,000 map of the island that was spread out over the desk was his bible. Over the years he had added his own notes and notations about local conditions. Photography was his passion. He had images of all the mountain paths and used these to show his clients what to expect before they began their treks.

A founding member of the La Palma Ramblers' Association, he knew the importance of not just knowing the lie of the land but how to navigate along the mountain ridges, forest tracks, volcanic craters and cones as weather conditions changed – as they did all too frequently. He also had to be acutely aware of the different skills levels of those in his charge.

'This will be a trek in every sense of the word. It is downhill from the starting point. We've a four hour walk ahead of us. I intend to do it in three slow, easy stages.'

Pointing to the coloured photo on the left he said: 'Here is the view of the crater of the Volcán San Antonio. During stage one, we'll visit the observation deck high on the top of the volcano. In parts, the path is very narrow, no more than two metres wide. A railing will help you with your balance. Once we descend further along, we'll pass by Volcán Teneguia; that's to the right of the trail. It is a riot of colour with its rim a blaze of mauve, cream and orange gravel. It erupted in 1971 – and has been inactive since I should add. Walking conditions will deteriorate in this area as the surface is loose stones and fine ash gravel for the most part. The good news is that the decline is very manageable all the way to the exit of the volcano field, three kilometres above Faro de Fuencaliente. All going well, we'll have a late lunch there before the coach collects us in the mid-afternoon.'

Some of the more eager members of the group started to move off.

'Just double check that you've all your kit as we'll be over four hours on the mountain,' said Damian. 'It will be a clear day until the early afternoon but very windy, so come prepared. And Judith, there is no need to fret about lunch. I took the precaution and asked the hotel last night to provide everyone with sandwiches, fruit and water.'

'That's great,' whispered Judith to her friend.

Damian suspected that she had taken a big shine to him. After seven years as a professional mountain guide on La Palma his rugged looks, tanned physique and Roman nose seemed to attract the more active twenty-something young women that preferred mountain hiking to sunny beaches.

'All set?'

He didn't need a response. They all had the full gear: long trousers to dissuade the mosquitos and ticks, faces well protected with high factor sun cream, the latest designer backpacks with multiple pockets for water containers and maps, army-standard walking boots, thick socks, light rain-proof jackets, gloves, bottles of filtered water, wide-brimmed hats – some declaring support for their football team, self-adjusting alpine walking poles, cameras – many with DLSR features, and essentials such as food, insect repellent and sun block. A small army duly provisioned.

'Any more questions?'

No more needed to be said. The walkers had done their own homework. They all had maps and knew what conditions to expect. They were in a state of eager anticipation.

Damian's company, Palma Walks, a family business, had grown to become one of the most popular on the island. Consistent high ratings with Trip Advisor, not unrelated to his very sociable personality, provided Damian and his business partner and fellow guide, Margarida, with a good living during the nine-month tourist season. What Judith and his other female admirers didn't realise was that they were happily married.

Before they got on the coach, he phoned Margarida on his mobile. She was leading a large group of twenty German walkers who were staying in self-catering casitas near the southern coast.

'Cherie, we're doing the south *Ruta* trek today,' said Damian. 'Where are you going?'

'Cherie' was his pet name for Margarida: a term of endearment. He rarely called her by her Christian name unless he was grumpy or had something urgent or important to communicate.

'My group is not as fit as yours,' replied Margarida. 'So, I'm taking them around the base of the Caldera de Taburiente. They seem more interested in fauna and flora than walking over rocks and lava. We'll be on the move within the hour. I expect we'll be able to join you for a late lunch at the lighthouse at Fuencaliente.'

'Weather conditions appear to be stable, so I expect it will be a routine day,' said Damian.

'See you for an early Aperol around three o'clock. Ciao.'

The one weakness Damian and Margarida shared was their daily treat of Aperol. The Italian aperitif made from bitter and sweet oranges was quite nice on its own. When local Cava was added, the worries of the day disappeared after a few glasses.

What a wonderful woman thought Damian. He was blessed that the love of his life shared his passion for walking, photography and good wine.

The coach reached the car park at the Volcán San Antonio Visitors' Centre just after 9 a.m. as the facility was opening to the general public. As Damian did with all groups about the set off on a mountain walk, he called them together beside the coach.

'Let's assemble in the café of the Visitors' Centre so that I can brief you in more detail. Our starting point is just to the left side of the Centre. I can't start a walk without my obligatory double espresso!'

'What should we expect today, Damian?' asked Judith, who was clearly keen to get started.

Damian knew that this walk was one of the most popular, but also one of the most challenging given the steep descent of over a thousand metres to their final destination, the abandoned lighthouse at Faro de Fuencaliente. He dunked his ginger biscuit into the bitter tasting coffee as he eyed the eager group, who ranged from their late teens to a couple who had just retired.

'The hike is over seven kilometres long. Given that you all seem quite fit and managed the Caldera de Taburiente valley trek yesterday without a bother, it should be manageable within four hours. The good news is that there is a great restaurant at the Faro – that's Spanish for lighthouse by the way – so we can have a late lunch once we arrive. As I explained back in the hotel, we'll trek up to the peak of the Volcán San Antonio first. From the viewing platform you will get stunning views of the south side of the island, including the vineyards and banana plantations of Las Indias at sea level.'

'Is this an active volcano?' Judith continued.

'No, it last erupted in 1677. The only damage it did

was that the lava buried the revered holy spring of Fuenta Santa that flowed out at the lighthouse. This spring is believed to be the origin of the name Fuencaliente (hot spring).'

'Alright,' said Judith.

'The walk to the observation deck is narrow and it will be windy, so we'll need to be careful. If any of you have vertigo this walk will test how bad it is.'

The group managed the short side trip in under thirty minutes. There were a few heart flutters as strong winds lashed the sides of the steep volcano walls and buffeted the walkers on the two-metre-wide path along the rim to the observation deck at the top of Volcán San Antonio. As Damian had predicted braving the vertiginous path was rewarded by stunning scenery. Their cameras and videos captured the vista along the sheer slopes of the western escarpment down to the town of Puerto Naos.

They re-assembled at the Visitors' Centre café. Many had a precautionary rest break before descending the GR131. There were no toilets on the *Ruta*.

The first part of the descent wasn't easy. It tested everyone's fitness and dexterity. The alpine poles provided balance over the uneven path down irregular steps. The path that started to the left of the car park comprised ash dust that had the consistency of soft sand over a base of jagged and stepped volcanic rocks. Within twenty minutes they had descended 300 metres. They stopped to gather their collective breath. More selfies were taken.

Four walkers, French from their accents, arrived from the opposite direction and started without hesitation up the steep path back towards the Visitors' Centre.

'Good decision Damian to suggest we go down and not up,' said Judith. 'They must be exhausted having hiked up from the lighthouse at sea level.'

'They look fit enough,' replied Damian. 'That said, mistakes are usually made when legs are tired and when calves ache. Let's go. The next section is along a flattish track that 4x4s can use.'

The group didn't need any encouragement. Once told what to do they sauntered off in single file. There were short stops, more photo opportunities, as the scenery was quite unlike what they had experienced over the past days. The desert-like terrain had no tree cover and there were numerous cinder cones speckled with isolated bushes that somehow managed to survive in these exposed harsh conditions.

'We'll divert down here. It is a short cut to the Roques de Tenenguia. This hunk of rock is not large but is a prominent landmark.' said Damian. 'It's ideal for all you camera enthusiasts.'

Many photos later they re-joined the GR131 and zig-zagged over a narrow ash path in the direction of Volcán de Teneguia. Damian halted the group a hundred metres in front of the volcano. At this stage they had been walking for just under two hours.

'Anyone interested in climbing a volcano? Not every-one will be able, but those of you who are can climb the stupendously high left-hand narrow rim of the island's most recent volcano. The deep brown colour rocks may be pretty, but they still emit hot gases.'

'Are you sure it is safe?' Judith asked – another obvious question.

'Absolutely. This volcano has been inactive since it erupted in November 1971. Two vents along a 300-metre fissure emitted lava to a depth of 12 metres in some places. The eruption ceased abruptly.'

'Why?' asked Judith.

'To be honest, I don't know. The lava flows stopped a few hundred metres away on this side of the mountain, see the limit of the brown ridges over there, but flowed down to the sea – so much so that over two square kilometres of lava were added to the island. It was a short eruption that lasted a few days. Only one person was killed. A fisherman who inhaled the sulphur gases. Since then nada.'

As they were fidgeting with their provisions, it was clear to Damian the group had limited interest in volcanoes.

'OK, let's have our picnic here. We're more than half-way to our final destination.'

Many sandwiches, protein bars and apples later, and all rubbish carefully returned to the rucksacks, the group descended past one of the secondary craters and onwards to a somewhat level pathway that was carved through the remnants of the 1971 eruption. It was eerie walking in between twenty-metre tall lava pillars. Shortly afterwards the path started its slow but steady descent to the sea.

'A glass of cava for the first person to catch a glimpse of the lighthouse,' said Damian, in a jest that was designed to lighten the mood and distract attention from heavy legs and ankles under pressure.

The group was crossing the narrow ridge just beyond Volcán de Teneguia when the first mild tremor started.

Judith was a few metres directly behind Damian,

walking slowly given the rough terrain that passed for a footpath. She screamed. Everyone gasped.

Damian too was startled. He had never experienced an earthquake, never mind one on a mountain ridge just four metres wide with severe drops on both sides.

'Sit down,' he shouted. Sit down now,' he roared. All obeyed, instantly.

The light gravel around them shimmered and jumped, but no ground shifted. The black ash dust rose slowly and eerily. The track remained stable.

'I know it wasn't in the brochure, but that was a seismic tremor.' He smiled with confidence and that seemed to bring about an element of calm.

'What do we do?' asked Judith.

'Just in case there is another aftershock, I suggest we remain seated for a while.'

On cue, the second tremor arrived. It rolled through in a matter of seconds. There was no panic as they were all seated on the ground and somewhat prepared. Being covered head to toe in a film of black ash didn't spook them too much. However, they were all clearly apprehensive.

Dust particles from the gravel track and along its length rose some metres into the air. It was strange to see a hazy cloud of red and orange dust appear and then dissipate in the breeze as if it was instructed to vanish.

'Honestly, this is the first time I've ever experienced tremors on the mountain. I'm assuming there may be more aftershocks at some stage.'

He could see that the group was getting increasingly agitated exposed as they were on the high and open ridge.

Initial calm was being replaced by growing apprehension. What had happened began to sink in.

'It's best that we continue to descend slowly,' said Damian. 'It's less than an hour downhill to the Fuencaliente lighthouse. Once we get off this ridge the track is well defined, wider and far less rocky for the most part. If there is another tremor you know the drill: sit down, keep calm and observe your surroundings.'

Dusting themselves off, and with determined strides, the group did what they were told. While the small tremors had everyone startled, the landscape around them was stark and remarkable. The trail meandered through a series of undulating small black hills windswept clean. In the far distance the red and white tip of the lighthouse, their end destination, was, figuratively as well as literally, a beacon surrounded by the ocean's spray.

When the GR131 met the main road above the lighthouse they abandoned the walking trail for the security of tarmac. There was another gentle tremor when they were two hundred metres from the lighthouse. This caused the group to stop, but as the shaking was barely perceptible a sense of self-preservation took them forward.

Damian knew Margarida would be at the lighthouse with her group. He was eager to compare notes.

Margarida's German group were also taken by surprise. While they were on a small rise in the National Park, the first of the two tremors loosened a lot of ash off the steep banks on both sides of the road they were walking on. The result was an avalanche of black soot that covered everyone and dimmed the sunlight. They panicked and scattered in a disorganised manner. Despite Margarida's best attempts at keeping them together, instinct kicked in. Without any prompting the group made its way back to the car park in rapid time. They lost their interest in any more walking and once on the coach were not shy in telling Margarida that their holiday was over.

The two groups ate their pre-booked lunch in shocked silence at the Faro de Fuencaliente 'El Jardin de la Sal' Café in front of the red and white lighthouse. They tried to forget what had happened. Bottled water washed down a variety of cheese and ham sandwiches, bananas and fritatas borrowed from the hotel buffet.

Damian and Margarida sat at their usual table, in a corner out of hearing of their respective clients. They treated themselves to a plate of La Palma soft cheese with coriander and marmalade sauce. The plat du jour was swordfish steak in parsley sauce. The Aperol did the business.

'Claudine phoned me a short time ago.'

'Where is she?' asked Damian about his niece.

'She and Maria were at their research station when the first seismic reading came in,' said Margarida. 'Claudine said that while the tremors were below two on the Richter scale, they were very shallow and as a consequence affected most of the island.'

'Goodness! What next?' said Damian, puzzled.

'Claudine is in touch with the Rodriquez brothers who are based at the Caldera de Taburiente. They are monitoring seismic activity too, but also unusual sulphur dioxide data. She promised to phone me this evening with an update. Today's walks are over. We'll have to do a rain check – or should we call it an 'ash check' – tomorrow and maybe in the days ahead. My German group will be on the first flight out of here in the morning, if they can get it.'

'We better get our troops back to their hotels. The buses have arrived.'

On the short walk to the car park eyes were drawn to the high mountain trail that they had descended not an hour previously. As the tremors had loosened the earth, a deep but low cloud of black and brown ash particles hovered in the air. It still covered the entire width of the mountain to a height of about fifty metres.

The video cameras were out. What the pictures showed was a weird phenomenon. The dust ascended and descended like a flock of swallows at dusk swirling in thick and varying patterns before the strong winds scattered the evidence.

Summit Station

The Summit Station was the only high-altitude, inland, year-round multi-disciplinary observation station devoted to science in the Arctic. The facility was located on the apex of the Greenland Ice Sheet at an altitude of over 3,000 metres.

Greenland, nearly four times the size of France with just 56,000 inhabitants, is the world's largest island. Some 95 per cent of the land mass is covered in ice so Greenlanders, mostly native Inuits, as well as a fair share of Danes, whose Government still controls and subsidises large parts of the economy, inhabit the coastal areas. The Inuits, the first Arctic explorers, are hunters, an ice age, ice-adapted people with a boreal culture. Their mind is sharpened by vulnerability. It shows them how to live.

Ice is what Inuits long for and love. They call their country 'Kalaallit Nunaat', the White Earth. Erik the Red, the Viking who was expelled by his family from Iceland in the year 986 had a clear sense of humour when he named the territory 'Greenland' in an attempt to persuade his clansmen to migrate and inhabit this new land. The sixth-century Irish monk, Saint Brendan, used an ox hide covered willow boat to search for an island sanctuary far to the west, where he might set up new monasteries. He described his first sighting of an iceberg as 'a floating crystal castle the colour of a silver veil, yet hard as marble, and the sea around it was smooth as glass and as white as milk.'

The Summit Station facility was based just inside the southern boundary of the North-East Greenland National Park. Built in 1988 by the USA's National Science Foundation, initially to house the Greenland Deep Ice Core Project that drilled to the base of the ice sheet far below, its remit expanded over the years and it now supported a wide range of research activities, including meteorology, glaciology, astrophysics and atmospheric chemistry. Senior researchers from Denmark, Norway and many European countries work alongside their US counterparts, all ably assisted by eager young undergraduate students.

The current summer population was thirty-two. The five permanent residents, hardy souls, the core boys as they called themselves, did two-month rotations throughout the year.

During the summer months sub-zero temperatures were made worse as strong winds increased the wind chill factor. The Summit Station had long challenged the physical fitness of its research community.

Access was provided by a Hercules C-130 military-standard aircraft operated by the New York National Guard 109th Airlift Wing. The C-130 transported light equipment, general cargo and personnel from Ilulissat Airport, some two hours flying time due east. Two ski-equipped Twin Otter aircraft operated by Norland Air were also used to transport personnel to the remote and smaller research stations such as Eismitte and the Zackenberg Station to the north-east whose work was coordinated by the Summit Station. The aircraft were also used for aerial photography. The snow runway, twenty metres wide and 1,500 metres long was groomed by two Bombardier B2 model ski-cats before every flight to remove surplus snow and to facilitate the ski-equipped aircraft. Tall red topped poles delineated the parameters of the landing zone. The Summit Station had just taken delivery of three high-powered two-person Yamaha snowmobiles. These latest toys were being tested for short duration assignments.

A dog sledge team comprising a dozen eager huskies was available for shorter trips within a five-kilometre range of the Summit Station. The huskies were smaller in stature and more fine-boned than their Alaskan counterparts. They had the same shaped head, ears and up-turned tail. Given the elevation of the facility, the use of the huskies was new and experimental. The basic idea was that the sledge used no fossil fuel and was therefore climate friendly. However, the effort required to feed, manage and water the huskies had been underestimated.

The fact that they barked incessantly night and day didn't endear them to the Summit's residents. When they slept in the used packing crates provided, they did so with their noses tucked under their tails. All except the lead dog, the ginger-coloured 'boss' of the pack, who usually busied himself burying a bit of seal meat under the snow with his nose. He understood the concept of the future. The Inuit team in charge trained the pack and exercised them on a daily basis, not least because the dogs hated being tethered all the time. Once they realised they were going to be harnessed the pack yelped even louder with excitement. Each sledge was capable of dragging a load of 200 kilos of equipment and three people with ease. The Summit Station residents soon learned the key instructions:

ah ta ta ta ta ta (faster, go faster), *arittet* (stop), *haruuu, haruuu* (go right): and, *attuk, attuk* (go left). Once on the move, the driver limited use of a coiled 5.5-metre whip made from a single strip of seal hide.

The original building structures were designed to provide basic comforts over a short summer. The Big House, the centre of all social activity, consisted of a five-by twenty-metre elevated building, designed to minimise the impact of snow drifts, supported by ten poles. It housed the central meeting room, the base kitchen, dining area, communications office, bathrooms, showers and laundry facilities. The adjacent Green House comprised connected modules, including laboratories, a science room, a small kitchen, and the main living quarters of sixteen bedrooms for the senior researchers.

A sprawl of Arctic geodesic tents was constructed around the compound each summer season to accommodate the students who actually enjoyed spending their spare time on poorly funded research in sub-zero temperatures. The tents were self-supporting and once securely staked down they coped with strong winds, flexing to resume their normal shape. The guy lines were anchored by being attached to a bag filled with snow, which was buried where it quickly froze solidly into place. Inside was a wall-to-wall sheet of closed cell foam, which provided insulation from the underlying cold surface of the snow. The tents and other basic creature comforts are perfect for resilient, young and keen researchers.

Today, just twenty of the team were in the Big House for what was called 'the melt season'– the four summer months from June to September at the top of the world's largest ice sheet. Smaller two- to three-person teams were scattered over an area of 200 square kilometres making observations, including measuring meltwater flows and areas of dark ice, or low albedo.

Lars Brun opened the briefing session.

'These video images were taken yesterday by Phil Teahon on the north end of the Jacobshavn Glacier about fifty kilometres due north-east of Ilulissat.'

The day room in the Big House at the Summit Station was lit up by the large TV screen; it was the centre piece of the room. The screen showed in vivid colours a cascading thirty metre waterfall of pure blue ice water. The flow was intense. The glacial river was exploding, roaring and pounding the perimeter of the sinkhole.

Phil was fully equipped for the cold outdoors. He needed to be as the wind chill felt like minus ten degrees Celsius. He wore multiple layers under his black and white parka and had long thermals pants under his heavy trousers. His ski hat, goggles and cotton scarf kept his head protected. And the ski gloves he used every year in Colorado's skiing resorts were the final touch. Fully protected he could only be recognised by his perpetual smile. You needed to have a good sense of humour to endure the trials and tribulations at the top of the Greenland Ice Sheet.

Lars paused the presentation. He took another sip of the bitter Turkish coffee that only he had a taste for. It was his morning ritual. Some people exercised, but Lars made his coffee. Using a blend of arabica varieties he ground the beans to a fine powder using a grinder purchased while on a business trip to Ankara. He brought the mixture to the boil, added a spoon of demerara sugar and poured it into a traditional cezve coffee pot. Once frothed to his required taste Lars supped his nectar. He repeated the exercise as and when required during the mornings. No caffeine after midday for him.

The small group of scientists had seen similar images during the previous year's summer research programme but none as dramatic in terms of the strength of the flow of the meltwater.

'Something must be changing,' speculated Lars.

Alice Kidney, who was doing a second summer tour at the Summit Station as part of her studies at the Geology Department of the University of California in San Diego, chipped in. 'I was at that same location last year. It was a small crevasse with a low flow of meltwater. Now look.'

She used the pointer to highlight where the ice water fell sharply under the surface. 'It's barely recognisable. There was a small sinkhole of, perhaps, two metres with a slow ice-melt flow. And that was at the end of the summer. It seems that the area has ruptured in quite a pronounced way during the winter. If that's the case, what caused such a gaping hole? By the looks of it, Phil is observing the creation of a really deep chasm chamber.'

She was a clever student whose outgoing personality had identified her as a leader. She was never shy of asking questions. Unless she got an answer she understood the questioning would continue. Her level of inquisitiveness was like that of a small child discovering the world for the first time. A charming trait in a child but a bit over-powering in an adult student. Her casual multi-coloured attire mostly dated from the late 1960s. She wore her signature bright red knitted beanie all the time. She was a Bohemian spirit whose thesis on the formation of ice caverns had brought her to the attention of Lars as a potential research fellow. She survived on black tea and biscuits of various hues and shapes.

'We're seeing the same picture at most of the other locations where we're taking observations,' remarked Lars.

Lars switched the camera feed to Per Jan Landshurst, a colleague from the Geography Department of the University of Oslo in Norway who shared his passion for exploration and research. Per Jan was tall at over two metres and his strong beard and prominent features made him look quite distinguished, a trait Lars never noticed, he knew him so well. He and Lars had known each other since they attended kindergarten school in rural Norway deep inside the Arctic Circle. They played in the snow. They understood snow. They respected snow.

'Per Jan, we've just seen footage from Phil Teahon showing a huge deterioration in surface conditions. What's the story with you?' asked Lars.

Per Jan and his team were located some fifty kilometres due west of the Summit Station in an area that until recent years had not experienced any thawing. They were accommodated in temporary canvas tents for the week they expected to be on location. They were using one of the Station's Bombardier ski-cats for transport, storage of supplies and as a communications hub.

'More or less the same,' replied Per Jan. 'The chasm is not as developed as the one captured by Phil, but the ice-melt flow is at least double what it was this time last year. We need to assume the worst. There seems to be a uniform structural pattern of accelerated ice melt at all the locations we're monitoring.'

'I had a gut instinct that this was where we were going, Per Jan,' said Lars. 'So much so that I've made arrangements to do something quite radical to get to the bottom of this. Please return to the Summit Station as soon as you can. I will call all the teams back to base to discuss our approach for the remainder of our summer work programme.'

A week later the Big House was packed. There was a noticeable buzz that had much to do with the rumours circulating about a new research project. Many of the summer students had had enough of staying in a tent for weeks on end without wi-fi and with nothing to do but talk, listen to music on a crackling radio and play cards. The importance of the ice-melt flow readings was, of course, fully appreciated. But they yearned to do something different.

Lars had their full attention. He had hinted over the past days, through a throw away remark here and there, that the next phase of the Summit Station's work was imminent.

As the lead scientist, he called for attention.

'When we left the Summit Station last year there were clear signs of significant flows of ice water melting at all the locations we monitor. Initial inspections over the past weeks suggest the extent of ice melt activity has greatly accelerated even at this early stage in the season. Many surface areas are slushy for the first time.'

He paused for effect. He looked out across the room and saw that everyone was in eye contact. Perfect. He had their full attention.

'The Greenland Ice Sheet, along with its Antarctic counterpart, contains ten percent of the world's fresh water: some three-million cubic kilometres. If it all melted it would raise sea levels by over seven metres. Worse still, the flow of meltwater into the North Atlantic would probably stop the Gulf Stream: not good news for Northern European countries that have a temperate climate, at least for the time being.'

He supped his coffee, paused to draw his breath and then continued.

'We know already that Greenland's lower peripheral glaciers at sea level have lost most of their refreezing capacity. Most of the meltwater at the top of the ice sheet is contained in what is called the 'firn layer' – a hundred-metre thick layer of compressed snow that acts as an efficient buffer for the meltwater that's produced at the surface.'

'That layer seems to be melting away?' asked Alice.

'You're right, Alice.'

She smiled at him and he responded with a look that went beyond a formal acknowledgement. She knew she was one of his favourite students, despite her never ending questions.

Lars continued, 'The latest evidence from the microwave imagers on the Oceansat-2 satellite suggests it takes over a week between meltwater generation at the apex of the glacier and its discharge at the ice sheet's margins. I believe that this transition is in fact much shorter as deep rivers beneath us are hollowing out much of the ice sheet. The faster the speed of the transition the higher the probability that the ice sheet is fractured at multiple locations.'

The Summit Station scientists saw the reality of climate change every day and didn't need to be converted. Their job was to assess the pace and the impacts of the ice sheet melt. There was no dispute about the phenomenon. Yet there was limited evidence about what exactly was happening. NASA satellite images could not map the layers under the ice sheet. What happened a hundred metres below was largely a matter of speculation.

'Our research programme for this year is going to be quite different, thanks to a meeting I had – on a golf course of all places,' explained Lars. 'I met a guy – an Irishman – called Sean Pitcher at the Masters a few months ago. He and I have been in regular contact since. I believe we've found a unique way to do our work to better effect.'

Sean was dialled in on Skype Business. His face appeared on the large screen. He sat upright at his cluttered workstation with several colleagues peering over his shoulder.

Lars noted immediately that he wore the same maroon sports shirt as when they'd first met, as did his colleagues. A very relaxed approach to 'business casual', he thought.

'Team, this is Sean Pitcher, head of research at the Nova Marine Institute based in Oranmore, which is just outside Galway City in the west of Ireland. He and I bumped into each other at a certain sporting event I attended in late March in the USA.'

'Hi Sean. How's the game? I see you are still wearing your uniform!'

'Just middling Lars. I've not played a round of golf since we met. Besides it rains here a lot as you may be aware. I'm a fair-weather devotee of the game. Anyhow, you and your project have kept me and my team busy. Immediately after this call we're off to watch the Galway County Gaelic football team, hence the gear.'

'OK, let's get started, Sean. I haven't told my colleagues in any great detail about what you and I've been discussing over the past weeks. So please give us an update.'

All eyes were on the TV screen. Sean rubbed his ginger beard vigorously with his ruddy hands. A gesture he made when he wanted to settle his nerves before speaking.

'I've designed a golf ball with an in-built tracker device that has all the functions we discussed in Augusta. Here it is.'

Sean held a golf ball between his thumb and index finger.

'Neat, eh?'

'Sean, you might explain what you have done,' said Lars.

'This for all intents and purposes is a golf ball. But a golf ball with a difference. It has an external hard core that's resistant to severe impacts. It should not, if our tests prove accurate, crack or disintegrate if it hits hard rock, or indeed hard ice.'

Sean had barely got into his stride before he was interrupted.

'Sean, Alice Kidney here. How do you track these golf balls?'

Ever the eager student, Alice asked the obvious question.

'Alice, the prototype only had a basic electronic tracker device embedded. Lars persuaded me to add enhanced speed, height and distance reading features. This means when the golf ball enters the meltwater you will be able to track its progress – what I call its flow rate – as it descends through the ice sheet. Not only will you be able to monitor the speed of the descent but to plot its course until it stops moving, wherever that may be.'

'Pretty neat, if it works,' said Alice.

Lars had forewarned him to expect a robust question and answer session. Sean continued.

'Each ball has been implanted with a powerful microchip with an individual identity that can be linked to a satellite-based GPS platform such as Google Maps or a bespoke system that you might wish to use. It can also be tracked by a standard iPhone. I'll provide the unique frequency signals that will allow you track every golf ball. Tell us your precise requirements and we'll do what is necessary.'

'Lars briefed me about last year's communications upgrade at the Summit Station. You need high capacity broadband to link to the satellite that will be geo-tracking the golf balls.'

'But golf balls are hard and can't float.' Alice continued the cross-questioning after a short pause.

Lars was impressed with his star pupil's ability to probe the claims that were being made. Sean's patience was wearing a bit thin, however.

'Good question Alice,' he lied politely. 'When Lars gave me his specification it was easy enough to substitute the hard rubber compression that you find within a standard golf ball with a softer filler. In addition, we used a thinner 'Surlyn' hard resin outer mantle to reduce weight. Believe you me, the engineering involved in producing a high-performance golf ball that floats is quite complicated.'

'Sean, I'm more than impressed with your work,' said Lars. 'So much so that I would like to confirm the order of 1,000 of these wonderful devices.'

'I had assumed that, so we've already made the necessary arrangements to get production going,' replied Sean.

'Actually, we've re-calibrated the assembly line and production equipment. I reckon it will take us three weeks to manufacture and test and another week to get the materials to you on location. Plan for a delivery around the middle to the end of August.'

'Perfect. That timeline suits us Sean.'

'Before I sign off, I've two surprises for you Lars. I'm making no promises, but we're at the stage of advanced testing the option of inserting a camera feature into the golf ball. It's a bit more complicated, as you can imagine, but we'll try to supply you with twenty of these special devices. Should they work, not only will you be able to monitor the progress of the meltwater flow through the Ice Sheet, but hopefully you may be able to see what is happening deep within the ice.'

'Sean, if you can do that for us it could transform the value of our research. You're a star! I hope we can get a round in Galway Bay Golf Club in the autumn.'

Lars was more than comforted that Sean had a clear grasp of the brief.

'What's the second surprise?' said Lars.

'To honour your country, we'll print each ball with the red and blue flag of Norway. When they appear in the Greenland Sea, or wherever, it will be clear who put them there!'

'That's a lovely touch, Sean. You are a character!' said Lars.

'Just doing my job,' replied Sean.

'Let me know when you have everything ready. I need to arrange shipment to the Summit Station via Ilulissat airport – no easy task.'

'*Slán*, Lars.'

'Guys, that's the Gaelic for "goodbye",' said Lars by way of explanation to his colleagues.

'You're learning fast Lars. I'm impressed,' said Sean, with a wide grin.

The video link went dead before Lars could respond.

Sean was in a rush. He and his colleagues drove as quickly as they could to the GAA stadium in Salthill where his beloved Galway team were playing their arch-rivals Dublin in the quarter final.

Galway Harbour

'You'll have another one?' He could not see the barman behind the partition but knew the voice well.

Without a thought he replied, 'Sure, why not.' A few minutes later a hand appeared through a small service window and placed his pint on the wooden ledge beside him.

Enda Killen, a veteran sea captain, had plenty of time off between voyages. It was one of the perks of the job. When not at sea, his preferred form of relaxation was an afternoon drink or two in the back snug of Doheny's, a small family-owned pub on Shop Street, the main thoroughfare of Galway City in the West of Ireland. He liked Doheny's because, unlike most other public houses in the area, it was quiet – a fact not unrelated to its dilapidated state. There were empty beer kegs scattered everywhere and many were used as seats. The owner thought hygiene was an unnecessary luxury and his premises bore witness to that. The restrooms were basic at best. The proprietor's broken nose was indifferent to the many smells that blended in the air. He, like Killen, was set in his ways. He too didn't have a particular liking for people. A strange affliction for one whose livelihood depended on the goodwill of his customers. As a consequence, students and locals avoided the place. That suited Killen as, with one or two exceptions, he preferred his own company when drinking.

He had left school early to go to sea: an ambition shared by many of his friends in the small town of Spiddal at the edge of Connemara. It was a pretty coastal village that was home to some near-shore fishing trawlers. A short, physically-demanding stint as a crew member on one of these boats convinced him that he should move to a bigger vessel and study for his marine qualifications. His slight frame didn't suit the duties expected of a fisherman, where brawn was more important than brain. Hard work, long hours, practical experience gained and a risk-averse frame of mind saw him progress slowly but surely up the chain of command.

He looked the part and took pride in his appearance. If he could, he would wear his beloved captain's cap and uniform at home. He had a ruddy, freckled face that was weather beaten from years exposed to Atlantic gales, and almost sallow skin, thanks to constant exposure to the sun reflecting off the water. In his earlier career he had smoked like a trooper, but doctor's orders and an enlarging tummy convinced him that one of his bad habits had to stop. Captain Killen was comfortable in his own skin: until now.

In an exception to his daily routine he had invited his wife Orlaith to join him. He was so traditional in his views that he usually disapproved of women in pubs, never mind the privacy of the snug at Doheny's, which he had frequented for the best part of forty years. The snug was his refuge.

'Why am I here?' His wife was a straight talker.

She was an affable Mayo woman with a strong rural background who, unlike her husband, was extroverted and optimistic. She enjoyed company and being sociable. It was these characteristics that had attracted him to her.

Given his job, Killen knew he would be away sometimes for half the year, or on monthly rotations. He needed someone dependable to look after the children and their modest house in the outskirts of Galway. She didn't disappoint in that regard.

'The first time you brought me here was the time we went to see the movie *Grease*. I think you had a fancy for the young one, what was she called? Yes, Olivia Newton-John: I remember, see?'

Killen decided he had no option but to put his cards on the table before a predictable rant developed. Orlaith never stopped talking. He used to joke that she was vaccinated with a gramophone needle.

'As you know, the research vessel I captain does really routine stuff. I enjoy the work. It is a stress-free job navigating scientists around Irish waters. However, my next voyage has me puzzled and a bit apprehensive.'

'Puzzled? You? I've never known you to worry about work. Why?' His wife certainly cut to the chase. 'What's that got to do with my rare invitation into your downtown residence?'

Killen took a large single sup. Almost half the black and creamy contents of the glass disappeared. He loved his pint.

'I can't put my finger on it, but I've a sense of unease and foreboding about this trip. Call it my sailor's instinct, but I feel apprehensive and I never felt this way before. I feel it could be my last voyage.'

'You're not thinking of retiring? That would be awful! What would you do rattling around the house all day? Far better for both of us that you continue at sea.'

'No, you misunderstand. I'm worried I may not return. Would you miss me if I was lost at sea?' asked Killen.

'Don't be so melancholy Enda,' replied Orlaith, showing the sense of frustration she usually experienced if they discussed anything serious for any length of time.

'Sure. But remember my words should anything happen,' said Killen.

'You're being a bit melodramatic. Buy me a brandy and ginger and stop talking nonsense.'

'Barman, the usual for the wife please,' said Killen with a touch of irony.

The following morning, just after dawn, Killen was the first to board the RV *Celtic Explorer* – the Irish Government's multi-purpose ocean research vessel – at its berth on Mulvoy Quay, in Galway Harbour. At seventy-five metres in length, it could accommodate twenty-five crew and twenty scientists. The ship was equipped with a full complement of survey equipment, communications and navigation systems, dry and wet laboratories, cranes and winches suitable for coring, trawling and camera operations. It also had the latest dynamic positioning system that was critical for the deployment of the state-of-the-art remote operation vehicles (ROV) that were used for deep dive research activities. The vessel had been modified in a recent re-fit to facilitate the launch of both an ROV and a manned submersible. At sea the RV *Celtic Explorer* was a busy place with various research projects being carried out at all hours of the night and day. The crew and the scientists typically worked twelve-hour shifts.

He went to the galley, as he did early every morning to brew a pot of Barry's loose leaf tea. He poured the tea through a strainer into a china cup, one of his small luxuries. A drop of milk, no sugar. Perfect! He climbed the steps to the bridge and sat on the captain's chair. This seat was the centre of activity when at sea and it had the best view possible when in harbour. He watched as Galway woke to a new day. He loved the peace and quiet of the early morning.

He looked out forlornly across the harbour and further to Mutton Island and the expanse of Galway Bay. There was a light wind and good visibility to the far horizon. This was where he felt most comfortable. The harbour was small – it served a regional hinterland – but had all the modern facilities, including a heavy-duty mobile crane, tugs and storage. The Port of Galway Company gave the RV *Celtic Explorer* first preference as Galway Harbour was its home base. Killen and the Harbour Master were drinking buddies in Doheny's, so he usually got what he asked for.

The day before he had studied the mission brief on the conduct of seawater salinity tests with growing concern. Its contents prompted the conversation with his wife in Doheny's. He was suspicious. An experienced mariner with twenty years' experience with the Irish Marine Institute, and before that in ships of varying characteristics and sizes all over the world, he knew this voyage was going to be quite different. Over the past days, not only had new scientific instruments been loaded, in sealed unlabelled cases but the usual mix of Irish scientists and young enthusiastic marine researchers had been replaced by new older faces and, judging by their accents, they came from several countries.

Also, without consultation, two burly new crew members had been added to the passenger manifest. With their casual clothes, they looked more like boxers than sailors. In fact, he wasn't too wide off the mark. They were experienced (and armed) navy marines as he would soon discover. Two other uniformed and armed navy marines stood guard at the gangway to the ship. All very strange. This was a research vessel not a navy ship.

Someone – he was told not to ask questions – had installed an upgraded communications package the previous week. The perennial problem they'd had with poor internet connectivity over many years had been resolved in less than a day. Bandwidth was no longer an issue.

'Why all this investment?' he wondered.

He was due to sail on the full tide the following afternoon and so had limited time to get the vessel ship shape.

A crew member approached him. 'The Chief Scientist, Professor Gerard Gilmore, has boarded and wants to speak to you.'

He wasn't on the passenger manifest either, nor did he know why he wasn't told about his presence. As a point of principle, he ignored his mobile phone when not on active duty and never checked his voice messages, so had missed the call the evening before from the Marine Institute's Chief Executive that would have alerted him to the arrival of his VIP passenger. He didn't know Gilmore but had seen him on television whenever there was a scientific problem that needed a plausible explanation. The puzzle got ever more mysterious.

'Thanks. Please bring him to the bridge after he settles in.'

Gilmore was brought to his quarters, a small functional single berth cabin – the only suite on board – and, having unpacked quickly, he made his way the bridge.

'Can I have a quiet word, Captain? Preferably in your cabin,' said Gilmore.

'Sure, come with me,' replied Killen.

Killen's cabin – located directly under the bridge – was also modest. He had a small desk, TV and a bookcase where he stored his precious library of books and maps. The walls were decorated by the ensigns of the many ports the ship had visited.

'Sit down please, Professor. To what do I owe the pleasure of your company? Cup of tea?'

'No thanks, Captain. Call me 'Gerdy' as we're going to on board for quite a few weeks.'

'I gather.'

The Professor opened a map on the table showing the eastern side of the Atlantic Ocean.

'I'm afraid that I can't tell you much more than what is in your mission brief.'

He put his finger at a point that was circled in red. 'We're to sail around four hundred kilometres due west to the edge of the Irish Continental Shelf, beyond the Hatton Bank to the Eriador Seamount, south-west of the Rockall Plateau.'

Rockall, whose ownership was still a matter of dispute between Ireland and Scotland, was a Norse name meaning 'spraying stormy sea'. It was a single rock atop a vast submerged plateau, some four hundred kilometres in length. The waters around Rockall are relatively shallow at between five hundred and a thousand metres. It is separated from Scotland by the three kilometres deep Rockall Trough.

'We'll be operating along the one-hundred-kilometre-long mountain that comprises the Eriador Seamount.'

'Why the Eriador Seamount?' asked Killen.

Gilmore explained. 'It's an extinct underwater volcano. The seismic activity around this area is the main focus of the mission. I know you were planning a short research voyage to test seawater salinity levels at more or less the same location. These experiments can proceed but the main job at hand is quite different.'

'I just knew something was up,' said Killen.

His instinct had been right. A knot started in his stomach as his anxiety mounted.

'We won't be returning to port until the scientific observations that I've been asked to supervise have been completed,' added Gilmore, in a by-the-way fashion.

'I should also tell you that the naval vessel LÉ *Michael D. Higgins* will rendezvous with us once we're clear of the coast and will escort us to our destination.'

'I never had a navy escort in all my life,' laughed Killen nervously. 'And what about the equipment and the strangers that I've taken on board?'

'At this stage, I'm not at liberty to tell you more than you and your crew need to know to get us to the first identified rendezvous. Be prepared not to ask too many questions in the meantime. I've hand-picked the scientists and will look after that side of things. I assume we can rely on you, Captain, to do the sailing bit of the business.'

'All a bit of a mystery, but that's in order. I will talk to the crew.' Killen was frustrated by the lack of information. He accepted that there was nothing he could do about it.

Within the hour Killen briefed his small team of senior officers as they stood around the worktable that was the centrepiece of the bridge.

His Chief Engineer, Vinnie Crowley from the seaport of Malahide, a prosperous suburb north of Dublin, was less than impressed that a two-month mission was in prospect. He stood out with his shock of thick blond curly hair. He was the tallest person on board at almost two metres. As the ship's ceilings were not designed for his height, he spent most of the time he was indoors in a crouched position. He and the regular crew of the RV *Celtic Explorer* were used to shorter scientific trips of no longer than a month. Like Killen, he was also uncomfortable with so many new faces settling into their quarters in the lower and mid-sections of the ship.

'Captain, the vessel is at its limits; we're packed to the rafters. Should I install bunks on deck?'

His poor attempt at humour went unnoticed.

'Vinnie, there is not much I can do about it,' said Killen. 'My hope is that we're not stuck in the middle of the Atlantic for an even longer period.'

The chef spoke. He was a man who clearly liked to taste what he cooked. 'But we're not provisioned for a long voyage captain. I only have four week's supplies.'

'I asked that question and was told the Irish naval vessel that will join us once we cast off is fully stocked with fuel and supplies for six months.' responded Killen.

Crowley muttered and growled as he tried to digest the information. 'What's the weather forecast?' he said.

Gilmore responded and tried to sound confident. 'Not too bad over the coming week, with two to three-metre swells but, as you know all too well, we can't be certain beyond that. It may be the middle of summer, but we should be prepared for the worst.'

'Jesus, I fear we're in for a long haul,' said Crowley, as he filled his pipe expertly for his second smoke of the day. The more agitated he was, the more he smoked. The ship's rule was that smoking wasn't allowed, except for the habit of the Chief Engineer, a veteran smoker since his teens, and only on the bridge near the aft door.

'Aye to that,' said Killen.

There was a routine to be completed before every research voyage and the crew knew their respective roles and responsibilities. Machinery had to be repaired. The sonar equipment was re-calibrated. The laboratories, stores and works areas had to be restocked and provisioned. The winches were oiled and tested. They got on with the tasks to hand unsupervised.

Twenty-four hours before the scheduled departure a large transport truck arrived at the berth and parked noisily beside the ship. Captain Killen was on the bridge talking to Gerdy Gilmore as the driver and his three passengers dismounted from the high cabin and walked towards the gangplank.

'I don't have space for any more scientists,' snapped Killen, his sense of frustration boiling over.

Killen knew he was wasting his time complaining.

'They are the most important of all your passengers, believe it or not,' said Gilmore.

'What do they do?'

'They dive,' replied Gilmore with a smile on his face. 'Watch.'

Killen looked out to see the two navy marines taking off the tarpaulin covering what turned out to be a three-person manned submersible: a twenty-tonne underwater behemoth. Painted bright yellow with black trim and the size of a large SUV, it shone like a beacon in the afternoon sun. It was like a giant bumble bee. He had never seen anything like it before. A large steel box the size of a garden shed was also positioned on the trailer.

Seeing his quizzical look, Gilmore explained.

'It's called PLU. Why the name I don't know, but it is the very latest in underwater technology. It can descend rapidly to fifteen hundred metres in under two hours, which is perfect for what we've got in mind. Our American friends lent us PLU and its experienced operator and support technicians for a few weeks. It needs to be handled with care so the plan is to store it at the stern of the ship where it can be winched into the sea using the ship's main crane.'

'What's in that big black box?' asked Killen.

'That's the PLU shack. It contains the controls and all the monitoring equipment for the PLU's operations.'

'OK, get it all aboard,' he sighed, resignedly.

The Galway Harbour Company did a great job lifting the PLU and the steel box off its transporter onto the ship. The PLU and the shack control centre were expertly positioned and secured at the stern. The deck hands could only stare at the PLU in awe. It dwarfed their ROV.

As he watched the winching operation, Killen's sense of foreboding went up a notch.

The following late afternoon, as planned, they sailed west on the high tide. Having passed through the lock gate, the RV *Celtic Explorer* was soon sailing into the vast expanse of Galway Bay at a steady pace of ten knots an hour. Killen was in his element: steering his ship out of port was one of his few remaining pleasures in life. 'And I get paid for this,' he smiled to himself.

Later, he watched the sun go down on Galway Bay, humming the song of the same name to himself. The coastline of Ireland soon disappeared as night shadows fell across the skyline.

The corvette LÉ *Michael D. Higgins* appeared off the port side as they went around the Aran Islands and was soon a few hundred metres astern. Killen used his Steiner binoculars to study the navy ship. He could not see anybody on the sleek grey deck. There were several people on the bridge, including one who was viewing him with a pair of binoculars. Officers are always on duty.

The LÉ *Michael D. Higgins*, named after Ireland's recent President, was the newest patrol vessel of the expanding Irish navy. At 100 metres, she was the largest and most modern of the fleet and had a helipad platform astern that was also used to deploy surveillance drones. She carried a small remotely operated submersible and a decompression chamber for the navy divers. Her twin 16-cylinder W16V26F Wärtsilä diesel motors gave her a top speed of 23 knots.

Over the following two days, the crew of the RV *Celtic Explorer* went about their daily chores. The scientists spent the time unpacking, testing and installing their equipment packages. The vessel's soft rolling as it made its way into the Atlantic didn't appear to bother anyone.

The *Holland 2*, the ship's newly installed state-of-the-art ROV, named after John Philip Holland, Ireland's unique submarine engineer, was the centre of attention. From what he could make out Killen reckoned that new sets of sensors had been added. Judging by the manner in which they were handled this was expensive stuff, or at least the type of equipment that could not be replaced easily.

The crew of the RV *Celtic Explorer* were experienced in handling an ROV as unmanned underwater research was their bread and butter. They had already navigated the ROV to a depth of over 3,000 metres, off the Irish Continental Shelf during a recent mapping survey. Weighing in at five tonnes, it required a careful hand at the tiller. The re-kitted *Holland 2* came with additional features, including high quality Pegasus still and video cameras, enhanced Lumen lighting, an upgraded USBL positioning system, new and larger storage buckets, electronically controlled grabs and a variety of chemical sensors.

Seated in the cramped ROV operations room, located midships at eye level to the main cranes, Paul McCrossan, the ROV's operator for the past few years, was having great fun exploring the new features of his favourite toy. He started his career a long time back as an accountant and thanks to a recession or two he had re-skilled into his current role. McCrossan was fascinated with technology and once he mastered it he knew he could do anything he liked with the ROV. His dexterity at manoeuvring the ROV's arms and gadgetry was legendary. Its arms were an extension of his own. McCrossan was supported by two technicians who shared the task of monitoring the ROV's movements, communications and experiments.

The crew were fond of McCrossan as he made no demands on them other than to ensure nobody ever went into the ROV's operation room without his permission. McCrossan sported a thick deep beard in a blend of grey and black, that identified him as a sailor.

Killen detected at least three American voices, two English and a few bearded types with less distinctive accents busying themselves around the PLU. The age profile was much higher than usual; he was used to seeing fresh, just-out-of-college faces. The Irish scientists aboard bade him and his colleagues the time of the day and were polite but conversations with the newcomers never got beyond the basic formalities. This was all strange to a captain that was used to the relative routine and casual nature of marine scientific research. He knew instinctively that something serious was afoot. Why else was he sailing to a destination much further west than they had in many years, and with a navy escort?

After three days of sailing, Gilmore made it his business to meet Killen the day before they were due to arrive at the appointed initial location. They met in the scientist's cabin.

'As we're about to start work, I thought I should give you a bit more detail,' said Gilmore.

'That would be helpful,' said Killen without revealing his increasing levels of frustration as his ship was all but commandeered by strangers.

'Vice-Commodore Noel Brennan, captain of the LÉ *Michael D. Higgins*, will be joining us within the hour and will be assuming command until our research mission is accomplished,' said Gilmore.

'Command? I beg your pardon, but on whose authority am I being stood down?' Killen let his anger spill over. He was genuinely stunned, and it showed. His high cheek-bones reddened instantly. His freckles flushed. He got a lump in his throat. His voice was stressed. His hands waved in all directions. His blood was roaring in his ears.

While acutely aware of the captain's obvious state of unease and discomfort, Gilmore continued unphased. 'This is a scientific mission of strategic national importance and, depending on what we find, the security of the State may be at risk.'

'Please explain,' said Killen, instinctively looking for a cigarette. Fidgeting in his pockets, he forgot that he gave up smoking twenty years before.

'Put another way, for a short while and under Government orders, the RV *Celtic Explorer* will be part of the Irish navy. As a consequence, full military discipline applies once Vice-Commodore Brennan takes control.'

'I deserve a better explanation than that,' said Killen, struggling to control his temper.

'I agree, you do. Let me put it this way: we'll be under-taking a series of underwater experiments over a period of weeks or thereabouts that will seek to prove emerging theories that major changes to the volcanic structure of the Irish Continental Shelf are happening much more quickly than could have been anticipated. If the findings are as bad as I suspect they will be we need to keep a lid on this before the results are made public.'

Gilmore paused before delivering the final blow.

'We can't afford to have loose tongues. We're relying on you and your crew to provide every assistance to the Irish

Navy and to the visitors on board. I can't afford to have sulky and uncooperative crew interfering with, or worse obstructing, our work. Is that clear Captain?'

Killen nodded. He didn't have a choice. 'OK, I'll do my duty to the best of my ability.'

'Thanks Captain. That's what I expected you to say. Please join me for the research mission briefing.'

They made their way to the mess hall, which was the largest room aboard. It was packed to capacity.

'Welcome all,' said Gilmore as soon as he walked in the door. He saw thirty sets of eyes questioning him. Some were friendly. Others less so.

'Barry, please start,' said Gilmore without making any introductions.

Barry Carew was both excited and apprehensive as he started the briefing, targeted specifically at the scientists he had hand-picked at the request of the Irish Marine Institute.

Carew, who wore designer stubble to match his grey sleeveless designer bomber jacket, had been observing weather patterns across the Atlantic for decades, long before issues such as climate change had made the headlines. He didn't allude to his long friendship with Gilmore, it wasn't relevant. They both had a job to do regardless of their relationship.

'NASA and NOAA satellites have shown increasing volumes of melt ice from the Greenland Ice Sheet flowing into the North Atlantic. This phenomenon is starting to disrupt the weather-mitigating effects of the Gulf Stream. Until a few months ago there was no cause for alarm. However, we now have new data from our satellites that suggests the situation is far worse than we realised.'

Several of the researchers shifted uneasily in their seats.

Carew continued. 'Once this data was confirmed, NOAA alerted the Irish Marine Institute because Ireland is one of the countries likely to be most affected by any significant shift in the pattern of the Gulf Stream. We're here to find out the extent to which the satellite images and data can be matched with sea level and underwater observation. I would like to show you what we can do.'

He tapped instructions into his PC keyboard and the large high definition TV screen on the wall of the mess hall lit up. He zoomed in. In the centre of the screen was a crystal-clear image of the RV *Celtic Explorer*.'

There was stunned silence.

Vinnie Crowley spoke, reflecting the views of his colleagues. 'We're being watched by a spy satellite.'

'Not so, Mr Crowley. NOAA's assets are not owned or operated by the military. We're watching ourselves so to speak thanks to the state-of-the-art technology built into our low orbit GOES-S Series satellite. It is this satellite that has detected wide variations of sub-surface temperature to a depth of nearly five hundred metres. Let me show you.'

The screen switched to an image of the surface.

'The outer area highlighted in blue is around 4 degrees Celsius. The light red area in the centre is fifteen degrees due to the eddying effect of the waves. This sharp difference in temperature shows us where the apex of a water column is located.'

Carew pressed ahead.

'Eugene Carroll from the Irish Marine Institute will explain what we're looking for and how we intend to get the data. Eugene over to you.'

He was glad his part of the briefing was over. It was never easy to break bad news.

Carroll was clean-cut, shaven, and dressed smartly with ironed trousers, leather belt and white shirt. As a retired captain of the elite commando wing of the Irish Rangers, he knew how important it was to set sartorial standards as a reflection of his general approach to his work. He was a stickler for detail. He had a limp, related to a wound he got when on duty with the United Nations in Mali. His walking stick, carved from bush mahogany with an artisan silver handle, was his pride and joy.

'Thanks Barry. My colleagues and I have been monitoring the daily feed from the Gravity Recovery and Climate Experiment, or 'GRACE', satellites for over a year. As you know the Atlantic Meridional Overturning Circulation, the AMOC as we call it, is part of a complex circulation of currents that take the warmer Gulf Stream waters across the Atlantic.'

He spoke calmly and assuredly with an easy-to-listen-to accent. The only other sound was the constant creaking of the research vessel as it ploughed its way through the Atlantic seas.

'The theory is that if the AMOC slowed down, or – Heaven forbid – if it stopped altogether, this would give rise to colder winters and summers, in particular in the British Isles and in Denmark and Norway. The evidence had suggested this phenomenon could take decades, even centuries, before a noticeable and permanent effect could be detected. That was before the Zachariae Isstrom Glacier in Northern Greenland became detached and started crumbling into the North Atlantic. Almost immediately we noticed much colder fresh meltwater moving south.

The scientists present nodded their heads in agreement. After all, they understood the science of climate change and the absolute need to have primary and irrefutable evidence to support their findings. On the other hand, the crew of the RV *Celtic Explorer* listened in silence not fully grasping the impact of the briefing.

Carroll continued. 'The volume of fresh water off the Zachariae Isstrom Glacier on its own should not cause such a pattern unless other outflow sources were combining to effectively flood the central part of the North Atlantic Ocean with melted ice. In the past months, our satellites have identified widespread areas of meltwater spreading as far south as the waters off the south-east of Iceland. We've asked Lars Brun and his colleagues at the Summit Station in Greenland to test the outflow levels. As we start our tests, his team is in the process of doing their own research.'

The crew started to pay attention as it became evident that this research trip was going to be a bit different. They could feel a growing sense of anticipation among the scientists and researchers.

Carroll too was aware that his briefing was now being listened too by all in the room with heightened attention. He continued: 'As you know, a rapid decrease in the salinity of the ocean waters resulting from its displacement by freshwater from the Greenland Ice Sheet prevents colder waters sinking down columns that spiral close to the ocean floor. What seems to be happening is that twenty of the seventy-eight known giant 'chimneys' of cold dense water that comprise the AMOC have stopped functioning. If this can be proved – and this is what we're here to do – it represents a startling acceleration of one of the most worrying changes to the earth's climate.'

Carroll pointed with his walking stick to the large map of the North-East Atlantic that hung on the wall of the mess hall. He loved showing off his African souvenir.

'We've been asked, as part of a much wider endeavour involving three other marine research vessels from Denmark, Norway and Great Britain, to test the salinity of the waters in the area of the Eriador Seamount. Here what is called the 'Irminger Current' transports relatively salty and warm water offshore from the East Greenland current. Between the four countries we'll test the salinity of the seawater along an arc from Rockall to Iceland. The Norwegians are coordinating the collective effort. I should add their Government is providing the funding for the research.'

He then pointed to an area shaded in red lines.

'This is our zone of activity.'

He paused to drink from a glass of water. This gave his audience time to grasp the importance of what had been said.

'We've re-equipped the *Holland 2* with new instrumentation to test seawater salinity levels, its density and to measure the flow of the sinking circulation. I reckon we need to take measurements at ten locations to a depth of two kilometres. This will take us at least four weeks, by my reckoning.'

Several people had their hands raised.

'I see a few of you have some questions.'

Crowley was undaunted. He puffed out another halo of dense sweet-smelling smoke. He wasn't aware that navy rules didn't allow smoking even if, as he jokingly argued, it was for medicinal purposes. Killen wasn't looking forward to telling him he had to quit his habit.

'Where does the PLU fit into all of this? Are there two projects going on at the same time? Who is in charge?' demanded Crowley.

'When Vice-Commodore Brennan comes aboard later, we'll set out how both teams of scientists will be managed to carry out their respective research projects. For the time being we just need to ensure that all equipment remains ready for use.'

'There is no need for all this mystery stuff you know. You are talking to adults.' said Crowley. Crowley's training as an engineer made him intolerant of waffle. He ran his life based on discernible facts.

As the scientists and crew dispersed after the briefing, Crowley and Killen stayed back a while.

'Enda, what's going on?'

'I wish I could tell you more, Vinnie. I'm as frustrated as you are that we're being kept in the dark about the real purpose of this voyage. We just better get on with our jobs and when they want to tell us more, I'm sure they will. My focus, like yours, is to run a safe ship.'

'Fair enough so. Cuppa?'

Over several cups of tea in the comfort of the staff room they spent an hour discussing a variety of sport and political stories, relatively uncontroversial subjects for seasoned mariners. Both decided to park their concerns about the issues raised at the briefing. After all there was little they could do to change matters.

It took a further day's sailing to get on location. They sailed across the Porcupine Bank, over the Rockall Trough and the shallow Rockall Bank, where the seabed was just 300 metres deep in parts, to a location 54° 50' north and 25° 20' west, a distance of four hundred kilometres from Galway.

They were well on the way to America.

CHAPTER 3

Instituto Volcanológico de Canarias

'Aren't we lucky – The Caldera de Taburiente must be one of the most stunning workplaces in the world!' As they approached the second measurement site, Ros looked around and took in the panorama.

'I agree,' said Simon. 'This is a stress-free zone. It sure beats working in a factory packing fruit or being in an office.'

The small stones that comprised the rough footpath where they stood moved ever so slightly – they shuffled – and this was immediately followed by a small but noticeable jolt under their feet.

'Am I dreaming, or …' Ros stuttered in disbelief.

'It's a seismic tremor,' said Simon calmly.

When it stopped, after ten long seconds, the brothers instinctively sat down and stared at each other. While this was their first experience of a tremor, they knew the consequence of such a mild movement.

Simon's mobile phone rang, and this startled them.

'Simon, did you experience what we've just felt?' said Claudine.

'Yes,' responded Simon. 'Let's hope it's a one-off. How bad was it where you are?'

'We were reviewing your sulphur data measurements when the seismometer beside us started to register,' said Claudine. 'It was a 1.3 Richter scale tremor. But what worries me is that it was a shallow tremor located equidistant between where you are at the Caldera and here some thirty kilometres further south. It could be located at the base of the Caldera.'

'We're not at the research station but on the other side of the Caldera, close to La Roque,' said Simon.

'Wow, here it goes again,' said Claudine in a matter-of-fact voice.

This time they were prepared and soon the short shock had passed.

'Another 1.3 and from the same location,' said Claudine.

Simon stood up. 'Claudine, Ros and I need to get back to base pronto to alert the Instituto Geográfico Nacional. Two tremors within ten minutes is far from normal. I will call you later.'

The brothers knew immediately that what had looked to be a routine and carefree few weeks until the end of their contract at the Pico de la Nieve research centre was going to be somewhat different. The fact that the network of seismic sensors had all recorded the event pointed to a potential shallow fault developing about half a kilometre south of the research station at the base of the mountain range. This was the point where the greatest energy release could be expected. The priority was to determine how shallow the fault was and then to detect the pattern of waves.

They gathered their kit for the long hike back to the Pico de la Nieve research centre. They walked in silence in single file on the narrow mountain path for almost an hour. When the path widened, they paused to catch their breath, sat down on a rock and drank some water. They knew regular rests were essential at this altitude.

'Do you remember what Professor Laffino told us about Charles Richter when we were in first year at college?' asked Ros.

'Sure do, as if it were yesterday,' said Simon. 'Way back in 1935, he defined the Richter reading. For each number up the scale the intensity increases ten-fold. As the Richter measurement increases so does the severity of the quake. What we felt, a 1.3, was comparable to a small quarry blast. Anything over a 5 would cause severe damage, like the impact of a major nuclear explosion. A magnitude 6 quake would cause widespread damage over a hundred square kilometre area.'

'Where was the biggest recorded earthquake?' asked Ros testing his brother's knowledge.

'In Chile in 1960, and it registered 9.5. Happy?' Simon had an encyclopaedic memory. His brother could rarely catch him out when it came to scientific facts. On the other hand, his awareness of general knowledge was poor. Too much time spent reading books rather than newspapers had taken its toll. Their training told them that a Richter measurement didn't tell the full picture when predicting the impact on volcanic activity. Seismometers close to an epicentre can't record reliable readings if the earthquake is too big. Neither can the Richter scale show how much damage a particular earthquake is capable of causing.

'Ros, do you recall what we were told about earthquake prediction methodology?'

'This was Laffino's speciality,' replied Ros. 'He was strong on the theory that the business of predicting earthquakes should be based on the study of an active fault and, in turn, on an assessment of the seismic patterns before incidents. That means, we should plot the readings at and around the epicentre.'

'Yes, it's coming back to me,' said Simon. 'He also said that only ten per cent of large earthquakes are preceded by smaller foreshocks. Do you remember we studied the 2010 Haiti earthquake in detail? It was so catastrophic because its epicentre was only about ten kilometres from Port-Au-Prince and at a depth of only thirteen kilometres. Before that there hadn't been an earthquake in Haiti since 1860.'

'Gosh, I wonder if this is what is happening here?' mused Ros.

Simon continued. 'We should try to find the files covering the 1949 and 1971 volcanic events. The records are stored in boxes somewhere back at the research centre. We dug them out a few years ago as part of the programme to locate the seismometers that were previously installed across the Caldera.

'That should help us pinpoint where the stresses were on previous occasions and the location of the epicentres,' said Ros.

'Exactly,' replied his brother. He continued, 'Our event will be one of dozens of earthquakes being monitored by the US Geological Survey and other international bodies. We need to brief Carmen Ortiz at the Instituto Geográfico

Nacional. She is probably as surprised as we are that this is happening in a hitherto inactive volcanic region.'

'Didn't Carmen work on the Canary island Volcano Monitoring Programme a few years ago?'

'Yes, and she did the same job that we're doing now. Carmen and her team developed the geochemical monitoring network that we rely on. She is the national coordinator for the ShakeAlert earthquake early warning system that's being pioneered by the US Geological Survey.'

'ShakeAlert? Is this a new cocktail or what?' said Ros.

'Where have you been? Not reading your scientific journals? This software is designed to give us advanced notice of seismic tremors. Such an early warning system could save lives.'

It took two hours of fast walking for the brothers to reach the safety of their base camp. There were no further aftershocks. They had a late lunch of hard bread and soft cheese while they pondered the events of the morning and what the Caldera de Taburiente was trying to tell them. They would find out soon enough.

When the brothers returned to their base it was no surprise to discover an email marked 'URGENT' on the centre's main computer. It was from Mark Doyle at the Global Seismographic Network (GSN). It read:

Simon, Ros,

I see you've had a busy day. When you get a chance please call me as we're getting other seismic readings in and around the other Canary Islands and in the mid-Atlantic. Actually, call me immediately.

Mark Doyle was the academic equivalent of a pop star in the small world of volcanologists and had two big fans in the brothers Rodriquez. A Canadian, he was Head of Volcanic Research at the Global Seismographic Network, which is a network of 150 stations that collects real time data on earthquakes and manages emergency responses. Run by a consortium of 120 American universities, it provides free real-time data to many governments, academics and research centres, like the one on Pico de la Nieve.

Doyle was called on by the major TV networks when volcanoes threatened local populations and wider communities as was the case when the Icelandic earthquake Eyjafjallajökull disrupted European air travel. Mark explained the volcano jargon that his fellow volcanologists took for granted but which was impenetrable to the general public. As a result, there was better public awareness about such things as vents, craters, cones, fissures, dykes, magma, lava and even pyroclastic flows, a fast-moving current of hot gases and volcanic matter that can reach speeds of over 700 kilometres an hour.

Simon called him as another brief tremor rolled slowly through the building.

'Mark, it is Simon and Ros here from the Pico de la Nieve research station.'

'Hi there,' said Mark in a friendly tone.

While they had never met Mark in person, they detected a slight nervousness in his voice, though he was doing his best to sound calm. Mark Doyle was the most senior volcanologist at the GSN and was well-known in the volcano community as a quiet and cautious person. When he had something to say, it paid to listen.

'I know you are trained volcanologists, but I think it

would be helpful if I gave you a head's up as to what we think might be happening. Is that ok?'

'Sure, Mark. Go ahead,' said Simon.

'La Palma may appear to be a calm and picturesque island and a haven for hill-walkers, but it has a volcanic sting in its tail. Until about fifty years ago the island was one of the most active in the world. All the attention, and budgets I might add, have switched to Iceland and Hawaii given what we're experiencing there on an almost daily basis. The Caldera de Taburiente and the fissures along the Cumbre Vieja ridge have been dormant for quite a while. We've perhaps taken our collective eye off that particular ball.'

'What does that mean, Mark?' asked Ros.

'Since 1430, or thereabouts, the many eruptions on La Palma were explosions of ash and cinders with emissions of fluid basaltic lava. In the main, the cones that were formed were quite small, at least that's what we can observe. Each eruption was preceded by earthquakes of increasing vigour and frequency that were felt all over La Palma. It appears that this pattern may be about to repeat itself. In fact, during the 1971 eruption at Teneguia there were almost one thousand tremors of varying intensity over a two-month period before the main eruption. Thankfully, that incident was relatively small and as early warnings were to hand there were no fatalities.'

'You mean that what we felt earlier is a precursor to an eruption?' blurted Ros.

'I can't say for certain, but you will need to be vigilant. On the basis of previous observations, we can expect small vents and fissures to open at random and at many locations.

No doubt many more tremors will occur. What concerns me most is where the epicentre will emerge and more importantly the potential scale of a possible eruption. The readings we've to hand don't give a clear enough picture as there are multiple possible sources. The volcanoes on La Palma have the potential to cause significant collateral damage if the eruptions are of a sufficient scale to cause major landslides and tsunamis.'

Mark paused before he continued. 'And to complicate matters, in the past twenty-four hours there have been many other low-level seismic readings along parts of the mid-Atlantic Ridge, and on the Canary Islands of La Gomera and El Hierro. All these zones have been stable for decades.'

'What can we do?' asked Simon.

'You will need to cover quite an amount of territory over the coming weeks,' said Mark. 'Do you need additional help?'

Simon spoke. 'As it happens, two colleagues from our university are working not thirty kilometres south of us. After this call I'll be speaking to Carmen Ortiz who heads up the Instituto Geográfico Nacional. She too will have seen the readings and will, no doubt, want to be on the island before too long.'

'That's a good start,' said Mark. 'We'll have to set up a plan to observe all the dormant volcanoes on the island. I'll talk to NASA and see if we can get satellite capacity. I'll also trigger the local earthquake alert response plan. If there are any more significant tremors expect a call soon from the Guardia Civil. Why don't you talk to your colleagues and try to map out the areas across the Caldera and down the length of the Cumbre Vieja that you might cover. I'll call you in the morning to review progress.'

'That's a plan Mark, or at least that's the start of a plan,' said Simon.

'OK so, let's talk tomorrow.' Mark signed off.

Simon grasped the import of the call and it scared him. 'Ros, I think we've landed ourselves in something that's going to develop into a major incident. I'm not sure we're in any way equipped to deal with this.'

Another mild tremor rolled through the building to support his observation. Ros's phone rang. As their stress levels were rising, they both jumped.

'Ros, this is Carmen Ortiz.'

'Hi Carmen, we were just about to call you. Hold on while I put you on speaker. Simon will need to listen in.'

'Hi Simon,' said Carmen.

While she was a good bit older than Simon and Ros, they knew her well as she was their PhD supervisor. As a result, they talked as colleagues rather than as juniors might to their seniors.

'What's your assessment?' asked Carmen.

Ros took the lead. 'We've just come off the phone from Mark Doyle who told us that there has been seismic activity in a number of areas and La Palma may be part of a wider phenomenon.'

'That's true.' Carmen was fully aware of what was happening.

'He was being cautious of course', said Ros. 'There is no evidence to suggest there is any reason to escalate matters, but we need to assume the worst and be somewhat precautionary. What are your plans?'

'I'm on the next flight to La Gomera as the research centre there is experiencing similar activity. When I arrive tomorrow morning we should talk further.'

'Before you go Carmen, we may need support if matters start to escalate. Any chance of some reinforcements?'

'Rest assured Ros. The main reason for my travelling to La Gomera is to get an overview of all the readings. We'll focus our limited resources where they are most needed. The team here in Madrid has been put on twenty-four hours' notice to travel and once I press the button we could send you a support team within five or six hours. I reckon between you and Claudine and Maria we've enough boots on the ground for the time being. OK?'

'Fine, Carmen. Talk Later. Bon Voyage.'

Ros put the phone down slowly. 'Let's talk to the girls and see what they have to say.'

Maria and Claudine were expecting the call. They recapped the day's events.

Claudine suggested, 'We could cover the ridge line south of Refugio El Pilar and I'm sure my aunt Margarida and her husband Damian will help. They know the mountains, and especially the National Park, better than anyone else on the island.'

Simon interrupted, 'We'll need much more help. It is possible that several sites may need to be observed at the same time.'

Maria joined the call, 'Until we get resourced up, I'm sure Uncle Damian will allow us use his drone. He uses it all the time for his photography in the mountains.'

'In the absence of a NASA satellite, a drone will certainly be useful. Please ask him to contact me as soon as he can. We'll need to get images of any vents and fissures that may rise to the surface over the coming days and weeks.'

'What do we need to do exactly?' asked Maria.

'Monitor, monitor and monitor,' replied Simon.

'What exactly?' probed Claudine.

Simon explained, 'We're fortunate that the island is peppered with a network of seismic monitoring devices, albeit some over thirty years old. They will help us pinpoint the centre of activity and, more importantly, the depth of seismic activity. I expect if the current tremors intensify, we'll know very soon where we need to focus our attention. The added complication is that there may be offshore as well as onshore incidents.'

'Our new sulphur dioxide devices have the potential to give us another layer of data. If magma starts to rise, as the plates beneath the island appear to be shifting, we might soon see new fissures. The devices will tell us the strength of the flow of one of the main gasses associated with initial volcanic activity.'

'But what will happen if your fixed devices are in the wrong location?' Maria knew the answer to her question before she got a reply.

'They won't be. The brothers Rodriquez are smart. You know that by now,' said Ros.

'We used the records of the previous volcanic episodes over several centuries to select where to locate our devices,' said Simon. 'Anyhow, we've a small stock of mobile devices that can be deployed wherever we decide.'

'Providing you can get close to the source of the emissions. Volcanoes can be hot you know!'

'Yes, of course. But given the current low-level nature of the seismic readings we're a long way off a volcanic eruption. So please rest easy,' said Simon trying not to worry the sisters. He continued. 'The one caveat is that we've limited cover in the National Park because there has been no volcanic activity there for as long as records have been kept.'

'That's encouraging,' remarked Claudine.

'It would be, but for the fact that the initial seismic reading suggests the source of the problem lies deep beneath the National Park,' replied Simon.

'Don't forget to ask Damian to phone me as soon as he can. The thermal imaging feature of his drone could prove to be valuable.'

'Will do,' said Claudine.

Minutes later Damian called. 'Hi guys. I gather my latest toy may be of some assistance. How can I help?'

'Damian, I've a hunch,' said Simon

'I thought you scientists only did evidence!'

'Ha Ha. While everyone assumes that our problem may manifest itself close to the old Cumbre Vieja volcanoes, I've a suspicion that the real source may be closer to the base of the Caldera de Taburiente that has been inactive for tens of thousands of years.'

'I'm listening. Where do I fit in?' Damian was impressed that the brothers were taking the initiative.

Simon explained, 'It could be days, months or maybe never before an eruption starts. If the patterns that we know about from Hawaii's experiences are replicated here on La Palma, the first evidence of an eruption will be a gradual phenomenon. What we need to detect are any rises, however small, in the surface temperatures.'

'That's where my drone's thermal imagery feature comes in, right?'

'You've got it in one,' said Simon.

'To be honest I've never had reason to use this feature,' said Damian. 'Whatever about checking body heat at night, the drone wasn't designed for volcanic surveillance.'

'Could you test the drone this evening? Once you get used to the controls let me know. If you could transmit the data to us using the drone's Wi-Fi; that would be a great help. It would be better if we could see the data in real time.'

'Ok Simon, I'll put the drone through its paces after dinner. Have you any specific locations in mind? You know the drone's range is limited. I reckon I could keep the beast in the air for no more than forty minutes.'

'That should be more than enough for starters. I suggest we focus our efforts at the base of Pico de la Nieve and the western end of the National Park. You might plot a crisscross grid that can be tested systematically. We can adapt the size of the sample area depending on developments. We can schedule a call once you have some results.'

'That suits me as I may be tied up with groups of hikers for the next two days.'

The River Corrib

As soon as Sean had signed off, Lars turned and spoke to the audience seated across the expanse of the Big Room. All available chairs and benches were occupied. There was a buzz of conversation as everyone tried to grasp the import of what they had heard.

'We need a plan.' While he was in marketing mode, he didn't really need to be. Whatever Lars recommended would not be challenged. His colleagues and the research students held him in the highest regard. His reputation as a fair, competent and professional project leader and world-renowned climate scientist didn't require elaboration or explanation.

'We'll take delivery of a thousand ice-melt monitors, for the want of a better term, in late August. Once they arrive, we'll have three weeks to get them into place before we close up shop for the season. We've worked at five principal sites for the past few years, most within easy reach of the Summit Station. To get the results we require, I believe we need to disperse the golf balls across a wider footprint of approximately 300 kilometres radius from here. I want twenty locations identified across the width and breadth of the ice sheet within that footprint. What we're looking for are large crevasses or sinkholes that have a good proven flow rate based on your observations. We need to select priority sites that have the potential to generate the data we need. That means we should split into several teams, with two or three a team. Can you break into five groups and talk through the logistics of doing what is needed in a safe manner?'

Before they set about this task, Alice, ever the enthusiast, chipped in.

'We already know some of the potential locations are unstable. If we can't get close to a crevasse could we use the drone to survey potential sites and perhaps more sophisticated equipment to deliver the payload?'

'That's a great idea,' responded Lars. 'We need to expand the coverage of the research over a much wider area. Let's see what the practical considerations are that we need to take account of in using this technology.'

In fact, Lars had already anticipated this option. As a master of detail, lots of phone calls had been made. He called in a long-overdue favour. As a result, he was hoping he would be provided with all the resources – including a pair of military standard drones – needed to deliver the research outcomes. Lars knew it paid to have friends in high places, especially a Rear Admiral of the Norwegian navy, a member of his regular four-ball.

Over the following days the researchers and scientists discussed, argued and debated where and how best to deploy the golf balls and who should lead each group. Gallons of coffee and mountains of biscuits and bagels were consumed.

The Summit Station's drone had basic features and was mostly used for aerial photography. It wasn't the latest model. In fact, it was quite out of date, but provided essential up-to-date details of the crevasses at distances that could not be accessed on foot. The drone was deployed, in turn, by the five teams with everyone getting some experience in flying this inexpensive but essential toy of modern earth sciences.

As images came in from a radius of some 300 kilometres from the Summit Station, the large map that dominated the common room at the Big House was dotted with colour coded stickers of all the possible drop sites.

Early on in their deliberations it became clear that the golf balls would have to be deployed in at least three locations quite a distance from the Summit Station. It was agreed that heavy-duty ski transport would be necessary if sites at a distance due east and west of the Summit Station were selected. The two ski-cats could not do such a job as they could only transport three people. This would necessitate the sourcing of Bombardier Humvee vehicles and provisions for an estimated two weeks period. Lars made calls to other research stations and used his influence to borrow some additional equipment and supplies. The wider Greenland research community had by now heard of the forthcoming experiment. All were eager to assist.

The Twin Otter could also be used. Lars had a clear preference for a location close to the Helheim Glacier, fifty kilometres up the Sermilik fjord from the small town of Tasiilaq on the east coast of Greenland, just under the Arctic Circle. The fact that there was an established research station in the area adjacent to a groomed ski runway was a factor in the selection of this location. While a decision in principle was reached to send one of the teams to this area, the exact drop location had yet to be decided.

There was a fierce disagreement about the best locations closest to the Summit Station. There was agreement, however, that the husky sledge should be used to get to a location ten kilometres to the south. And the skimobiles could be deployed to a second location. Who got to travel by sledge would have to be decided by lots as all the students wanted to have this special experience. The sledge and skimobiles could only be used if weather conditions were good because the teams would have to return to the Summit Station the same day.

Lars was made aware early on that Alice wanted to lead the field team that was going to the area of the Helheim Glacier. Her initial subtle hints were followed up by a direct and formal request. She was pushy and took advantage of his growing feelings for her. Phil Teahon was far more relaxed. He had a preference to lead one of the Humvee teams and once that was settled Per Jan would be in charge of the second.

Lars had to make allowance for the transport of the pilots of the military standard drones he hoped to procure and their analysts, as well as the drivers of two Bombardier Humvees that would be used to provide transport to the locations at the greatest distance from the Summit Station. Additional oven tents, assorted equipment and food was ordered, enough for a three-week period. It was going to get crowded. He felt like a Quartermaster General. The Excel spreadsheet he was using to manage the project was off the page and just about out of control.

Throughout Sean and Lars spoke at regular intervals. The production of the golf balls was on target and logistical arrangements were made to get the materials to the Summit Station by the agreed deadline.

The only last-minute glitch was with the acquisition of the drones. Despite an earlier promise, Lars had to follow up on his not inconsiderable contacts with the Norwegian air force to source these high-spec drones.

It took two further phone calls before the Norwegian air force's commander agreed not only to deliver the kit and the Humvees to the airport at Ilulissat on the west coast of Greenland, but also to facilitate the transport of the golf balls from Galway City Airport to Ilulissat. He also agreed to provide skilled drone pilots and the supporting computer system that would be used to monitor the progress of the golf balls. Given his initial reluctance, it was a Damascene conversion.

'Project Masters', as it was now called, was no longer a secret. On the contrary, given the potential impact of a more rapid melting of the Greenland Ice Sheet than had previously been understood, it had caught the attention not only of officials but also of senior politicians in Norway and, most importantly, within the military community. All of a sudden, and in contrast to earlier reticence, everyone wanted to help and have a slice of the action. There was disbelief that such a simple idea as using floating golf balls might be the solution to the information deficit.

Lars appreciated the willingness to help but was somewhat concerned that he might get crowded out. However, his contact in the Norwegian government made it clear from the 'get go' that he was in charge and that any military personnel and supporting technicians deployed to the Summit Station would be under his command. That made sense. As a quid pro quo, the Norwegian Government wanted immediate access to the data that would be generated. On this condition, they had no issues in meeting the costs of this part of the project. That also made sense.

A few weeks before Lars had met Benny Lundt, Norway's Chief Scientist, at a climate action conference. He shared his news with him. Benny had submitted a detailed report to the Norwegian Government about the serious consequences that could arise if the accelerated pace of the Greenland ice melt led over time to the collapse of parts of the glaciers into the North Atlantic. The main conclusion was that Norway's weather patterns, and its economy, would be brought back to the Ice Age. The evidence suggested this could happen within a few decades and when it did the phenomenon would be irreversible. One of the wealthiest countries in the world could not buy its way out of such a scenario.

No questions were asked when Benny arranged to have two of Norway's long-range military drones redeployed for a short period along with supporting equipment and operators. He didn't tell Lars, but he decided such was the importance of the experiment that he would travel to the Summit Station to lend support and to be there when the results came in.

Lars and his project team leaders decided, having reviewed the preliminary drone and satellite images, the precise locations of the five base stations that would be used. In the end, the five locations selected themselves as all had been monitored on a regular basis over the past years.

Allowing for the promised Norwegian air force drone pilots, each team would comprise three to four people. Additional tents to house everyone would need to be transported to the sites and assembled in good time. The two Humvees – also provided gratis by the Norwegians for the duration of the project – would have to be airlifted to the Summit Station.

Communications were tested. At a very early stage Sean shared the radio frequencies of the individual golf balls with Lars. These, in turn, were passed to the Norwegian military and programmed into their computers. In short order, the required telemetry protocols were completed and programmed. Sean didn't really understand why, but the Norwegians managed to get some use of a NASA polar orbiting satellite for the duration of the experiment. Despite some reservations, the American Department of Defence had released one of their most recently launched satellites, which had advanced space-based infrared systems. This satellite was normally used for missile defence.

The Norwegian air force drone group did a series of tests using the early golf ball prototype on the River Glomma that flowed into the sea at Fredrikstad. They were impressed. While some tweaking was needed to address minor software glitches in the tracking system, Sean provided exactly what he had promised. The fact that the golf balls were embossed with Norway's flag didn't go unnoticed.

As the August deadline for the arrival of the drones, transport, additional personnel and golf balls approached there was a rising sense of anticipation. As there was little else to do at 3,000 metres, everyone available at the Summit Station put in all the hours necessary to prepare for the deployment of the golf balls.

Sean and his engineering team took on the task of designing and then producing the 'floating ice balls', or 'FIBs' as they became known, with their usual enthusiasm and skill.

Sean's was a start-up business and as a result there was no hierarchy within the ten strong work force. The average age was twenty-six. He was fortunate that the National University of Ireland Galway's Engineering Faculty had educated such highly motivated people. They didn't want to emigrate or leave the area preferring instead to work in a modern building within a short commuting distance of their families and friends. As long as he kept them busy, they would remain with the business. And busy they certainly were. The team was thrilled as online orders from a dozen countries for the original tracker golf ball were pouring in, despite the fact the ball itself was still deemed ineligible by the world's golfing bodies. Amateur golfers didn't care for such details. They didn't want to spend a fortune on replacement golf balls when they could use Sean's on multiple occasions. The revenue from these sales and the accompanying App exceeded all expectations. As a consequence, Sean was able to invest in additional equipment and testing facilities using the resulting cash flow.

When he met Lars at the Masters, he was confident he had the capacity to produce a thousand golf balls within a short period. He didn't tell Lars at the time, but his two-person innovation team had already tested a floating golf ball with the aim of identifying the inner core content materials that would give the ball the correct ballast without compromising its look and feel. They had also experimented with a variety of surface covering materials.

After the Masters meeting, Sean's innovation team started to explore the option of embedding a small camera into the ball. Again, nothing too sophisticated but a functional unit nonetheless.

Lars' technical specifications were challenging. The biggest problem was finding the most appropriate technology for the small enhanced transmitter that would be placed at the top of the golf ball. Sean had met the owner of another start-up company in the same business park who specialised in electronic gadgetry. He and Sean co-designed the chip that was capable of sending signals to a predetermined electronic reader. It wasn't unlike the technology used to track and fly drones.

As with most things that are innovative, a few ideas from other products were cannibalised, such as the inclusion of a small aerial protruding almost unseen through the core. Soft resin would surround the transmitter. The software code for tracking was written within a week. Writing the security protocols to comply with Lars' requirements took much longer. As they were already putting logos on the golf balls, adding the Norwegian flag wasn't an issue.

Within three weeks Sean and his team had the first prototypes ready for field trials. They decided the fast-flowing River Corrib which passed over several weirs as it made its way to the sea through Galway City was as close as they could get nearby to the conditions of an ice sheet crevasse. Sean and two colleagues set up their computers in the company's van at the edge of the river. The others involved with the trials were members of the local rowing club. They borrowed two four-seater boats and rowed to the centre of the river. Ten balls were dropped in the water. They floated, which was a start. More importantly, once they moved with the river's flow Sean's computer tracked and recorded their progress as was the intention. Each ball was displayed on a dotted red line. Minor tweaking to the tracking software was needed to improve the visual image of the reading. Otherwise everything was in order.

They did one further trial with a prototype camera golf ball and it performed as expected. Again, some adjustments to the code were needed to improve the clarity of the visual images.

It was time to make contact with Lars. They agreed a time for a conference call. After brief pleasantries, Sean got down to business.

'We did a final test on the last batch late yesterday evening.'

'And?' asked Lars nervously. He was excited but impatient.

'All the golf balls performed to the required standard,' said Sean trying to speak calmly, relieved that he could finish his sentence. 'The biggest challenge, as I expected, was to design an in-built camera with infrared and low light capacity. Thankfully the latest version of Apple's iPhone has somewhat similar features.'

'You didn't use their technology, surely?'

'Not exactly. Once we found out how the camera affected the balance of the golf ball, we set about adapting the camera kit we bought from a Chinese source.' Lars laughed.

'Sean Pitcher, you are a total rogue.'

He smiled.

'While we could only do a preliminary test of the golf balls with the added camera feature, they too seem to be finished to a high standard. Let me show you. Here is the recording of the field trial.' Sean activated the clip on his computer.

The TV screen in the Big Room lit up and showed the rapid movement of water.

'What we did was place these camera golf balls close to a weir on the River Corrib that flows through Galway City into the Atlantic. What you are seeing is the first ever view of the Corrib in full flow from the viewpoint of the riverbed. We know the floating golf balls work best in a fast-flowing current. We added a few grams to the base of the core. This had the effect of the camera recording images upwards at an angle of about forty-five degrees. If the camera golf ball settles, for example in a slow flowing cavern structure, you should be able to observe its ceiling.'

'Tell me more about the infrared ability. I didn't know that Apple's cameras had such a feature.' Lars was keen to get a complete understanding of what Sean had achieved.

'They don't, nor do android cameras. One of my engineers served in the Irish army's Ranger Wing with the United Nations. He had a lot of down time and with access to a work bench he managed to miniaturise the technology of his night vision goggles into the block that contains the lens of a standard iPhone camera. You should be aware that he has a patent on this invention and expects to make his fortune if Project Masters does the business.'

'More Irish ingenuity,' laughed Lars.

'What hasn't been tested is the range of the infrared images,' said Sean. 'If the deep caverns are penetrated with even the smallest amount of ambient light, even light from a safety lamp, this will greatly enhance the visual images that the camera will transmit.'

'That's great,' said Lars.

'I'm also going to send you the programme software that you should use to track the golf balls. Let me show you a camera shot of a replay of the data that the Corrib golf balls generated. We used ten golf balls so expect to see a plot for each one.'

With Sean's support they tracked the first golf ball to start with. The PC monitor showed it moving at fifteen kilometres per hour for the first ten minutes and as it approached the first weir the speed doubled. The red tracker line was crystal clear. As it went over the weir, it reached a speed of forty kilometres before it slowed down to a stop, then it started moving at just two kilometres per hour as it bounced slowly off the riverbed, reflecting the river's current as it approached the next weir. After it passed through this drop it stopped altogether. Unexpectedly, and to everyone's amazement, Sean turned on the camera feature and the screen showed what appeared to be a thick clump of reeds. The golf ball had lodged there and would not be moving any time soon.

The demonstration was exactly what Lars wanted.

'The Norwegians will love this Sean. Their monitoring equipment is due to arrive in a few days and is ready to go using the radio frequencies you provided.'

'Lars, I should have explained that the camera images can be captured using the same software we've designed for the golf ball tracking. It is a simple matter of selecting the 'Use Camera' button.'

The entire team in the Big Room was more than impressed. They applauded spontaneously.

Sean continued with a greater degree of pride.

'When you deploy the golf balls into the ice-melt sinkholes, I expect there will be no vegetation to block their progress. As you can see, the software allows you to graph the speed, direction and descent of every golf ball. Assuming the majority of the golf balls work, and you should factor in a failure rate given your conditions, within a day or so the golf balls should be able to tell you whether your theories are correct by how close they are to emerging somewhere on the coast of Greenland.'

Lars knew he had to factor in a failure rate. A thousand golf balls seemed a lot, but he needed the majority to produce the scientific data they were designed to deliver.

'What might go wrong Sean? We need to talk through all these issues before the balls are deployed.'

'One precaution would be to deploy a small sample in the first instance and depending on their progress and feedback proceed to a full deployment. As you will only have twenty camera golf balls, I would not use them until you are getting good readings from the test batch.'

'That makes sense, and all project leaders should adapt their procedures accordingly,' said Lars. 'Any questions for Sean?'

'Will the ice water temperature affect performance?' said one of the researchers.

'I don't know to be honest. We were told that the temperature of the meltwater was above freezing at the surface – otherwise there would be no movement. We placed a sample of the golf balls in water that was frozen to minus twenty degrees Celsius for forty-eight hours. Eight of the ten golf balls tested failed. The camera function had deteriorated quite significantly in all the golf balls. How frozen meltwater two thousand metres below the surface will affect performance is one of the lessons to be learned. However, if the golf balls are moving through currents under the ice they should perform better than if they are stuck in frozen water.'

'To be honest, I'm not too bothered,' said Lars. 'If only a handful reach sea level we'll have achieved a major scientific breakthrough. The sites we've selected are flowing at an average speed of thirty-five kilometres an hour at surface level. I know it will not be a straight run to the sea. Many will be blocked by ice formations, but we might be lucky.'

The researchers kept asking questions.

'Will we be able to retrieve the golf balls once they enter the sea?'

Sean responded. 'You will have to ask our Norwegian partners if that's possible. Seriously though, they float so there is no reason why they can't be retrieved and even reused. Imagine the thrill of going through the Greenland Ice Sheet for a second time!'

With a broad smile, Sean concluded the conversation. 'Lars, I so like Project Masters that I've arranged to hitch a lift on the Norwegian air force plane when it comes here to collect the golf balls. All going well I should be with you within the week. How is that for a surprise?'

'Sean, you do know there are no golfing facilities up here at the Summit Station!'

RV *Celtic Explorer*

Killen and Gilmore were at the guardrail to greet the captain of the LÉ *Michael D. Higgins* as he climbed aboard the RV *Celtic Explorer* from a motor launch. Brennan was the most senior commander of the Irish navy. Tall and clean-cut with jet black hair and a seaman's tan, Killen reckoned he was in his late thirties. He wore his navy dress uniform square on his shoulders, bedecked with several medals to commemorate his missions served with the United Nations. He had won his spurs thanks to two high-profile tours of duty off the shores of Libya during Europe's refugee crisis. Killen assumed, correctly, that to get to this position at such a young age required excellent leadership skills as well as true grit.

Brennan saluted the captain formally. Killen tried to do the same.

'Captain,' greeted the Chief Scientist.

'Nice to meet you again, Professor.'

Killen shook hands with Brennan and noticed he was in a firm grip and that Brennan made direct eye contact.

'Can we have a word before we go to the briefing? Perhaps we might have a chat in your cabin,' said Brennan in what seemed to be a helpful manner.

The three of them walked silently to the captain's modest accommodation. Killen shut the door. Brennan didn't allow for any pleasantries and got straight to the point.

'Captain, thanks for having me on board. I think you

have been informed by the Professor about our mission and the role of your vessel.'

'In part, but I don't quite understand the secrecy,' replied Killen.

'As part of a coordinated international effort the *Holland 2* will be used to test the salinity of the waters in this area of the East Atlantic. You've also been told, in confidence, we've satellite evidence that the Gulf Stream is slowing down due to the melting waters off the Greenland Ice Sheet. But the situation is a bit more complicated.'

'Complicated?' said Killen.

'Let me spell it out,' said Gilmore. 'Ostensible we're seeking to verify oceanographic data. However, we've preliminary evidence from our British friends of recent seismic activity on the ocean bed at locations on the edge of the Irish Continental Shelf, at the eastern flanks of the Eriador Seamount to be more precise. We need the manned PLU to get close to the seabed to allow us get a better picture of what is actually happening and to take some rock and gas samples.'

'What does this mean?'

'The scientists are concerned that unusual seismic activity might be a pre-cursor to a significant volcanic eruption possibly generating a tsunami that could do serious damage to the British Isles. They have asked us and the British Navy and a government research vessel that are some one hundred kilometres north of this location to get measurements and visual evidence of whatever is happening.'

The penny finally dropped. Killen composed himself.

'That certainly adds a new dimension to what we're

about and explains why everyone is talking in hushed tones. It's about time we got a clear indication as to why we're so far off the west coast of Ireland whistling in the proverbial wind.'

Killen wasn't so much angry as unsettled by his role and the involvement of his ship. As the reality of the Eriador Project unfolded, he was experiencing both emotions. A ship's captain can't function properly unless he has access to all the facts that might affect the performance of his ship. It wasn't possible to steer a ship with one's hands metaphorically tied behind one's back.

'But there has never been volcanic activity along Ireland's Continental Shelf?' Killen posed the question to himself as much as to his visitors.

Brennan responded. 'Captain Killen, like you, I'm not an expert regarding such matters. We need to plan for several dives by the ROV and the PLU and to hand over this task to those who are best equipped to do the work. Everyone is waiting for us in the mess hall so let's see what the teams need from us. Fine?'

'No problem.'

He meant the opposite. He always had a problem with lying. In truth, that's why his marriage had lasted so long. His darling Orlaith could spot a lie at fifty paces. He could never bluff.

Gerdy Gilmore took a moment to reflect before he briefed the crew and the scientists about what lay ahead. The past week was a bit of a haze, all as a result of his meeting with the enigmatic Billy van Os.

'If the news about the Gulf Stream stopping wasn't enough to keep one worried for a lifetime, what does all this mean – and just months before I'm due to retire?' He decided to keep this thought to himself.

As he entered the mess hall the room fell silent. The ship's mess hall was again packed to capacity as Gilmore made his way to a small table near the port side window. Before he started his presentation he noticed Captain Killen at the rear of the room sullen faced with his arms crossed.

'Captain,' he greeted him. A necessary protocol in front of his crew.

'Professor.'

The barest acknowledgement. His colleagues could sense all wasn't well.

Gilmore coughed to catch attention.

'Welcome everyone. Best I start.' He powered up his slide presentation. The introductory slide read 'The Eriador Project.'

'A few new introductions are needed. When you find out who's on board, you'll get a better sense about the nature of this research mission. At the outset I must make it clear that this is a joint operation involving the Irish and British navies, which has political support at the highest levels of both Governments. We had planned a four-week research programme to conduct deep water salinity tests. These activities using the *Holland 2* will go ahead as planned. The additional dimension is that we're going to use the PLU to explore the seabed to capture images of possible volcanic activity and to take rock and chemical samples. Hence the need to bolster our research crew.'

There was a clear sense of rising anticipation in the room as the primary focus of the research mission was unveiled.

'First of all, I would like to introduce you to Vice-Commodore Noel Brennan, Captain of the LÉ *Michael D. Higgins* who will give you more background.'

'Thanks, Professor. We've assembled a scientific team at under a week's notice for the tasks we've been set. Many thanks to everyone for dropping other priorities and getting to Galway at such short notice. My job is to provide you with supplies and communications as we expect to be on station for at least two months. It's also very possible that we'll need additional equipment, and perhaps a few more scientists depending on what we find. Our light Bell 206 Jet Ranger helicopter has the range to fly to Galway Airport should that be necessary. Before I ask members of the team to tell you what they will be doing, I would like to introduce you to Johnny Drew who works for British Military Intelligence. Johnny is our guest on the LÉ *Michael D. Higgins*.'

Drew stood up. Everyone knew he was a spy. He was the only one in the room other than the Vice-Commodore wearing a jacket and tie. Nobody on a research vessel ever dressed with such formality.

'I wish I could say it's nice to be here. The background is that two weeks ago we were tracking Russian submarine activity off the Rockall Plateau using our seabed sonar devices. This kit also has the capability to read and record seismic activity. While finding a Sierra Kondor class submarine on routine patrol wasn't much of a surprise, we were more than astonished that a 2.8 Richter scale earthquake was recorded close to the seabed in the Maury Channel as the submarine sailed by.'

Killen took an instant dislike to the spy. His plummy

Oxbridge accent concealed his Irish heritage. That didn't bother him. He was under instructions to do a job for His Majesty's Military Intelligence.

'There were many minor aftershocks before another shallow earthquake was recorded ten days ago, immediately beneath the eastern flank of the Eriador Seamount. We also have intelligence from our American friends that there have been a series of low volume tremors in other parts of the Mid-Atlantic Ridge as far south as the Canary Islands. An isolated small-scale sub-marine earthquake or two would not be grounds for concern, but when a pattern appears then it behoves us to check it out.'

Drew continue to deliver his script, 'Our satellite assets, as well as those of NOAA, are being deployed to support this mission. My job is to make sure you get access to our data. This will help you pinpoint the optimum search locations for the PLU and potentially the ROV. In an arguable breach of military protocol, I'm going to be based on the LÉ *Michael D. Higgins* as Liaison Officer. In that manner both navies and our collective scientific effort will be coordinated and put to best use.'

Drew didn't take any questions. Spies don't like to have to explain themselves after all.

Gilmore thanked him and then invited the next speaker. Tony Doherty took the floor. The crew knew he was a scientist: he fitted the stereotype perfectly. He clutched a file of papers wrapped in thick elastic bands that had multiple Post-it notes on numerous pages. His glasses, perched at the end of his nose, were ill-fitting. His doubled breasted brown cord jacket with multiple pockets contained at least ten pencils and pens. A small ruler protruded from his top pocket. He had numerous books, note pads and a small Apple laptop in front of him. He was set to lecture his students and not his peers, least of all the increasingly sceptical crew of the RV *Celtic Explorer*. He was out of his comfort zone.

He started nervously, handkerchief in hand. 'I'm the Professor of Oceanography at the University of Maynooth. Best if I give you a quick overview of the geology of the area we're in. The Rockall Plateau was once part of Greenland, about fifty-five million years ago and sank as North America separated from Europe. The seabed is shallow and comprises many narrow and wide valleys. At the time there was widespread volcanic activity so thermal uplifts grew the plateau's height while keeping it mainly below sea level.'

He paused for effect and to catch his breath. He blew his nose this time with a great explosion of air. 'Rockall itself, part of Ireland's territory, is the only place it rises above sea level. It has the same alkali granite composition as can be found on some islands of Scotland and on Greenland. To the north-east, there is a feature called the Anton Dohrn Seamount, which is an underwater summit that rises fifteen hundred metres from the seabed to some six hundred metres below the surface. It too was formed by volcanic activity many moons ago. Many of these sub-sea mountains are higher than some Alpine peaks.'

Much of the following detail went over the heads of the crew.

'The eastern margin of the Plateau, where we are now, is called the Feni Ridge and runs in a north-east to south-west direction for over six hundred kilometres. Here the

Irish Continental Shelf drops sharply. In fact, in some parts there are sheer cliffs over three hundred metres high.'

He moved the presentation forward to display a 3D map of the sea floor. 'Despite all we know about the marine environment of this area of the Atlantic Ocean, we've very limited scientific evidence of the behaviour of the North American and Eurasian tectonic plates that run the length of the Atlantic Ocean. And when we start seeing seismic activity after tens of thousands of years of stability, we've no option but to check out exactly what's going on. My colleague, Maeve O'Farrell, will lead the PLU research team. Maeve could you be so kind as to tell us what to expect.'

Whatever about paying attention to a grey-haired ageing Professor with a legacy cough from decades of smoking hand rolled cheroots, listening to an attractive, thirty-something with a West of Ireland lilt proved much more interesting to the crew. Her black hair was tied back in a neat chignon with red and blue bobbins keeping it in place. She wore a pair of bright pink granny glasses that balanced her subtly made-up face.

'I'm the senior researcher of the Volcanic Analytics Department at the National University of Ireland Galway, and an academic colleague of Tony. I'm so excited to be here! It's not often that we get the opportunity to monitor such activity in Ireland, or even offshore Ireland. Initially we were going to take the PLU submersible five hundred metres down the side of the Feni Ridge and later to explore the slopes that comprise the Eriador Seamount. In the light of the recent intelligence, we'll skip the first location and focus our attentions on the Eriador Seamount. This is where all the action appears to be.'

Vinnie Crowley chipped in. He was well-read and didn't hesitate to show off. He had an irresistible urge to try to impress any women that came near him.

'Eriador is a J.R.R. Tolkien *Lord of the Rings* character isn't it?'

O'Farrell smiled at him. He was old enough to be her father. Crowley blushed. He had not done that in quite some time.

'Yes, well nearly. It's the western part of his Middle Earth that lies between the Misty and Blue Mountains. In fact, the name is of Elvish origin and means "Lovely Lands".'

'Let's hope we don't run into the armies of Melkor then. I much prefer Hobbits,' Crowley continued his one-to-one conversation with Maeve, with everyone else listening in.

'I don't expect we'll find dragons or anything too fearsome in the depths. However, I do expect to detect some signs of seismic activity. That's why we've added a package of seismic and chemical detectors to the PLU. We've also taken the precaution to bolt on a sulphur dioxide testing kit.'

O'Farrell smiled again and continued. She accepted she was attractive and was happy to make the most of it when she was presenting. 'Andy Gallery is the best volcanologist we have in Ireland, so perhaps Andy you can explain what our instruments will be looking for.'

Gallery, weather beaten in appearance, had spent decades on the summits of ancient calderas all over the world. Like O'Farrell, he was keen to put his practical skills to good use close to his native land. He was a cautious man, small in stature with few words. Years spent in solo observations on mountain tops doesn't provide much opportunity for conversation.

'It's important to have access to detailed seismic data. This will tell us if the magma under the earth's crust is moving or fracturing. These may be signals that are symptomatic of background volcanic activity, which is likely to culminate in a major explosion. Another, far more vital, tell-tale sign is the change in the rate of gas escape, or variations in the cocktail of gases escaping. If we manage to detect, for example, an increase in sulphur dioxide at a vent this usually reflects the arrival of gas-rich magma not far below the surface.

The deep furrows on his brow of thinning hair indicated he was clearly concerned. 'The higher the level of gas emissions the higher the probability that an active lava dome is growing in size. We've installed what is called a COSPEC – a correlation spectrometer – on the PLU. If we manage to find sulphur gas leakage on the seabed and can take some samples, this equipment will give us the readings we need to make an assessment about the imminence and possible magnitude of any volcanic activity.'

Crowley, impatient as ever, wasn't at all impressed with the science mumbo jumbo.

He interrupted. 'How wide an area are you planning to survey, and how long will this take?'

'The two locations where the British satellites spotted seismic activity are well defined and only one hundred kilometres apart. I envisage a series of dives at these two locations initially. I expect we may have to stay on location for a while as volcanic activity can happen at great intervals between events. As everything is weather dependent, we've allowed a period of two months, or perhaps a little longer depending on what we find. As you have been told, we'll also get access to the output of the British Navy's array of seabed sonar detectors and will be working in close collaboration with the other assets that are being used as part of this wider research effort. Time, to be honest, is not the issue. Mother Earth will decide when and where we conclude our business.'

'But what about our salinity research programme?' demanded Eugene Carroll.

Silent until now, Carroll was also getting agitated. He had not been briefed in advance about Project Eriador and was annoyed his scheduled research was going to be jeopardised.

'We spent months preparing for the salinity test project. It now appears we'll be playing second fiddle to your endeavours.'

He didn't aim his comment at anyone in particular.

Gilmore saw that both research teams were taking sides. It was like the period just prior to a football match. He needed to defuse the situation before a few foul tackles went in. After all, he had overall responsibility for ensuring that everyone remembered the importance of teamwork in such a small vessel. His scientific passengers were still finding their feet in very cramped conditions, so some element of crankiness was inevitable.

'Eugene, I can assure you we've enough space and equipment to conduct both projects simultaneously. We may be a bit more cramped compared to what you were expecting, but with a bit of patience we'll all get our respective jobs done. The more we cooperate and coordinate the sooner we can all go home.'

Brennan was also aware of the rising sense of unease. He too wanted to calm things down. 'I expect our Bell helicopter will be on regular trips to Galway so if anyone has to leave a bit early, I'm sure we'll facilitate that.'

Many heads nodded approval.

To distract from the situation, Gilmore clicked on a hyperlink on the slide deck.

'Here's a live feed from a British ROV of shallow sub-sea volcanic activity on the sea floor close to Iceland, just five hundred kilometres north-west of here.'

Images of molten deep red lava and lava bombs lit up the room.

CHAPTER 4

Roque de los Muchachos

A LOT HAD HAPPENED by noon the following day.

Within an hour of the brothers' call with Mark Doyle, Marco Lesle, the head of the island's Guardia Civil, was in touch by phone. He had consulted the La Palma Earthquake Emergency Response Plan that had not been used in decades. He was keen to find out how serious the threat was. It became very clear that a series of minor tremors wasn't going to force him to trigger the Plan. This would have required all hotels and other accommodations across the island to evacuate their clients at the peak of the tourist season.

Lesle liked the quiet life, in so far as that was possible for a part-time police officer. His office on the pedestrianised Calle O'Daly in Santa Cruz de la Palma, while modest in terms of furniture and decoration, was a sanctuary of peace. Apart from an occasional gorse fire and the odd mountain rescue the Guardia Civil didn't really do too much. And that's the way he wanted it. His team had other jobs to attend to after all.

'Señor Lesle,' said Ros. 'I really must stress that we need to have a channel of communication 24/7 with your team. The mountains don't work nine to five. We need at least a dozen members from the Guardia Civil to be based at the locations we believe to be at most risk.'

'Let me stop you there. I've just twenty officers to cover the whole island and this is the busiest time of the year. The best that I can do is to ask the mountain rescue volunteers that have two off-road jeeps to contact you.'

'That would be helpful, Señor Lesle,' said Ros, somewhat dismayed by Lesle's failure to accept the seriousness of the situation. 'Please instruct these teams to locate themselves in the National Park's visitors' centre. You might also prepare contingency plans to have the Guardia Civil resources coordinated from this base.'

'The emergency plan hasn't been activated. You need to realise that the part-time mountain rescue volunteers can only do their best. They are trained to take injured hikers off the mountains. They know nothing about earthquakes.'

The head of the island's Guardia Civil believed he was one of the most important public servants on La Palma. A man who demanded and expected respect. And here he was taking instructions not only from an outsider, but from a young man who clearly had no idea how the chain of command worked. He was about to speak but was interrupted.

'Señor Lesle,' said Ros in a firmer tone. He could barely control his temper. 'You need to tell all your colleagues in the Guardia Civil to expect a deteriorating situation. It's highly probable that, if matters get worse, the Director General of the police in Madrid and not I will be directing you. All that I'm doing is letting you know what will be necessary. Be prepared to comply or justify, Señor Lesle.'

Ros hung up. The head of the Guardia Civil was incandescent. He threw his hat on the ground and screamed to himself. Nobody else was there to listen. 'That stupid boy. Telling me my business.' Lesle's blood pressure rose. He paused and reflected on the conversation. He was an ill-tempered bombast, but a good listener underneath it. He had a gut instinct that before too long it would be 'all hands on deck'. The dozens of pages of guidance in the Earthquake Emergency Response Plan would be of little use. Maybe the scientist was right to be cautious. He called the mountain rescue unit and without question their two jeeps drove to the visitors' centre as instructed.

Simon and Ros reviewed the locations of all the remote monitors during the night and into the early hours. All were silent and not a quiver registered. They divided the mountains into six areas, each centred around a dormant volcano. The plan was that six teams would need to be ready to move once increased seismic or volcanic activity became apparent. They caught a few hours' sleep.

True to his word Mark Doyle called as they were finishing up their breakfast. They put the call on speaker.

'Guys, I've some good news and some bad news.'

'Go with the bad first,' said Simon.

'NASA can't commit any satellite support unless there are clear signs of a major emergency situation. Something to do with budget cuts and a higher priority being given to security surveillance in and around the Gulf of Hormuz.'

'And the good news?' asked Ros.

'I believe you got a less than enthusiastic response from the Guardia Civil. I had anticipated that, so I spoke directly to a contact of mine who runs the defence air base next door on the Island of Tenerife. Should the mountains start shaking, as I suspect they will, then three military Sikorsky helicopters with paramedics and a team of a hundred marines will be provided for medevac and general support.'

'Señor Lesle will be pleased,' sniggered Simon.

Mark continued, 'I'm making arrangements to have two of our state-of-the-art thermal imaging kits that are mounted on commercial drones couriered to your part of the world. I expect you'll have delivery within thirty-six hours. Constant monitoring of the footprint of the National Park is the priority. When this kit arrives, we'll need to deploy it immediately.'

'So much for Damian's drone,' said Ros.

'We're ahead of you,' said Simon. 'We've procured thermal imaging capacity from a local tour guide who has just purchased what he believes is a state-of-the-art drone. This could be a good interim solution.'

'Well done. Glad to see you are using your initiative.'

Ros slapped Simon on the back. 'Now who's a clever boy?'

'There's more news lads,' said Mark. 'You two, Maria and Claudine are to move immediately to the Observatory at Roque de los Muchachos that's only a few klicks from your rather primitive base. I need our best assets under the same roof. I briefed Antonio Farillo, the Director at the ORM, about what we might expect. He was more than willing to help. If nothing else, it's a safer environment and one that's fully provisioned. He will provide you with access to his communications network, so we'll be able to keep in regular touch on secure links. We need to set up a situations room and the ORM's boardroom fits the bill quite nicely. In addition, the ORM's logistics support crew will be at your disposal so straight away you have a small transport fleet at the ready.'

'I've spoken, as you have, to Carmen. I expect she will travel from La Gomera to La Palma on the afternoon ferry tomorrow. She will join you within twenty-four hours at the ORM.'

'What about back-up?' said Ros.

'Will the girls be joining us? asked Simon softly.

'Carmen assured me that she has access to a support team from the Instituto and once she deems it necessary, they will join you. That's why I want you all under the same roof at the ORM. I'm packing my gear and expect to be on site within a day or so. It's a long way from Hawaii to La Palma.'

'Does all this suggest we're in more serious trouble than we realise?' said Simon.

'Guys, if a series of minor tremors on La Palma was the only story, I would treat this as routine. But overnight we had more sea floor seismic activity out in the Mid-Atlantic Ridge. There's on-going low-level readings on the other Canary Islands. Like you, I wouldn't rule out that Mother Earth may be getting ready to give us a surprise. I hope she is not too angry. And I hope we've time to organise a response.'

After he rang off, Ros and Simon made silent eye contact. They too knew that the dormant volcanoes of La Palma were about to make the news.

'It is only a matter of time before Fox News and Sky will be broadcasting live from the island,' said Simon.

'Your amateur acting experience will make you a great spokesperson,' replied Ros.

'By the way, what is the relationship between the Instituto and GSN?' asked Simon.

'Simple. The GSN has clout, resources and global expertise. They call the shots when a pending global emergency is in the offing. Can you imagine what Carmen would have to do to get Sikorskys deployed here! Donkeys: yes, helicopters: no! The GSN has global experience so if activity escalates, they will know best what to do. Don't forget there hasn't been a serious earthquake or volcanic eruption in all of Spain for over a hundred years. We've a theoretical knowledge of our environment. Mark and the GSN deal with these natural events all over the world every day.'

The brothers knew that a move to the ORM made a lot of sense. It was an added bonus that it was a lot more comfortable and would mean a reunion for Simon and Maria. The ORM also had skin in the game because it was located at the edge of the Caldera de Taburiente at an elevation of 2,400 metres. The vast investment in this state-of-the-art astronomical facility was exposed. Its high-resolution telescopes provided one of the best places in the world to experience clear skies and to stargaze, but when it was built a gamble had been taken. It was known the facility was located close to a set of dormant volcanoes that could put the entire complex at risk.

Hotel Icefjord, Ilulissat

Lars Brun decided that it would be best if he was present when the Norwegian Air Force's Lockheed C130 Hercules transporter landed at Ilulissat airport.

The recent extension of the runway at Ilulissat to accommodate wide bodied aircraft had an upside and a downside. The downside was that the quiet and quaint town of Ilulissat was now inundated – snowed under so to speak – with tourists. Direct flights from JFK, Toronto and European cities other than Copenhagen were a good idea in theory but, in reality, the local population could not cope with mass tourism. The indigenous Inuits, hunters by nature, now felt hunted.

As summer conditions were good, one of the De Havilland DHC-6 Twin Otter ski-planes that serviced the needs of Summit Station was pressed into action for the 382-kilometre journey to Ilulissat – a distance it would cover in a little under ninety minutes. It was an ideal transport option as it could take both cargo and fifteen passengers. Its powerful Pratt & Whitney turboprop engines allowed it to take off and land on short runways. It might be a noise bucket, but it provided basic comforts to research staff who were more than used to rough conditions.

At the Summit Station's high elevation, the plane's capacity to take off and the fuel it carried was very much determined by the weight of the passengers and cargo. Lars knew the drill. He stood on the weighing scales as the two Canadian pilots observed.

'Ninety-one kilos. You have put on two kilos since you last flew.'

Patting his belly, one of the pilots joked, 'Is this your eskimo bank account? Your hedge against hunger?'

Lars responded to the good-natured banter, 'What do you expect when all we eat is meat and carbs! When is the last time we saw fruit in this place?'

'That's a feeble excuse! We'll trim the aircraft to take account of the excess personal baggage.'

The pilots and Lars boarded the Twin Otter.

As the plane prepared to take off down the runway at the Summit Station Lars asked himself if this was a total waste of time, money and effort. Although he had to admit a bit of bias, the conclusion he reached was 'no' on all counts. For over a decade, scientists had been aware of the extent of the Greenland ice melt but could not predict patterns nor the impacts of what was happening, literally under their feet. Within two to three weeks they would all be wiser.

One of the benefits of heading up the research team at Summit Station was that he could take full advantage of every opportunity to fly on the Twin Otter. Wrapped in a wool blanket, he sat on the jump seat in the main cockpit, immediately behind the two pilots. He put on his oxygen mask, checked the radio communications and looked out. It was a rare clear day with excellent visibility. There were basic flight preparation routines and rules. The pilot confirmed the flight details with the control tower at Ilulissat. Once that was done the Twin Otter took off down the groomed runway. They were off the ground in under a hundred metres.

The scenery at 3,000 metres above the ice sheet was stunning.

Across the horizon to the south there were over fifty white peaks, many unclimbed, protruding above a hazy dirty cloud base. Only the highest peak wore a cloud cap. A crown for the king towering in his turret over his troops. This was God's place, where mountains, summits, rivers and lakes had no names. Undiscovered remoteness. Wide open nothingness. Pure beauty. An untamed and untended land. While a lot could be seen, he knew there was much more that lay beneath.

Just after take-off the terrain below had been full of ridges of what can best be described as dirty ice. There was growing evidence that the top layers of the ice sheet comprised deposits of volcanic dust from Iceland's volcanoes as well as brown industrial particulates pollution from Canadian and American cities. How this affected the snow-white colour of the surface was no longer a matter of debate. Lars was more surprised when he noticed small but identifiable pools of deep blue water at regular intervals. As far as he could see from 2,000 metres up, there were channels of water spreading out from these pools.

As the Twin Otter descended into Ilulissat airport over the ice sheet, the views were nothing short of spectacular. What struck Lars, when they were still some distance from the coast, were the great number of blue lakes dotted all over. Many of the larger lakes were over two hundred metres wide and had what appeared to be tails – rivers of azure blue meltwater that disappeared under the ice sheet.

The morning fog that usually hung thick over the low-lying coastal areas had been burnt away. The jagged high edge at the rear of the Jacobshavn Glacier was the dominant feature as they approached the airport. Behind the glacier lay a thirty kilometre stretch of icebergs waiting their turn to join the warmer waters of the Baffin Sea to the west. Tides arm-wrestled the pack ice. The land and the frozen sea were as still as a painting.

As the plane flew lower over the side of the glacier the scenery changed dramatically. One thousand metres below the landscape was radically different. The brown clay, fields of moss and creeping white lichens and soiled grey boulders defined the seashore. The fields were infused with Niviarsiaq, the 'Young Girl', Greenland's national flower and other perennial flora. There was a veritable palette of vegetation. The freezing blue-black Arctic waters were full of icebergs of all shapes, hues and sizes playing with each other in slow motion. Calm but voracious sentinels. The light winds blew chunks of blue-white ice across the bay. The high sloping mountains close to the shoreline were mirrored in the water. It was hard to believe that once Greenland was lush with ancient poplars, chestnuts and conifers.

I should have brought my camera, thought Lars.

Apart from the small town of Ilulissat some five kilometres ahead, there was no visible sign of habitation. This part of Greenland was barren. The nearest Inuit village, Qaanaaq, was seventy-five kilometres to the north. This was a traditional Greenland settlement, where people depended on what nature afforded them. It was a slow way of life where few Western influences penetrated.

The Twin Otter glided in like a large snow albatross. Lars pushed back against his seat and the plane landed with a bump, lurched, slowed and slid to a stop, and in doing so pushed the limits of luck and physics. This was just another effortless, routine school run for the Canadian pilots. Although they didn't let Lars know, their priority was to catch the second half of an ice hockey play-off in the airport crews' TV room where their team, the Toronto Maple Leafs, were locked in mortal combat against the unfancied Ottawa Senators. Professional hockey, after all, was a religion that demanded total devotion from its believers. The post-flight de-brief could wait.

Later, Lars supped some hot vegetable soup in a mug with the base manager in the control tower as they watched the C130 Hercules loop over the airfield against an almost clear blue sky. This four-engine turboprop transport aircraft, much favoured by the military across the world, was as comfortable landing on unprepared runways as it was on a fully tarmacked one. The Air Traffic Controller gave permission to land. It wasn't as busy as Heathrow or JFK, but standard operational protocols had to be respected. The plane taxied up at a distance from the terminal building and the piercing roars of its engines subsided. It was a behemoth beside the much smaller De Havilland DHC-8 200 series aircraft used by Greenland Air and Air Connect Iceland.

Soon after the immense rear cargo door opened.

Sean strolled out as if this was something he did every day of the week. As he sucked in his first lungful of cold clean Greenland air, he began a conversation with a tall civilian who Lars reckoned was a Scandinavian about fifty years of age. He looked learned and carried his weight well. He wore a grey padded waistcoat and sported Chinos. His

Ray Bans and the absence of a hat suggested he was aware of his appearance. As they got closer, he recognised Benny Lundt, the man he had spoken with at the climate action conference a while back.

Lars walked out to greet them. The cold air hit him hard.

'*Tikilluarit Kalaallit Nunaat*, or Welcome to Greenland for the tourists among you.'

'Have you arranged a tee-time in this land of forty shades of white?' joked Sean as he gave Lars a hug.

'Yes, we've a four-ball arranged at the indoor pitch and putt.'

Benny spoke before more golf talk got in the way.

'I'm not on the passenger manifest but, like Sean, I couldn't resist travelling to observe this unique experiment. As you may know, it was me who arranged the plane, the Humvees, the drones and their operators.'

'You're most welcome Benny,' said Lars. 'Great to see you again. We've an interesting few weeks ahead of us. And many thanks for the transport in particular. Having access to the Humvees will make our job so much easier.'

Benny was quite proud that he had not only managed to borrow two Norwegian army Bombardier Humvees and experienced drivers but also had the opportunity to have them fitted out for the tasks that lay ahead. These machines could travel in practically all conditions in sub-zero weather over snow and ice terrain. They were designed to transport heavy equipment to remote destinations. Their Vickers aluminium suspension, driven by a sprocket on each side, gave its crew an easy ride. The airtight cabin could accommodate six people in comfort in sub-zero conditions.

'Let's get you and the equipment to the Summit Station,' said Lars.

'I've sorted that,' said Benny, with a wry smile.

'I have helpful friends in high places who, when they heard what you were trying to do, offered us the use of a heavy lift military Sikorsky helicopter. We can transport all the equipment to the Summit Station, weather conditions permitting.'

'Let's make a start then,' said Lars.

'Less haste, Lars. As the helicopter will not arrive until first thing in the morning, I've taken the liberty of booking us into the Hotel Icefjord, one of the better accommodations in this part of the world. Time for a bit of recreation, given that we'll be full on from tomorrow.'

Sean gazed out the window of their taxi as they drove through the town. He soon concluded it would never win the Tidy Towns Competition. Arctic clutter was everywhere: sledges in various states of disrepair, drying racks hung with halibut, seal and polar bear skins pulled taut on stretchers, construction waste, abandoned children's toys, broken ladders, bottles, cans, containers, plastic and cardboard packaging, wires, rope and cabling, and drying clothes flapping frozen on lines.

Ilulissat's residents kept over four thousand huskies on the perimeter of the town. The associated acrid smell of their waste permeated everywhere. Outside most houses, skimobiles lay covered on packing crates awaiting winter.

They met up before dinner and sat out on the sun-filled balcony that looked out on the array of icebergs of all shapes and sizes that filled the expanse of Disko Bay. An iceberg the size of a tennis court floated gently fifty metres from their table. In the near distance the edge of the Jacobshavn Glacier could be seen. Speed boats zigzagged across the bay transporting tourists, mainly Danes, on whale-watching and other excursions. The small shrimp fleet out of Ilulissat's small harbour was scattered along the horizon with their brightly painted boats clearly visible amidst the icebergs. A great setting for a pre-dinner drink.

'Try Taseq, the local craft beer.' Lars' frequent visits to Ilulissat gave him critical local knowledge.

'I thought it best if we had an honest chat just among ourselves before we transfer to the Summit Station,' said Benny. 'Sean, once Lars told us about the features of the golf balls and their potential, we moved heaven and earth to mobilise resources to assist with the delivery of the project. In addition, and not unrelated to your meeting with Lars, our American friends decided to share some critical but unpublished data about the Greenland Ice Sheet with us.'

As he spoke there was a sound like a gunshot followed by a loud growling sound with a low pitch that seemed never ending. 'What in the name of the Lord is that?' exclaimed Sean.

'Calving glaciers,' replied Benny. 'Get used to the constant noise. It never stops at this time of the year. You will hear the sounds of glaciers big and small cracking, splicing and falling into the sea as small icebergs day and night. We are, after all, looking at the world's largest graveyard for maritime glaciers.'

'What have the Americans told you?' Lars interjected. He wanted to talk shop.

'You were right all along, Lars, said Benny. 'Your theory about the hollowing out of the Greenland Ice Sheet is shared by our American cousins. They base their findings on seismic records but, like us, they need to get the data that we hope Sean's mobile friends will produce. Thankfully, they have agreed to leave us to our own devices and will not interfere with our work – even though we're using their precious Summit Station, as I was reminded constantly!'

'There is no such thing as a free lunch,' chipped in Sean.

The conversation continued with a large Greenland smokehouse plate, including whale, seal, musk ox, caribou and halibut, being plenty for all. Tapas Greenland style. Several Taseqs loosened up the conversation.

'What a sight,' said Sean as the sun slowly lowered its yellow glow over the skyline.

Sean noticed that the 'tennis court' iceberg that was in front of them when they arrived had moved over the horizon on the tidal current.

It was close to midnight and still the sun shone bright. He was tired. It had been a long day. Not many people travel from Galway to the west coast of Greenland in one day.

'You know I've never experienced a day when the sun shone for a full twenty-four hours. It must be near midnight. When is it time for bed?' said Sean.

'Later', said Benny. 'Our turn to give you a surprise.'

'Explain please.' Sean put an empty bottle of Taseq on the table.

'We're going on a midnight trip to the Jacobshavn Glacier,' smiled Benny.

'Is this some kind of a joke? I'm usually tucked up in bed at this hour.' Sean feigned a yawn.

On cue, a skiff with 'World of Greenland Tours' on its prow drew up at the dock beside the hotel. Powered by twin Yamaha engines it had the speed and agility to manoeuvre in all kinds of sea conditions. Tonight, though, only a light breeze blew.

'Lets' go then,' said Benny.

'But I'll freeze. I don't have any suitable gear,' said Sean.

'All will be provided. The boatman has head to toe survivor suits – and you can borrow my beanie!'

Within minutes the private tour to Jacobshavn Glacier and the floating city of icebergs, began.

'Sean, we decided to show you the practical side of the melting of the Greenland Ice Sheet at this most prolific of maritime glaciers. Sit back and enjoy the scenery and the experience.' Benny knew this midnight trip would help Sean better appreciate the importance of Project Masters.

Around the bend from the hotel they met the first colossus: an iceberg almost four hundred metres long and as high, which had multiple jagged edges and crack lines where gravity and erosion were working their way through the ice faces. Its neighbours, hundreds of them, were of all sorts, shades and sizes. The ice comprised several layers reflecting various shades of light testifying to their different ages and qualities.

Behind the first line of icebergs others were stacked up as far as the eye could see far out to the edges of the Baffin Sea. The skiff slowed down as they went through brace ice, the small remains of what were once large icebergs.

The brace ice was everywhere as were smaller icebergs that moved at remarkable speed with the tide. They moved further out and sailed alongside icebergs that towered into the sky. The larger ones were stationary. Their base was lodged against the seafloor. They were mainly white, but most had noticeable lines of what appeared to be black soot along their columns. Some had thin layers of a brown substance running in parallel. The biggest, a tabular iceberg, was shaped like a large box with squared features and sharp perpendicular edges almost a hundred metres high. Sean remembered that only ten per cent of icebergs were visible above water.

He could hear the delicate sound of the melting ice dripping from sharply angled bergs. The common feature was the growling, groaning noise that filled the midnight air as calved sections crashed into the sea. The rolling and turning plates of ice made louder, angrier noises as they scraped against each other.

Sean stared in silence at this never ending and ever-changing vista that defied description. The geology and white landscape made a deep puzzle.

How could words be used to describe a wonder of the world?

Little auks, hundreds of them, soared above the frozen icebergs. They came to Greenland each year to breed, nest and fledge their young on south-facing talus slopes. The sound of the beat of their wings competed with the growling of the icebergs.

The boat man steered the skiff slowly into Kannia Bay. On the shore side one could make out the board walk into this UNESCO site. Even at midnight there were hikers on the trail taking advantage of the full light under a high cloud ceiling.

'Look, starboard side!' shouted the boatman.

To Sean it looked like a puff of smoke. Then a broad black back appeared with a triangle tail some two metres out of the water. Another puff, then another.

'Humpbacks. I think we've six around us. They come into this bay as it is shallow and full of fish and squid, their staple diet. I'll cut the engines so that we can observe them in silence.'

The following twenty minutes left Sean in awe. The whales, part of a small family pod, drifted at slow speed around the bay within a short distance of the skiff. They were chasing their supper and were in no hurry. At regular intervals they surfaced and expelled air. They glided majestically from one side of the bay to the other as the bay was full of food. The male, all of thirty tonnes and some twenty metres long saluted the boat as he breached just twenty metres away from them. Sean could see the creature's eye and wondered if he returned the stare. As quickly as they appeared, they disappeared.

Sean's senses were in over-drive.

They were not the only people to witness the passage of the humpbacks. A two-person kayak moved at a more relaxed pace off their bow. The person in the front held a small harpoon that's always thrown from the right. They were fishing for seals. The paddles dipped effortlessly without stirring the inky blue water.

Anticipating Sean's concern for the fragility of the kayak in the presence of the world's largest mammals, Benny explained. 'Don't fret Sean. These are Inuit 'umiak' kayaks and are made of sealskin. These kayaks are perhaps the finest craft that mankind devised. It is less a boat or a canoe than an extension of man himself. For generations their basic design has allowed hunters successfully navigate across turbulent waters, through waves and around surly bucking ice masses.'

As the boat turned back towards the hotel a loud shot gun sound echoed around them.

'Wait. Eyes left, quickly.' The boatman was again on alert.

Turning around, they witnessed a large blue-white section the size of a double decker bus calve off a tall iceberg in front of them. As it began its collapse from the top of the iceberg, it shattered with splinters of ice and snow flying in all directions. It hit the water with a loud thump.

'Brace yourselves,' roared the boatman.

He had no sooner spoken than the huge chunk of ice that had split re-emerged from its dunking in the dark blue sea. Such was its size that the waves it generated tossed the skiff like a kite in the wind.

The short return to the hotel's dock was uneventful. Sean slept in fits and starts as the summer sun poured into his bedroom all night. The body in daylight wanted no rest. His understanding of the power of ice was enhanced. It gave his contribution to Project Masters a context. That's exactly what Benny and Lars had intended.

The arrival of the helicopter 'first thing in the morning' required them to return to the airport for 7 a.m. They were joined on the apron by the airport dispatcher, a small man, an Inuit, who knew not to ask too many questions.

The familiar distant roar of helicopter blades slowly filled the air. To the south, what turned out to be a Sikorsky

S-64 Skycrane twin-lift helicopter grew from a dot in the distance to a giant of the skies. It landed a hundred metres from the rear open door of the Hercules C-130. Its six-blade main rotor, powered by Pratt & Whitney turboshaft engines, blew all dust and loose rubbish to the extremities of the airfield.

Two Arctic adapted Bombardier M15 model Humvees, four-tracked, quarter-tonne utility vehicles, were driven out from the plane's interior. These were going to transport goods and personnel to various sites located within a medium range of the Summit Station. In addition, Benny had procured two of the Norwegian military's drones with their support crews and an array of accessories, which soon followed.

Proud of his toys, Benny beamed. 'This is the best flying crane on the planet. Yesterday it was servicing oil rigs off Ekofisk in the North Sea. Today it is at your disposal for forty-eight hours. I reckon two round trips to the Summit Station will have everything on location before close of business tomorrow.'

'Lars, Sean, you have a choice of transport for a change! Twin Otter or Skycrane?'

'Skycrane,' they replied in unison.

'Hey guys I've never flown in a helicopter before,' pleaded Sean.

'This is another Greenland experience for your memoirs,' said Lars.

In short order the support personnel were transferred to the Twin Otter.

Later, as the noon bell rang at the Summit Station, the Sky Crane was already in the air on its way back to

Ilulissat. It would be back on station at the Ekofisk oil platforms the following day, its job done.

Once the visitors had settled into their Arctic tents, Lars convened a meeting in the Big House.

'Benny, I want to put on record how really appreciative we all are. We've been struggling for years to get resources to carry out our research. In the space of a matter of weeks you have mobilised all the kit we need to deliver Project Masters. Best if I give you the floor. I know you wish to share some thoughts with us about the strategic importance of the task ahead.'

Benny put the project into context.

'We've known for some years that the hot summer extreme melt event of recent years impacted almost the entire of the 1.7 million square kilometres surface of the Greenland Ice Sheet. The likely cause was an anomalous ridge of warm air, acting as a strong heat dome, that became stagnant over Greenland. Data from the QuickSCAT scatterometer revealed that the pace of the ice melt has accelerated in recent years. The eastern region of Greenland, just north of the Arctic Circle appears to be the worst affected.'

'What's a scatterometer?' asked an inquisitive Sean. 'These things are above my pay grade!'

'It's a device that transmits electromagnetic waves and measures the returned power of the waves scattered back from the snow and ice on the ice sheet, which is quantified by a radar parameter called backscatter,' replied Benny. 'Clear?'

'I guess so.' Sean smiled, embarrassed for having interrupted Benny's presentation, but really none the wiser.

Benny continued his talk.

'To date, most of the research has concentrated on reconstructing the extent and the dynamics of the Greenland Ice Sheet during the last ice age. What we've been trying to do is to predict how the ice sheet may respond based on evidence of landforms left behind during the last ice age. We know that the ice sheet covered the continental edge when it was at its largest extent. It then retreated eight kilometres to the middle shelf, during a period that's called the Younger Dryas some twelve thousand years ago. It was stable for a while until it retreated a further hundred kilometres during the final deglaciation. This dramatic collapse has possible implications for our understanding of the future evolution of the Greenland Ice Sheet.'

'Forgive me Benny, but where does Project Masters fit into the scenario?' Sean's second interruption was more serious.

'The ice sheet contains enough water to raise global sea levels by some seven metres. We've, unfortunately, been fixated by the impact that this might have on coastal communities. Specifically, we've spent a lot of research effort to date trying to predict scenarios of sea level rises. All doom and gloom stuff.'

'That misses the point. Significant sea level rise is not an immediate prospect, or at least I hope it isn't,' added Lars.

'Got it in one,' responded Benny.

'What has become the number one research priority is the extent to which the increasing evidence of significant fresh off-flow from the ice sheet is impacting on the Gulf Stream, the upper limb of what is called the Atlantic

Meridional Overturning Circulation – AMOC in our jargon. As we all know, salty water sinks at high latitudes, it pulls warmer water from lower latitudes to replace it. There is evidence that some of the columns close to the south and south-east of Greenland that move warm water across the North Atlantic have weakened by as much as forty per cent in the past five years. Earlier this year a US submarine under the Arctic Ice Sheet east of Greenland tried to measure the giant chimneys of cold dense water that normally sink down to the seabed to be replaced by warm water. Of the ten giant columns that had been there during a previous research visit only two remained.

'Lars, is that the Gulf Stream problem we spoke about at the dinner we had after the Masters?' said Sean.

'Sure is. One and the same,' replied Lars.

Benny paused ahead of revealing the main reason the Norwegian Government had decided to fund and support Project Masters.

'The Gulf Stream moves a prodigious amount of water– more than 5.6 million cubic metres every second – and it is very sensitive to changes in water density. The conveyor belt effect means that, as it reaches cooler waters in the North Atlantic, it sinks into abyssal depths and flows southwards as the lower limb of the conveyor. However, if significant volumes of meltwater off the Greenland Ice Sheet mix with saltwater, this reduces the density of the flow and can, and it appears has, stopped some of the columns of water that return south to warmer waters. What concerns me is not only the increasing evidence that the off-flow from the ice sheet is accelerating, but the volumes of freshwater are such that it would not take too much more for the Gulf Stream effect to slow down and eventually stop.'

The researchers and the scientists in the room deduced the practical consequences immediately.

'Sorry, but what does all this mean?' Sean was a bit slow this morning, despite his on-going consumption of double espressos. He had not grasped what Benny was saying.

Benny concluded his briefing.

'If the western boundary current of the Gulf Stream pumping mechanism stops because of the release of huge quantities of ice-melt off the Greenland Ice Sheet, then Norway, Iceland and the British Isles will become a frozen tundra. The ice cover will gradually extend southwards to cover all of Northern Europe, as it did around twenty thousand years ago. We need to know not if, but when, this phenomenon will start to impact on our climates and economies. The Norwegian Government is most concerned that Project Masters delivers the goods so to speak. Sean, your golf balls may provide us with the insights that are urgently needed to help us put a timeline on our adaptation preparations.'

And if the golf balls fail to perform …? Sean thought to himself. He felt a deep sense of foreboding. He had not fully appreciated the enormity of what the researchers were seeking to prove. The stakes were truly high.

Holland 2

Just after dawn the *Holland 2* was launched into the blue-grey waters off the stern of the RV *Celtic Explorer*. The ROV crew expertly positioned the umbilical tether. They knew if it twisted the ROV would have to be retrieved.

Its thrusters were controlled by Paul McCrossan who used the joysticks like a professional gamer. Once the ROV was in position any variation from that position was indicated by the sensors. Sitting in front of several display screens, McCrossan drove the ROV as if he were onboard it. His job was to deliver a payload to a pre-determined location and once there, to execute certain tasks. In this case to test the salinity and temperature of the columns of seawater that were the motors of the Gulf Stream.

Seated close behind him, two technicians monitored the ROV's vital functions.

The ROV deck crew had completed standard pre-dive safety operating procedures on dozens of occasions. The day before the ROV had been given a full physical examination. All the equipment: the frame, specialist instruments, cameras, communications and the tether were tested. One or two technical adjustments had been made. All systems had been tested and cross-checked and double cross-checked. It was expensive to make a mistake. A shorter checklist was completed in the period immediately before the ROV was expertly winched into the water using the research vessel's Triplex crane.

The surface directed ROV was capable of descending to two thousand metres. It was the pride and joy of the Irish Marine Institute since its purchase for €2 million a year before. It gave marine research an entirely new dimension. The biggest advantage was its advanced submersible technologies. It was chock-full with the latest gadgetry. It had successfully been deployed on a variety of research tasks: hydrographic tests, fishing surveys, seabed mapping and recovery tasks.

With the support of the Chief Engineer, Paul McCrossan had set the coordinates for the dive. With his team, he had also prepared the scientific instruments that were ready to detect the smallest changes in the salinity of the ocean and the speed of the currents. He was especially pleased with his innovation in assembling and installing electro-connectivity devices that didn't require a flow of water to take a reading. These could – in theory at least – measure the salinity of water by testing the electrical conductivity of the water. While the sealed bottle canisters had worked well near the surface, this was the first time they had been tried at significant depth while secured to an ROV. He spent a lot of time ensuring the devices were correctly calibrated and that the stainless-steel electrodes were cleaned with pure alcohol to improve performance.

'What do you think we'll find?' asked Patricia Treacy, one of Tony Doherty's colleagues from the University of Maynooth, whose job it was to analyse the salinity test readings.

She stood at the science desks that were to the rear of the bridge. The Chief Scientist and other researchers were also present to observe the first findings of the salinity tests.

An array of data monitors lit up the room as the ROV descended with the vessel's tethering providing power and communications links through a fibre optic cable.

'To be honest, despite what we've been told, the satellites can't give us reliable data,' replied Doherty. 'The water surface temperature has dropped. That's certain. A somewhat similar phenomenon happened ten thousand years ago when sea ice was found as far as the north of Spain. In terms of the earth's geology that was yesterday! Back then the Canadian ice fields melted and burst into the North Atlantic at what is now the Gulf of St Lawrence. Imagine the consequences if we find a comparable modern-day phenomenon is already so advanced as to be unstoppable. I can't begin to imagine the consequences if the pace of melting on the Greenland Ice Sheet and its frontal glaciers accelerates.'

The Chief Scientist intervened. 'Patricia, I should know, but please refresh me on the basics of these salinity tests that we're going to conduct.'

Gilmore wasn't in any way embarrassed to display a gap in his scientific knowledge.

She explained, 'The two largest dissolved components in seawater are chlorine and sodium. The total of these dissolved salts is expressed as salinity, which can be calculated from conductivity and temperature readings. What we're looking for are variations from the normal ratio expressed as the electrical conductivity of a standard concentration of potassium chloride solution. In other words, where meltwater mixes with saltwater this should be measurable by means of passing an electrical current flow through the seawater. One of the new kits we installed does just that.

However, this far south of the main source of fresh water – the Greenland Ice Sheet – and given the vast expanse of the ocean, I wouldn't expect to find any major changes. Does that make sense?'

Gilmore nodded. He knew that the most important thing a scientist needed to know was what it was that they didn't know.

Treacy continued her lecture to Ireland's Chief Scientist.

'Finding these chimneys or columns of dense saltwater that are up to a kilometre across is the first task. Not only do they plunge suddenly and rapidly, but they move randomly between Labrador, Greenland and the British Isles. But find them we must. That's where the satellites' thermal imagery helps us, as subtle differences in surface and sub-surface water temperature can be detected. We're at a location where the British Skynet 6 satellite has detected that water may be somewhat less saline. We need to observe and test the salinity of the seawater at different levels below the surface and should its descent slow down at what pace. If a dramatic reduction in this conveyor belt effect is found in multiple locations, it could be a long hard winter very soon.'

Gilmore understood. 'The geography schoolbooks will have to be re-written if the Gulf Stream decides to pack it in.'

Treacy continued, 'We just assumed that the Gulf Stream would always be there. This ocean river moves waters poleward at a greater rate than the combined flows of the Amazon and the Mississippi rivers. Its flow has been threatened: that's for sure. It is a sort of meteorological battlefield, except everyone is on the losing side. We and the four other marine research vessels being deployed on a similar exercise have to provide the evidence.'

They both turned to the monitors on the science desks with a growing sense of foreboding.

The ROV was easy to control in expert hands. It was in stationary mode ninety metres astern of the ship at a depth of six hundred metres. The instrumentation showed there was a small but noticeable reduction in salinity levels. As the ROV moved away at the same depth this reduction was also marked by red graphic lines on the main monitor.

'Let's go down another two hundred metres,' instructed Gilmore.

McCrossan responded. As the ROV dropped the intensity of the readings on the monitor continued to show a falling level of salinity and, more worryingly, a fall in the speed of the dropping column.

For the next three hours *Holland 2* was guided to greater depths within a circumference of half a kilometre.

The end result was that the water column that was being observed disappeared. They had real time evidence for the first time that one of the columns sustaining the Gulf Stream was on the point of collapse. Once the ROV was retrieved and safely secured on deck the water samples collected were transferred to the dry lab. Soon after, Treacy was able to confirm the other data. The salinity levels of the water column, especially near the surface, were a fraction of what would normally be expected.

A conference call was scheduled for that afternoon with scientists from the Woods Hole Oceanographic Institution in Cape Cod. These scientists tracked the Gulf Stream as it progressed into the North Atlantic. Over a year before, it had been their sub-sea buoys that had picked up small but subtle changes in the ocean's patterns at levels of latitude nearest to Greenland. This intelligence prompted a request to NASA to use its array of TOPEX (topographic experiment) satellites to measure the thermal differences in the North Atlantic Drift's rings, loops and splits.

The Gulf Stream had always split into two after it crossed the Mid-Atlantic Ridge, a chain of volcanic mountains that ran the length of the Atlantic Ocean. It was the width and pace of the northern current, the North Atlantic Drift that continued past Iceland towards Ireland and Scotland that had everyone at Woods Hole preoccupied.

The conference call began with the ROV's scientists standing in a circle at the rear of the bridge.

'What do you read from the data?'

The question was directed to Tony Doherty.

Patricia Treacy had asked an open question, but she knew what the data meant. Out of courtesy to her Irish colleagues, she didn't wish to impose her view but wanted to encourage a discussion.

Doherty had struggled earlier to cope with the consequences of the rapidly changing data sets. He spoke with an edge in his voice.

'The column we analysed appears to be almost non-functional. What concerns me most is that its flow has changed so dramatically from what our sensors had been telling us a month ago.'

'Are we in trouble?' asked Gilmore. He had spotted the body language of his colleagues while observing their monitors as the data built up a complete picture over the past hours. The more experienced scientists seemed to be resigned to the findings. It was as if they expected the results that had been confirmed.

'We can't be sure Professor,' said Doherty.

A Woods Hole scientist spoke. 'One bad outcome can't be described as a pattern by any stretch of the imagination'.

'We reckon there are over thirty columns like the one we've just analysed across five hundred square kilometres of ocean,' said Treacy. 'This one is near the southern limit of the North Atlantic Drift. We need to get data from columns north of us. As you know, the Brits are working on this area. I guess we should proceed to review the limited information we have on our next priority location.'

Gilmore interjected. 'We'll prepare the *Holland 2* for another dive once the deck crew have caught up on their sleep.'

'Yes to that,' said McCrossan as he faked a yawn.

'I hope our need to move further north coincides with whatever the others want to do with the PLU submersible,' said Doherty. It was a statement and not as a question.

'Please send our data findings to the British research vessel located north of us,' instructed Gilmore.

'Will do, Professor,' replied Doherty.

Gilmore left the room and retired to his cabin. He called the Minister on his encrypted mobile to brief him about the findings and their implications. That done, he picked up the phone on his desk and dialled an internal number.

'Barry, Gerdy here. Whiskey?'

'Sure. My room in five.'

CHAPTER 5

La Cumbrecita

OVER DINNER WITH THEIR Aunt Margarida and Uncle Damian, Claudine and Maria discussed the events that had literally and figuratively rocked them earlier. They sat on the wide veranda as the red rimmed sun was setting to the West. The tapas had hardly been touched. The wine was poured but the glasses were full. Nobody had an appetite. They all felt the tension.

The family's villa was a basic two-story over basement wooden structure with a large living-cum-dining room but, more importantly, it had a wraparound veranda that caught the sun from dawn to dusk. Called Haciende del Molino, it was located high on a hill near the townland of Fuencaliente at an elevation of over nine hundred metres. All the houses on the island were painted with almost luminous colours. Their hacienda was bright turquoise. The garden was full of exotic plants, fruits, herbs and vegetables, their colours contrasting with the dominant hue of the walls.

From the veranda there were stunning views of the abandoned lighthouse, with its red and white tower, and of the vast expanse of the island's black ash beaches along the southern coastline. However, enjoying the scenery was far from their minds.

The girls had spent all their summers since their early teens holidaying on La Palma with their aunt and uncle. They were the daughters they never had. There was a special close and trusting bond between the four diners. Margarida and Damian were very protective of their young charges.

Margarida broke the contemplative silence that would have befitted a closed order of monks.

'Did you know your late granddad was in the Guardia Civil and helped with the evacuations of the local villages around us when the Teneguia volcano erupted in October 1971? He told me that they got a lot of warning. There were minor local tremors for months before the main eruption. When the lava started to flow it was gradual and took place at remote locations. This house, and the others around us, were built afterwards as this site wasn't affected. I hope we're still in a safe zone.'

'Aunt Margarida, don't fret,' said Maria. 'While volcanoes are still fairly unpredictable, we should get plenty of warning signs before anything major happens. The science of volcanology has improved quite a lot since 1971. I don't expect anything too dramatic to occur any time soon. Here on La Palma there are dozens of remote monitors scattered across the mountains with arrays located on what are considered be the locations at most risk. That's what Simon and Ros are doing: keeping us safe. You should also know that NASA has a satellite capacity to provide real time thermal images and data, so we'll know if matters are going to get out of control.'

'Sure, I could do the same with my latest toy,' chipped in Damian. 'I just got a top of the range DJI Phantom ready-to-fly GoPro camera drone with great camera and video resolution and a flight range of fifty kilometres. I bought a thermal imagery add-on feature too, not realising that I would be using it so soon. I told Simon and Ros earlier that I can help if they need an extra set of eyes. I could also use the older drone, but its range is more limited.'

'Let's talk about the practicalities once we finish this excellent Albariño. The vineyards of Galicia sure know how to produce a world class product.' Margarida tried to lighten the serious tenor of the conversation.

The conversation switched quickly to the subtleties of La Palma's wines, but Margarida soon brought it back to business.

'Damian, you never told me about your new purchase. I hope it wasn't too expensive.' Margarida as guardian of the family's purse didn't like surprises.

Damian had anticipated this interrogation and had his lines well-rehearsed. 'No need to concern yourself, Cherie. It'll pay for itself within months. I intend to fly over all the island's walking routes and do a commentary describing what our tourists can expect to see. I'll start with the GR 131. Once we upload these videos on our website, we'll become the go-to guides that everyone will want to hire.'

'Uncle Damian, that's a brilliant idea. Young people like to research their holiday experiences online. Your recordings of the top hiking trails will attract a lot of attention. Can I be your marketing manager?'

'Maria, I will appoint you Chief Executive Officer once we make our first million!'

Margarida yawned. She was exhausted and troubled by the day's happenings. 'Time to stop daydreaming. I'm off to bed. Good night.'

In the morning over breakfast the conversation was all about family matters: favourite uncles, doddery aunts, black sheep and their mischiefs, and who would inherit what from an eccentric great uncle. Inevitably, however, the situation on La Palma was soon back on the agenda.

Damian and Margarida were booked to escort walking groups over the coming days and debated long and hard before deciding to go ahead but choosing the least risky routes.

'As I suspected, my German group has cancelled. They are already on their way to the airport despite the fact their flight is not until this evening. Total over-reaction, if you ask me! One of the group who could not cope with the heights – Herr Vertigo I called him – spooked them all. If matters get any worse there will be media attention and that will be bad for business.'

'Do they know something we don't?' asked Damian.

'I very much doubt it. They were hill walkers and not high mountain hikers, so the terrain was far too difficult for them.'

'On the other hand, the Malmesbury orienteering group clearly have far more grit and determination,' said Damian. 'I spoke to one of them last night before dinner and they seemed keen to continue. I've arranged to meet them at their hotel within the hour to take stock and to plan a low risk walk if they want one.'

Damian was about to leave the table when Claudine said out loud to nobody in particular. 'We might as well trek to the ORM as it is a manageable distance. We could be there by tomorrow afternoon.'

'No problem with me,' replied Maria, a bit too enthusiastically.

They had discussed this option into the early hours.

'In any event Ros and Simon will need someone to support them with the monitoring of the devices along the *Ruta* and who better than us to assist,' said Maria, her face flushed.

Claudine thought, she can't wait to meet up with Simon. How lovely! Her aunt and uncle also spotted their niece's noticeable change in demeanour once Simon's name was mentioned.

The girls were delighted to get the call to move to the ORM as part of the wider effort to monitor the island's volcanoes. The fact that Ros and Simon were going to be there was an added bonus. The chemistry between Simon and Maria had nothing to do with basalt rocks and lava flows. Maria had confided in her sister about the relationship, without going into too much detail. Of course Claudine saw the signs: the jitters when the phone rang, the blushes when she spoke to Simon, every call on Facetime that went on far longer than purely practical updates would require. How can people talk for so long, she wondered. Does conversation never run out? As the pair had not held hands for two months, she dared not imagine how they would behave when they met again.

The girls had hiked the famous *Ruta de los Volcanes* dozens of times. The trail may be arduous to most, but they were fit and mountain aware. The girls were not only trainee volcanologists but also expert mountain climbers. Even if there was a repeat of the tremors they would press ahead.

'Maria, please keep your mobile on and activate the auto-find App,' implored her nervous aunt.

Margarida had a sinking feeling, a dull sense of foreboding, that the girls' bravado wasn't justified. Youngsters rarely considered the risks of the actions they took. Hiking the *Ruta* was a risk even on a bright summer's day. But with the events of yesterday it took on additional dimensions. Margarida knew she was a conservative person by nature, too conservative at times, especially in relation to routine matters, but when nature started to behave in an unpredictable manner, she instinctively knew it was time to be cautious.

'If you need drone support call me,' added Damian as he helped them put on their well-provisioned backpacks.

Once everything was organised, the girls headed out the door for the GR 131. Damian turned to Margarida.

'I best be off to meet my group.'

Damian searched for his phone, keys and wallet.

'Do you mind if I join you?' said Margarida, her protective instinct kicking in. 'Safety in numbers and all that.'

'No problem, Cherie. Actually, given the circumstances, it's best that the two of us accompany them.'

They set off for the Hotel Taburiente.

At the hotel, which – in contrast with the previous day – was almost deserted, the Malmesbury group were ready in their mountain gear. Their backpacks were provisioned with the day's essentials. They were waiting in the reception area with an air of calm. Damian sat them down around a coffee table. He introduced Margarida.

'Same as before guys: I'll give you a full briefing about the route before we set out. It's important that you not only know the route, but that you can visualise it.'

He opened up his trusty map and his selection of photos.

'Today's target is the observation point called Lomo de las Chozas, close to the car park at La Cumbrecita. It's within the Caldera de Taburiente National Park and is accessible on a tarmacadam road from the Visitors' Centre. It's a seven-kilometres uphill walk through one of the prettiest forests on the island. It may not be as dramatic as yesterday's barren volcanic scenery, but your effort will be worth it as we transverse through the valley into the centre of the island, at the base of the Caldera de Taburiente. I'll arrange for the bus to collect us at the information point at La Cumbrecita. This is a one-way walking adventure.'

'Sounds like a plan,' said Judith. Her group all nodded approval. They set off calmly.

As in previous days, walking conditions were perfect. It was around twenty degrees Celsius with a light breeze. As they were using a paved road and were largely in the shade of forest, they progressed at a good pace.

Judith peppered Margarida with questions as they walked along beside each other.

'Yes, we're in the Riachuelo valley. Over the peak to the left is the ascent to the Pico de la Nieve. Only mountain goats and experienced and fit hikers would ever attempt that trail and only in the best of conditions.

For much of the trail, the path is barely a metre wide, with almost vertical sheer drops. Having a parachute would be an idea.'

Another question.

'Yes, the Canary pine forest catches fire every few years, and yes fire breaks have been built to minimise the damage. It's the only tree variety that puts out new shoots from its trunk and branches after a fire.'

And another.

'Yes, there have been heavy storms down this valley. When it rains there is severe flooding and erosion. The culverts at the side of the road are designed to prevent the road being washed away. When it is damaged it is re-built.'

Judith paused for a while, perhaps taking in the panorama of the rising forest against the backdrop of brown and black coloured cliffs of basalt lava. The hills of the Cotswolds had a lot to offer but the guidebooks didn't do this place justice. It was a hiker's paradise.

She walked up beside Margarida.

'He is really cute, isn't he? Damian. He's gorgeous.'

'Is that so?'

'Well I wouldn't mind if he swept me off my feet!'

'Really?'

'I bet you he has a girlfriend.'

'No, he hasn't.'

'That's promising then.'

Margarida smiled as she prepared to deliver her punchline. 'He has a wife.'

'So, he's off limits I suppose.' Judith was clearly disappointed.

With a beaming smile Margarida concluded the exchange. 'As his wife, I believe he is spoken for.'

Judith could only say 'Ah.'

Turning crimson with embarrassment she nervously rubbed her hands and walked ahead to join another member of the group. Damian caught up with Margarida.

'What was that all about?'

'You have one less suitor.'

He laughed. 'You've a way to dissuade my admirers.'

She smiled.

After walking for about two hours Damian called the group to a halt.

'Best we take a rest here for five minutes as the climb up to La Cumbrecita is quite steep.'

The final ascent took just twenty minutes. The view surprised the group. The cliff tops of the ridge of the Caldera de Taburiente towered as far as the eye could see. There was a blanket of thick white cloud above them. Without warning a fully formed rainbow emerged and joined the floor of the valley five hundred metres to the left. The cameras were soon clicking. WhatsApp messages were sent far and wide.

'This is one of the best views of the Caldera,' said Damian. 'But there is an even better viewing point at the end of the trail. Let's head to the Lomo de las Chozas. It's just over a kilometre to the left side of the car park.'

With the promise of an even better panorama they proceeded along a wide zigzag path.

'Look up high to the left. This is an old eroded dyke.' Damian began his tour guide commentary. 'Dykes are former volcanic vents through which the lava flowed when this area was active many years ago. See the dark-coloured edges? The minerals include black pyroxenes. Look up to the summit right of Pico Bejenado. The ochre-coloured soil lies beneath greyer soil. This is the dividing line between two periods of intense volcanic activity. La Cumbrecita is located in the area of La Palma's first volcanic period.'

The air was still. This added to the wonder of the track that had been carved out of the lava outcrops. Whatever about the barren mountains above the left side of the path, the steep ravines and gullies to the right were populated with the ever-present Canary pine with some trees rising vertically to over one hundred metres. They temporarily blocked out the view over the valley.

Rock plants were in abundance. Given the amount of rainfall at this height they thrived in what was otherwise a barren landscape.

'One unique feature of the Canary pine is that it has deep roots.' Damian pointed to a towering pine on the side of the track. Its base was eroded away exposing a massive tangle of roots to a depth of nearly ten metres scattered in all directions. The roots sought out water that was clearly in short supply.

'It's clinging for life,' said Judith.

They moved forward.

'Get your cameras ready,' said Damian. 'The Lomo de las Chozas lookout point is just ahead. As the rock outcrop is atop a sheer drop of five hundred metres, there is a rail to prevent you falling off. I suggest you descend the steps in small groups, as the space is tight.'

Ever to the front, Judith and three of her friends walked carefully, following the wooden rail, down a series of uneven stone steps that were carved out of the large boulders that comprised the Lomo de las Chozas. Within a minute they had reached the high wooden guard rail on the outcrop. They soon realised why the rail was an essential support. At the very rim of the Lomo de las Chozas they got a stunning panoramic view of the entire length of the Caldera de Taburiente and the valleys and smaller rises at its base. The drop to the valley floor was precipitous.

They started to take photos as the view was strikingly photogenic.

Judith turned on the video feature of her Canon EOS 80. The new DSLR was her pride and joy. She was a skilled amateur photographer and knew how to make the most of the 30 to 135mm lenses. She was so engrossed in doing a voice over for her video that she didn't notice the initial jolt, nor did she immediately realise what was happening. Her camera slipped from her grip. Tumbling to the ground, the live video continued to record.

She realised before she was knocked to the ground that a violent tremor was responsible. Her experience from the day before came back to her. She also knew this tremor was far more severe, although the time needed to process this information was brief, a fraction of a second. She tried to get to her feet and failed. Her friends were also struggling to keep their balance.

Damian and Margarida were making small talk when the tremor started. They were a hundred metres back on the track they too realised in an instant what was happening.

'Margarida, look.'

He had barely spoken before a large cracking sound could be heard. A noise that sounded like a muffled quarry explosion. It seemed to fill the entire space around them.

Judith and her friends were comprehensively startled by the tremor and the unnatural noise. They were rigid with fear as the wooden guard rails buckled, split into pieces and fell into thin air. They snapped out of their initial fright to try and compose themselves. They managed to get back to their feet and took two paces up the steps back to the main track where the rest of the group waited. In the distance they saw the fear in their friends' eyes. Not for themselves as they were on terra firma. The eyes of the unwitting spectators to the unfolding disaster also conveyed a sense of deep sadness.

The earth shook violently. A wide crack suddenly appeared in the front of their feet as if someone had shattered the rocky outcrop with a powerful hatchet. Brown dust particles shot into the air. In a split second the section of the outcrop where they were standing separated away from the walkway that lead to the path ten metres above them. Judith and her friends were left stunned momentarily as the platform broke away with a loud bang. It then fell into the valley far below like an elevator that's cable had been cut descending the exterior of a tall skyscraper.

If it had been recovered Judith's live video would have shown a party of four who had just a second or two to accept their fate.

They were the first casualties on La Palma.

There would be more – many more.

As Damian and Margarida were leading their group towards La Cumbrecita, Claudine and Maria headed out on the GR 131 north of the town of Los Canarios. After a gentle ascent they reached Volcán Martín, with its red-pink cone contrasting with the green forest pines on its flanks. The Atlantic Ocean was visible over the edge of the sandy volcanic slopes. It was calm and partly cloudy. Perfect conditions. There were no signs of any disturbance to the surface of the sea.

They decided it would be wise to phone Ros and Simon. Simon answered as the mobile indicated the call was from Maria.

Maria went crimson on hearing his voice. She sat down as the conversation started.

'You'll never guess where we are?'

'Surprise me,' said Simon.

'We're at over nineteen-hundred metres.'

'Eh? you're on the mountain?'

'Yes, we're two kilometres short of Volcán de la Deseada.'

'What are you doing there, or is that a stupid question?' Simon's voice changed. Gone was the soft gentle talk to his girlfriend. Instead, he switched tone to that of a worried parent.

'We decided to hike it to the ORM and what better way than on the *Ruta*.'

'You won't make it by sunset.'

'I know, so we plan to camp overnight at the visitors' centre at Refugio El Pilar. All going well we should join you for lunch tomorrow.

'Be careful!'

Simon stopped talking.

Although it was a solid and modern structure, the ORM wasn't immune to tremors and this one was sufficiently violent to knock over some furniture and cause storage racks to fall. Their precious – and near full – cafetière fell and broke into bits.

Looking up from his screen Ros shouted. '2.2 on the Richter and it was also shallow and not far from here.'

This was the same seismic tremor that shattered the outcrop at Lomo de las Chozas, no more than three kilometres, as the crow flies, from the ORM.

'Maria, did you feel that?' said Simon with a tremor in his voice.

'Sure did.'

'I suggest you hurry to Refugio El Pilar. I was going to ask you to check out the instruments at the Volcán de la Deseada but give it a skip. If there are more tremors, we can expect to see small vents blowing very soon. They could emerge anywhere, so you'll need to be on high alert for the warning signs. If the ground starts to bulge anywhere near you run away as fast as you can. You have your oxygen masks?'

'Of course.'

Claudine took over the conversation.

'Simon, I'm not at all worried about the tremors. We can manage a bit of rock and roll. Have you any insights from Mark about the likely strength, or the main source of the seismic activity?'

'No details yet, but he expects there may be several minor tremors across the entire range of the *Ruta*. You are in the middle of the danger zone. Be aware and behave accordingly.'

She handed the phone back to Maria.

'Keep in touch. Stay safe. Please phone in an hour or so,' concluded Simon.

'Will do. Love you.'

Maria and Claudine pressed on in silence and in the uncomfortable knowledge that something very dangerous might happen.

The track varied from black volcanic rock, well-worn from decades of walkers, to soft pine needles in the sections that went through the high forests. While keeping up a brisk pace, they paused at intervals to take in the vistas all around them. Isolated volcanic cones peppered the skyline. This was after all the Route of the Volcanoes. They didn't need a map to identify the surrounding terrain. As seasoned mountain hikers they knew every Pico, every Mirador (viewpoint) and could identify the small villages at the foothills.

'It's time to play our geography quiz.'

'Fair enough,' replied Claudine.

'Usual terms?'

'Of course. The loser prepares the dinner and does the wash and clean up.'

There was a huge incentive to take the game seriously.

The quiz was always spontaneous.

It could be short, or long and often went on for hours. Such was the extent of the geography and geology in these unique mountains. Maria started. She knew a new transmitter station had been installed since they last walked the *Ruta* and thought she could get one up on her sister.

'What's on top of the mountain ridge at five hundred metres?'

'Are we talking about Volcán Martin?'

'Yes, but the question is not the name of the mountain but what's on top it?'

'Sneaky, but within the rules.'

She too had a difficult question up her sleeve and had been waiting weeks to find the opportunity to test Maria.

Claudine squinted her eyes to focus on the mélange of mauve, orange and cream rocks and ash that shaped the rim of the volcano that lasted erupted in 1646. Its lava flows had reached the eastern coast of the island.

'Is that a radio antenna just below the right side of the rim?'

'What good eyesight!'

'No need for a visit to the opticians!'

'Ha Ha.'

'But I need a more accurate description otherwise you are on duty tonight.'

'Be reasonable sister. I can't possibly see anything other than the broad outline of what appears to be a device with an aerial.'

'Do you give up?'

'What do you know that I don't?'

'What you are looking at is a remote sulphur dioxide detector with a transmitting aerial.'

'You can't possible see that far.'

Then it dawned on her.

'I don't suppose that Simon told you about the location of one of his new devices?'

'I can neither confirm nor deny. You are on duty.'

'Hold on there. The quiz rules give me an opportunity to redeem myself. Let's walk on while I find a feature so far away that you will be unable to identify it.'

Maria set off. She was distracted as she knew Claudine could stop her at any time to pose the decider question. As a result, she was on high alert observing her surroundings. What an amazing panorama, she thought to herself.

They walked past the Cráter del Duraznero, a deep lake of old lava. The track dipped and rose as it followed the contours of the mountains. After about thirty minutes they were passing to the right of the Hoyo Negro, the suitably named deep black hole devoid of vegetation when Claudine exclaimed.

'Stop.'

'Ah, she has at last found her quiz question,' thought Maria. She expected the worst.

'It is a two-part question. When did Hoyo Negro erupt and what's the name of the eruption?'

'That's unfair. A two-part question is stretching the rules is it not?'

'If you know the answers that's all that matters, oh knowledgeable one.'

'We're in the midst of the remnants of the 1949 eruption.'

'Correct. Go on.'

'Three vents opened up along a two-kilometre fissure. I suspect we're standing on the very line of the epicentre.'

'Getting warm, figuratively and literally.'

'The episode started at the Crater del Duraznero that we passed a while back. I think it was in the month of July. As can be seen from the surrounds, there was a violent explosion and it stopped activity at this site. Days later, a new eruptive vent opened on the western flank of Cumbre Vieja, in the area of Llano del Banco. As it is three kilo-metres north of here we can't see it. Large volumes of lava flowed for over a fortnight and reached to three hundred metres short of the banana plantations at the coast.'

'Go on.'

'The third vent opened here at Hoyo Negro with strong explosions caused by the heating and expansion of underground water. That opened a large funnel in an old volcanic cone. At the time the mountain was covered in woodland, so forest fires added to the threat of gas explosions under great pressure.'

'Answer the question.'

'The answer to the second is San Juan as the eruptions started on the feast of the saint.'

The sisters smiled at each other. They loved their quiz sessions as it kept them alert to their surroundings. Both knew there was a kicker to the San Juan eruption event. After the volcanic eruption strong earthquakes persisted for several weeks. They were on a ridge that had history. That was best left unsaid. They picked up their back packs and headed further north on the GR 131.

They reached the serviced camp site at Refugio El Pilar an hour before sunset. They chatted nervously as daylight slowly disappeared. The visitors' centre was deserted because through the late afternoon mild aftershocks had been felt and dozens of intrepid walkers had bussed back to their hotels along the coastal towns. The abandoned mountain was theirs to enjoy.

It was strange to be in a very familiar location that was normally throbbing with activity but was now eerily empty.

'Let's have dinner,' said Maria.

The girls unpacked their drinks, bread and cheese and other eats and started what they hoped would be a leisurely early dinner. The plan was to set off to the ORM at first light, around 5 a.m.

The view was of a well-tended recreational area set amid tall Canary pines and cedars. The sun was setting on a bright clear evening, the light reflected off the brilliantly coloured rocks showing up reds, yellows, green and blues; in fact, every colour of the rainbow filtered through the branches of the forest.

This was an idyllic setting where they had camped on many occasions, enjoying the isolation and crystal-clear night sky.

The bang was loud, but not close. The earthquake was worse than before.

Not a kilometre away, to the left of Pico Bejenado, several surges of bright red lava flew high into the sky cascading its deadly rocks around. As hot rocks hit the ground, they set off a fizzing sound as they torched the undergrowth on impact. Red dots with varying intensity dotted a large area.

The first gush soon petered out and the lava flow almost stopped within minutes. The deep red of the lava bombs dimmed as they cooled. The fizzing sound also stopped. The ensuing silence was, in a way, more disturbing than the bang.

'Wow, that was a close call.'

'Too close for my liking.'

Their mobile rang. It was Simon.

'Maria, tell me that you were a safe distance away.'

'We were, but we got no warning. What happened?'

'We'll have to investigate the site and take samples to find out. I'm assuming that the magma found a weak spot and gravity did the business. How far are you from the ORM?'

'About a five hour walk along the Cumbre Nueva ridge route.'

'It's too dangerous to walk along the ridge,'said Simon in a firm tone. 'I know it will be dark soon,' but could you and Claudine try and make it down the path to the car park at the Reventon gap. You could be there in under an hour. I'll meet you there with the Mountain Rescue Unit of the Guardia Civil and drive you to the ORM. You know the mountain trails better than any of the locals and I, eh we, would feel much better having you with us. There is a near full moon so visibility should not be too bad.'

In the distance a muffled bang could be heard and to the right of the earlier blast bursts of deep red and black molten lava shot high into the night air. Any indecision about staying put or not was quickly put aside.

'We're on our way. Could you please phone my aunt and tell her we're safe and well.'

It was a steep climb down the Cumbre Nueva trail to the Reventon car park. This part of the GR 131 ran along an old Camino path that levelled out at 1,400 metres for most of its length. In normal circumstances, the views from the thin ridge of the Caldera de Taburiente were breath-taking. Scenery wasn't a priority. As it got dark, the sisters focused on their next foothold as the light dimmed. The light of moon at this elevation provided them with enough ambient light to continue, but they got increasingly unsettled and had a few missteps.

Within sight of the car park, just twenty minutes away, the earth shook, this time with a renewed ferocity. They were immediately thrown to the ground as the effects of the tremor made its way towards them. With frightened eyes, they observed that the ground was rising as it moved towards them splitting and gouging the surface in all directions. The rolling motion was moving too fast for them to take evasive action. They were propelled into the air when the earth hit them. Before they were knocked unconscious as they hit the ground their last memory was the strong pervasive smell of sulphur, with its characteristic smell of rotten eggs.

Sites ZX

'OK, we're almost ready to go,' said Lars. 'Sean and Benny have been briefed about what we've decided as part of our deployment plan over the past weeks. First, let's discuss the proposed locations. Alice, as you are the project lead in relation to the selection of the priority sites, please clarify who goes where.'

Alice displayed a map of the eastern and central side of the Greenland glacier on the TV screen.

'We took full advantage of the recent availability of a low orbit GEO-6 geostationary satellite that carries a space-based infrared system. Our friends in NASA gave us enough time to examine in detail ten potential sites where we knew significant surface melting was taking place. Not only can this eye in the sky measure heat differences, it generates visible images that penetrate to the bedrock surface some three thousand metres beneath us. Based on this data and our visual observations and knowledge of the sites over the past years, we shortlisted five locations with high potential.'

She used the cursor to point at the map.

'We've picked five sites where the ice melt rate at the surface has increased sharply over the past two years. More importantly, we've tried to pick crevasses that may feed into the bedrock canyons that have been revealed using 3D landscape imagery that has just become available. It's like viewing Greenland with the ice sheet taken off. We know there are hills, valleys and channels as deep and as wide as the Grand Canyon under the ice sheet. The liquid subterranean ice water flows around bends hundreds of metres deep.'

'How can satellites do this?' Sean was like the keen student at the back of the class who never allows his teacher to finish a sentence.

Alice smiled.

'Sean, ice is entirely transparent to radar. Let me show you.'

Alice switched to a map that for all intents and purposes was a traditional Google Earth view of a large land mass.

'This is what Greenland looks like stripped of its ice. Let me show you one of the 3D map's enhanced features.'

She brought up an animation that showed the projected movement of the glacier aquifers flowing into the waters all around the island of Greenland. The mass of bright red lines, with moving arrows to indicate direction, suggested where the ice-melt was flowing.

'What we can't find out is how and where these aquifers are interconnected through the mass of the glacier nor do we know the speed of the subterranean rivers.'

She flicked to another channel.

'Here is a video of the raging Qooqqup Kuua River that's 350 kilometres to the south-east of us here. See how it crashes with a hundred white fists of detritus into the Qooroq Ice Fjord? I've no doubt that as the ice we're standing on melts it ends up feeding into this river. All we need to do is to find the evidence.'

They all observed that the roaring river was carrying enormous amounts of sand and silt, turning the dark green sea at the edge of the fjord a thick brownish-grey colour.

'Pause there a minute,' interjected Lars.

'This is the key for our research. The weight of the surface meltwater is creating large cracks, or crevasses, and is forcing them deeper and deeper. How far, we don't know as remote sensing technology does not provide a solution. If we can find the main passages that these aquifers are taking, we can then begin to calculate the volume of fresh meltwater that flows into the waters around Greenland. The golf balls are as useful as the advanced satellite technology. I hope they will unlock the mysteries that lie within the Greenland Ice Sheet.'

The lesson over, Alice continued, 'Given the unstable nature of the surface in the immediate vicinity, I propose we deploy the golf balls by drone into a deep chasm at a location quite remote from the Summit Station. The first site – we refer to it as ZX1 – is ninety kilometres west-south-west of the Summit Station. We've had a small tent observation post nearby for the past three summers so we estimate it will take at least twelve hours to get on site using one of the Humvees.

'I would like to lead the group to site ZX1,' chipped in Phil Teahon.

'That's ok by me,' confirmed Lars.

Phil, having achieved his ambition, relaxed and observed the reactions of the other members of the group as the order of battle was set out for the generals of the ice sheet.

'The second site is almost in the opposite direction at a distance of over a hundred kilometres from the Summit

Station. Site ZX2 was picked because satellite images showed a huge lake, that wasn't there a year ago, has formed on the top of the glacier. This area hasn't been explored recently. I'm assuming it will take a day to get on site as the surface conditions appear to be slushy in parts. The other Humvee will go to this site.'

Alice was in her element. Telling people what to do came naturally. She would make a good project leader, mused Lars. Like me, she is a stickler for detail and uncompromising preparation. Not just an excellent scientist, he thought. She went up in his estimation even further.

'Last week, we got detailed satellite images of two potential sites beside the Knud Rasmussen and Helheim glaciers and took photographs of the proposed landing area for the team that will be transported there by the Twin Otter. Everything seemed normal. My team of five, including the second drone pilot, will fly to this site, coded ZX3, which is some 250 kilometres almost directly north-north-east of our current position. The largest sinkhole we've identified is adjacent to the landing strip. A second potential site is about half an hour on foot to the east. When we get there, we'll decide to deploy at one or both sites. I don't intend to stay on site for any longer than is necessary. Once we re-fuel – and there are adequate back-up supplies in the storage cabin – we'll head back to the safety and comfort of the Summit Station.'

'Is it really safe to land a plane there?' asked Benny, who was somewhat troubled that site selection seemed to have been a bit rushed. 'What are the risks?'

'Ok, we didn't have time to do a physical inspection,' replied Alice. For a change she was at the receiving end of the questions. 'Summit researchers were last here over two years ago and ground conditions were fine. I spoke to the leader of the group who told me that there was good firm snow underfoot. Provided we've high cloud cover, and the forecast over the next forty-eight hours is good, it should not be a problem to land as a snow runway is marked out about five hundred metres right of the crevasse. We've had a small Portakabin facility beside this landing strip for several years and our pilots have used it many times before. Just in case, we'll be bringing emergency rations and basic provisions for two weeks.'

'Ok then,' said Benny, but Phil and Lars noticed he was clearly not fully convinced.

Alice continued. 'Site ZX4 is just four kilometres to our east at what we've called 'the Big Crevasse'. We can get there quite easily on the ski-cat. The final site, ZX5, is five kilometres due south. I'm under pressure to agree that we use the huskies to get us there. This should be no more than a two-hour round trip.'

'Using the husky team is fine by me as they need a run out. If nothing else, we'll have a few hours peace from the barking.' Lars took over as he assumed that Alice had completed her part of the briefing. He paused and she began to bring the briefing to a close.

'The Summit Station will serve as the communications hub. All the systems have been stress-tested. We've set radio links to the Humvees and the ski-cat. The Twin Otter's comms will be used for the site ZX3 team. We're fortunate that the two drones have state-of-the-art communications capability, so they'll be our eyes and ears in the sky. As each project leader, including the driver of the dog sledge, have an Inmarsat Mini-M satellite telephone everyone will be in constant contact with each other and with the base here. And if we need extra support, NASA will lend us their eyes in the event of an emergency.'

'I drew the short straw and will oversee our communication,' said Lars.

Alice continued. She was in full flow and was eager to finish her presentation.

'We've programmed our computers at the Summit Station to provide live feed from all the golf balls deployed at the five locations. We've also developed software that by overlaying NASA images we'll be able to generate 3D images in real time. The data will be shared with NASA and the Norwegian Government, as will images from the camera golf balls.'

Lars stood up. 'Alice, many thanks for all the hard work you and your team has invested in this over the past weeks. I guess we're now ready to go.'

Sean interjected before Lars could continue. 'Lars, I've a proposition to make.'

'Go ahead.'

'I suggest we deploy six golf balls at the nearest site to the Summit Station to test the tracking software. In that way we can all benefit from the feedback before the larger deployment. I also suggest we hold back on using the camera golf balls until we're happy that my technology works. To have maximum impact, we should deploy across all sites more or less at the same time, say at midday two days hence.'

'That makes a lot of sense,' said Lars.

'Good. Here are the golf balls that we might test.'

'Perhaps the drone pilots who are responsible for dropping the golf balls at sites ZX1 and ZX3 might each be given the opportunity of testing their skills,' said Benny.

'No problem,' said Sean. He put his hand in his pocket and handed over three golf balls to each drone pilot. The two drone pilots, along with Alice and Lars and most of the remaining researchers, went outside to observe proceedings. It was windy, but no more than usual. The high cloud ceiling was a help as the pilots got their machines ready.

The on-site initial operational procedures were completed: the props were tightened, the carbon fibre propellers were checked, full battery strength confirmed, the lens cleaned, the GPS navigation autopilot was turned on, the radio and video controls were powered up, and a communications link-up established to the Summit Station base control desk. The on-craft remote control transmitter power switch was also checked.

The hand-held 'OpenPilot' flight controller comprised a standard configuration of four channels to control the rudder, ailerons, elevator and throttle. The drone pilots had learned their basic skills when flying remote controlled model airplanes as teenagers. It was easy to adapt to much larger and more sophisticated hardware.

Since the first multi-copter was launched in 2010, military and commercial drones had developed beyond everyone's initial expectations. Drones now had an impressive array of optional extras that could be attached to their basic airframe. The Norwegian drones were eight rotor MD4-6000 series models and of military standard.

Powered by a Li-Pod lithium battery, they could stay in the air for four hours in sub-zero conditions. They were capable of handling a payload of nearly twenty kilos. The drones had a motorised three axel gimbal supporting an advanced LUMIX GH8 DSLR cinema-grade digital camera. The operator was able to zoom the lens and take video as well as still shots.

A unique feature of the MD4-6000 series was the option to fly the machine using Wi-Fi enabled virtual reality goggles linked to a front-facing internal camera. The pilot could steer his drone visually as if on board, while observing the terrain below and the prevailing weather. Heavy rain or snow would render the drone useless.

The operators at the Summit Station launched the computer tracking programme on their PCs. Once the drones were powered up, and using the visual features of the pilots' goggles, they had the option of remote flying the drones independently from the on-the-ground pilots. The drone pilots and the base operators confirmed that all systems were in order and the drones were ready to fly.

The pilots placed the golf balls in a bucket box that was designed to open once a remote signal was sent. The Norwegians had built a bucket box that could hold a payload of ten kilograms, or some two hundred golf balls. Sean had told them that the rules of golf required a golf ball to be no more than 46 grams. Sean's adaptation was a third of that weight. The Summit Station PCs picked up the golf balls' unique signals using the software programme they had installed earlier.

Speaking into his satellite phone, Lars gave the order to start the test.

As if by magic, the two drones rose silently into the air. They hovered some ten metres apart about two hundred metres up. One headed east, in the general direction of the Big Crevasse, while the other flew south to site ZX5.

The Big Room was packed as the PCs showed the track of the golf balls as they rose in the air in the drones' buckets. As remarkable was the video feed from the drones' cameras of dark ridges of ribboned ice spread out as far as the eye could see.

After two minutes, when the drones were over a kilometre away, Lars called out. 'Pilot of the drone going to site ZX5 please stall, hover and zoom in so we can get a better look at ground conditions. Over. Please acknowledge.'

'Did you see something,' asked Alice.

'Wait and see.'

'Roger, Lars,' said the drone pilot. He did what he was told. Everyone stared at the TV screen as the images appeared crystal clear. The ice surface seemed to resemble a series of ripples like sand dunes buffeted by the wind.

'Zoom in as far as is possible.' Lars feared that he had spotted a potential problem.

The emerging image showed that beneath the surface there was a thin layer of slushy meltwater.

'Shit,' said Lars. Not known for bad language, Lars' loud comment turned everyone's head. 'This is the first time we've witnessed surface ice melt at this altitude. It may be an isolated incident. What do you think Alice?'

'This should not be a problem. The Humvees will plough their way through soft snow as will the ski-cats. The huskies have no preference for ground conditions. I don't want to over-simplify matters, but if we're careful and observe the terrain to spot slushy areas, the worst situation is that deployment might take a bit longer than we've planned for.'

'I go along with your assessment, but everyone should be mindful that ice conditions have clearly degenerated,' said Lars.

Soon after that distraction the drones were over the chosen sites.

'Drop when you are ready,' instructed Lars.

The drone operators duly obliged. The red track line fell sharply as the bucket boxes were opened. At the Big Crevasse, once in the water, the golf balls dropped sharply accelerating at twenty kilometres an hour in an easterly direction. What startled everyone was a significant and sudden boost in speed as the golf balls, all close to each other, sank nearly five hundred metres within the space of thirty minutes through a series of steep rapids and then slowed down to a stall before progressing in a north-north-west direction at a much slower pace of four to five kilometres an hour. While the descent at the second site was less dramatic, the tracking system worked as programmed. Dotted red lines showed the line of progress as the balls twisted and turned deep below the ice sheet.

'They work!' Sean was more than elated to see his invention in action.

'They do indeed. It was prudent to do a small test before we go to full delivery. I can't wait to see the camera feature,' replied Lars.

The drone pilots confirmed that their high-tech military flyers had no issues in deploying the golf balls from the bucket mechanism. Their only concern was what might happen in poor visibility.

'We're all set. Best of luck to everyone. Once everyone is on site and on my signal, we'll deploy at all five sites at midday the day after tomorrow.'

PLU

The PLU's first dive programme meeting started at 7 a.m. and lasted the best part of four hours. Chaired by Gilmore, the Chief Scientist, and attended by the PLU's crew, the Diving Operations Control Manager, a medley of scientists, and Vinnie Crowley every detail was presented, discussed and stress tested. The most immediate issue was the state of the sea bottom transponder network deployed overnight that would pin-point the final target destination.

Later, on deck, a separate team prepared the PLU for the first dive. The checklist was long. However, as they had a lot of experience, the dive crew visitors went through their checks as a matter of routine. Iron pellets were poured into linen bags and loaded into special compartments on the side of the manned submersible. Five of these ballast bags were secured to the sides of the vessel. The instruments in the PLU Shack, compressed into a room half the size of a box container, were also tested.

Weather conditions were deteriorating as the deck crew completed the pre-dive preparations. They were at the end of the long night shift. A three-metre swell was manageable and within safety limits. The PLU was securely anchored on deck and linked to a heavy-duty Triplex crane that would put the vessel into the water.

Because O'Farrell and Gallery had not been in a manned submersible before, they had had to go through intensive training in the simulator, based at the Irish Marine Institute, in the days before they boarded the RV

Celtic Explorer. It was just as well they didn't suffer from claustrophobia. Diving in a manned submersible wasn't part of their job spec.

They were in the capable hands of Mike Smith, the PLU's pilot. As a former Woods Hole staffer, he had over twelve years' experience of navigating and manoeuvring the most expensive bubble on earth, as he called it. Every dial, lever, button and stick was handled with skill and dexterity. The controls were an extension of his own arms.

Before they went out on deck the three crew members were weighed. Gallery's extended tummy was more than compensated by O'Farrell's slight figure. A good balance. A calculation was then made as regards the required level of buoyancy needed.

As the PLU's crew were kitted out with their jumpsuits, woolly hats and outer layers, the bridge of the RV *Celtic Explorer* was a hive of activity. The ship was manoeuvered to keep it aligned to the sea bottom transponder network. The transponder beacons mounted on acoustic devices sent signals of different frequencies to the submersible. Estimates were made of the surface and bottom currents as this would require adjustments to be made to the angle and direction of the PLU's descent.

Once the PLU was ready, the three-person crew walked out on the rear deck of a rolling ship a bit unsteady on their feet. They were the centre of attention as a large crowd had gathered at the upper guard rails to witness the first launch of a manned submersible from the RV *Celtic Explorer*.

Smith beckoned to O'Farrell. 'Maeve, you will need to take the seat at the rear that's located behind me. After you climb up to the opening step onto the door casing make sure you grip the handle that will allow you swing into position. As you know from the simulator we used in Galway, your monitors are to your left side as is your camera. No need for seat belts. I don't expect we'll be meeting much traffic where we're going.'

Nervously and awkwardly, O'Farrell climbed the curved steps to the top of the PLU. Keeping a tight grip on the rails, she installed herself into position in what was going to be home for the next few hours. She felt like a stuffed doll dressed as she was in a heavy jumpsuit to take account of the sharp fall in the submersible's ambient temperature as they descended.

Gallery did likewise, taking a position to Smith's left. 'It sure is a bit cramped, barely room to swing a cat.'

'Make room for a sea dog,' said Smith as he effortlessly climbed the ladder and sat on the edge of the hatch. He verified the seal and cleaned the grooves around the hatch with a clean rag to ensure the closure was airtight. He slipped into the cockpit and sat in front of the main control panel. He closed the hatch and secured it in an instant. The squishing sound confirmed an airtight seal had been achieved.

He turned on the PLU's communications system. The radio went live immediately.

'All safely interred, Eoin,' said Smith.

'Roger that Mike,' said Eoin O'Neill, whose job was to winch them off the ship. 'Let me know when you are ready.'

'Let's go through the last-minute checks before we get started,' Smith ordered, as he assumed the role of captain of his mini-ship.

'Paul, can we go through the final pre-op checklist, please?'

Working under the supervision of NOAA technicians, Paul McCrossan sat, legs akimbo, in the PLU Shack in front of what looked like the controls of a Dreamliner aircraft. The room contained the controls needed to monitor the PLU, which – unlike the ROV – had no tether as it operated independently using six high-capacity lithium batteries.

He and Mike Smith systematically checked battery levels, the sonar and side-sonar equipment, oxygen controls, the radio communications links, and the PLU's main and secondary grabbers. All the remote cameras and the 4K high definition video equipment were also checked and in order. The recently installed chemistry diagnostic kit was also approved for deployment. A series of control switches were activated. The main monitors at the centre of the cockpit panel lit up.

O'Farrell and Gallery sat in silence as the minutes went by while the safety and operational checks were completed.

McCrossan also linked the PLU's newly installed video and sound communications to the Skynet 6 satellite that had been assigned to the project by the British Government. Everything that was being said, seen and done would be visible to monitoring teams in the UK and the US. The team in the world's first underwater volcano research centre, the Hawaiian Underwater Geo-Observatory, was also on alert to give their expert opinion on whatever PLU found.

'OK, Mike, we're nearly ready to go. We just have to re-confirm the plot coordinates to the seabed,' said McCrossan.

'Roger that, Paul. I've these pre-programmed. In any event, I expect that we'll be moving about quite a bit along the edge of the target area.'

Smith took a deep breath. 'Maeve, Andy, are you all set?'

His crew nodded.

'Good, let's go then. Eoin, please winch us to the starting position at the stern of the ship.'

'Roger.'

The creaking of the main Triplex 'A' frame could be heard inside the cockpit as the PLU was lifted slowly off the deck and held steady by members of the deck crew. Expertly, the PLU was swung over the stern of the stationary ship and suspended briefly just above the water. Once it steadied, the winch lowered the PLU into the Atlantic. It was like putting a baby into a bath. The PLU's crew could hear the clips securing the vessel disengage. As soon as it floated the impact of the moderate swell could be felt inside. O'Farrell and Gallery hoped they would not be seasick.

'Mike, you are safely disconnected,' said McCrossan. 'Turn on the electric motor and take charge of the joy sticks. We'll let you descend in peace. Get in touch when you are above the designated position. Have a good dive.'

The scuba-diver released the submersible's umbilical cord from the 'A' frame, tapped the window, and gave a thumbs up sign. Smith reciprocated the signal. He turned on the electric motors, and the oxygen then clicked the switch for the reading and ambient lights.

'Permission to dive captain?' asked Smith.

'Roger that,' said Killen who had been observing the preparations with a sense of disbelief. Sitting on his seat on the bridge, he felt a degree of pride in being in charge of the first successful deployment of a manned submersible from the RV *Celtic Explorer*.

Smith expertly opened the valves to let water enter the ballast tanks. The PLU disappeared under the surface without a sound. It sank like a stone at a speed of thirty metres a second and in so doing rotated slowly like a spinning top. At a hundred and fifty metres below the surface, the last of the sunlight disappeared and the types of sea creatures that were visible also changed. PLU passed through a dense cloud of plankton, but very soon marine life was less noticeable in the chilling darkness. To save battery power he kept the arc lamps at low levels.

As he manoeuvred the craft downwards at an angle of about thirty degrees, Mike got a feeling his passengers, while pre-eminent scientists, were nervous so he started to talk out aloud.

'What persuaded you to study volcanoes Maeve?' asked Smith as they began their two-hour long dive.

O'Farrell was eager to talk. This was the distraction she needed. Her stomach had started to tense up. 'When I was sixteen, I was on a cruise holiday with my parents that took us to Naples. While they took it easy walking the streets and eating pizzas, I went on an escorted tour of the neighbouring towns of Pompeii and Herculaneum. I was fascinated by the guide's matter-of-fact account of one of Europe's most dramatic human tragedies.'

'The eruption of Vesuvius?' asked Smith.

'Yes, I was fascinated by the story of how in August 79 CE, all but one of the population of thousands in the wealthy Roman town of Herculaneum were incinerated by a violent blast of volcanic gases and ash that surged down the mountain as the fringes of the volcano collapsed. The lucky survivor was incarcerated in a cell under the town's prison and he lived to tell the tale. The Roman admiral Pliny the Elder was offshore on a rowing galley and he wrote a graphic account of the destruction of Pompeii, which he witnessed. The year after that holiday I persuaded my parents to holiday in the Bay of Capri area so that I could spend my time climbing and observing Vesuvius. At university I did a science degree and specialised in predictive volcanic analytics.'

'In your expert opinion, what will you be predicting?' asked Smith as he looked over his shoulder and caught Maeve's eye.

'Far too early to say. That said, if there are tell-tale signs, we might be able to provide alerts of potential activity in good time. What I have in mind is the placing of an array of sea floor sensors along the length of the area we're starting to investigate. There are similar sensors off the shores of Japan for instance, and at various locations in the Mediterranean.'

'But who will we be warning?' Smith was at this stage seeing the bigger picture.

'The countries that will be most affected by the resultant tsunamis,' concluded O'Farrell in a matter of fact voice.

That silenced everyone, including the many listeners to the PLU's internal conversations.

The PLU continued its downwards track without a sound. Its battery powered thrusters were designed to cause minimal damage to marine life. Without warning there was a short but very loud 'bang'. O'Farrell and Gallery simultaneously gasped and jumped out of their seats.

Before his passengers could ask a question, Smith explained, 'At around a thousand metres below the surface that bang indicates that outside pressure is compressing the sphere of the submersible.'

Time for more chat to distract attention, thought Smith.

He started to talk to himself. 'Why do we have water? One theory is that water condensed from the primeval atmosphere. Only earth has water in all three states: solid, liquid and gas. Some 2.5% is fresh water with 99% of that water found in ice and groundwater. A small amount is stored in the atmosphere in the form of vapour. Oceans cover over seventy percent of the surface of the earth, which to be honest as a planet should really be called 'Ocean'. Because it contains salts and minerals, seawater only freezes at minus four degrees Celsius. As the salinity of water increases, the freezing point lowers. Ocean water increases in density as it cools and sinks. The waters of the oceans contain 321 million cubic miles by volume. That's a lot. The circulation of the world's water is controlled by a mixture of gravity, friction and inertia. Winds push water, ice and water vapour due to friction. Water vapour, fresh water and hot water rises. Ice floats. Fascinating isn't it?'

'Interesting,' said a very disinterested and disengaged Gallery.

Smith continued with his information dump although he knew he was rambling and annoying his fellow passengers, it was distracting them from their nerves. 'Did you know that we've the equivalent of satnav on board?

Certain parts of the world's oceans, including much of the North Atlantic, have been surveyed by side-scan sonar. It may not be as good as Google Maps, but as soon as we're near the seabed I will be able to drive PLU along a predetermined route. Examining the Atlantic's volcanic rim started back in the 1970s with the French-American Mid-Ocean Undersea Study, or FAMOUS as it was called. More recently, the civilian version of the US Navy's Sound Surveillance System, or SOSUS, consists of a wide network of hydrophone arrays sited on continental slopes and seamounts that have the ability not just to detect submarines and whales but also volcanic eruptions.'

The Lumen arc lamps and the glass roof provided the PLU crew with an almost three hundred and sixty degree daylight view to a distance of ten metres.

'What can we expect to see?' asked Smith.

'It's not widely appreciated, but there are over ten thousand volcanoes below sea level. As a consequence, over eighty percent of the earth's volcanic activity takes place on the sea floor. There is a continuous chain of volcanic accumulations rising up to two kilometres from the ocean floor along a continuous line from the Arctic to Antarctica. Off the main mid-Atlantic chain there are hotspots, the Canary Islands being a good example. There are multiple fissures and dykes all along the sea floor.'

O'Farrell was becoming all too aware of the enclosed confines of the small craft, which seemed to get smaller all the time. Talking helped her manage her nerves. She completed the answer to Smith's question.

'I expect that we'll see many 'black smokers' as we call them. This common form of volcanism gives rise to basaltic pillow lava and minor gas explosions. These quieter eruptions are in contrast to what are called pyroclast events, derived from the Greek words *pyros* meaning fire and *klastos* meaning broken, that involve the explosive emissions of lava bombs and debris. Dozens of minor seismic events are recorded around and at right angles to the mid-ocean ridges. If not today, over the coming weeks, we should be able to use our seismometer to detect activity.'

It was Smith's turn to be at the receiving end of random information. He asked the obvious question. 'How will you know that a smoker is not a potential pyroclast event?'

'Our seismic readers will go off the Richter scale if a major eruption is brewing up deep within the sea floor. We'll also see the extrusion of large bubbles of gas prior to any explosion. Magma, a viscous mix of molten rocks that rises to the sea floor, that contains highly volatile elements such as sulphuric acid will be released if the pressure of the gases exceeds that of the surrounding material. Few such incidents have ever been observed.

O'Farrell was getting into her stride. She continued, 'In May 2009, an ROV witnessed two active sea floor volcanic vents near Tonga Island in the Pacific at a similar depth to where we are. This is the reference case history taught at university. Over a seven-day period, multiple small eruptions occurred at the main vent and at lateral locations. The ROV's video witnessed underwater fire fountains, billowing sulphurous gas emissions, bright orange lava and glowing gas bubbles as wide as a metre across.'

'Wow, let's hope we've a less exciting experience,' said Smith.

'Below the sea floor's surface, the rigid lithosphere is thinner and is closer to the earth's mantle where most of the transfer of matter and energy takes place. Only seventy percent of the sea floor has been mapped and explored. This is a major gap in science as the sea floor tells us so much about the internal structure and evolution of the earth.

'Look ahead,' shouted Smith.

Drifting into their vision from the chilling darkness was a pair of Minke whales about twenty metres long that seemed to pause in suspended animation metres in front of the PLU. The Lumen arc lamp highlighted their grey and black skin. Their eyes were enormous. Their wide stares unsettled everyone.

'No need to panic as they are just curious and will not come any nearer.'

'How do you know that?' said Gallery, who was frozen to his seat in fear.

'Their sonar told them we were here a long time ago. They made their way over to see what the noise was all about. Whales have never attacked a manned submersible and we're trained to move around them. As long as we give them space, they will not bother us. I would guess that this pair, judging by the blemishes and barnacles on their skin, are a male and a female at least thirty years old. They are probably migrating south. They eat krill and not humans, never mind humans in a protected shell. No need to worry.'

As Smith was talking, they disappeared into the dark abyss out of the range of the Lumen arc lamp.

Smith resumed his banter, erudite as always, as the PLU approached its target. 'The PLU's prototype dates back to Alexander the Great, who in 325 BCE descended into a harbour in a barrel and viewed his surroundings through a window made of the skin of a donkey. Fast forward to modern times, where manned deep-diving submersibles are constructed around a sphere made of an alloy of steel and titanium about two metres in diameter, which can resist the high pressure found at ocean depths. In most cases, manned submersibles have two pilots and one scientist on board. We had to cut corners for this voyage I'm afraid.'

Before he got a response from his passengers, Smith turned on the external communications system.

'Paul are you receiving us?'

'Yes Mike, clear as a bell. All ok?'

'Apart from a close encounter of the whale variety that spooked Maeve and Andy, all is in order. The sonar shows we're about fifty metres above the sea floor. I'm about to use the satnav to take us to our target area. Any more seismic readings from our British friends?'

'No, nothing since the last set we spoke about during the briefing.'

Smith expertly slowed the PLU's rate of descent and in so doing the main Lumen and secondary arc lamps began to illuminate the seabed. He was able to adjust the rate of descent and to obtain neutral buoyancy by releasing weights in the form of the iron pellets stored in six reservoirs on the sides of the PLU. He controlled the release lever mechanically.

'I reckon I'm about four hundred metres from the location of the last seismic reading. We'll proceed north-north-west to a depth of some fifteen hundred metres off the east flank of the Eriador Seamount.'

The main noise in the chamber of the PLU was the constant ping of the sonar. Casual conservation was put on hold as they glided over the sea floor.

Smith was careful not to drive the PLU too quickly. That would have the effect of stirring up a lot of sediment. Through the wide front porthole, they could see solidified deep grey layered lava tubes and lava pillows, some as high as twenty metres: remnants of volcanic activity that ceased a long time ago. These dark lava structures dominated almost the entire seabed with the only noticeable feature being higher ridges at irregular intervals. There was almost no vegetation on the barren sea floor.

'Is that a basalt formation Andy?' asked O'Farrell pointing to a low ridge of rock.

Basalt is the most common type of volcanic rock found on the sea floor.

'Yes, it is. I wasn't expecting to see …'

He didn't finish his sentence as coming into the light were two three-metre tall active vents side-by-side. They spewed a yellow gas and oozed dim red lava.

'My God,' exclaimed Gallery.

Smith halted the PLU a safe distance away as the scientists observed all before them in amazement.

'Not exactly what I was expecting to see, guys. Let the video roll so that we can transmit pictures up to the control room. Mike can you please zoom the main camera into the apex,' said O'Farrell.

As the camera brought the mini-eruption into better view, McCrossan came over the communications link. 'Mike, the Woods Hole team want you to take samples of the gas and the lava. Be very careful. They think this is an unstable fissure and you should keep your distance. Use the probes on the mechanical arms to get the samples.'

Smith turned on the light projectors located on top of the portholes and on the ends of the mechanical arms. They too were turned off during the descent to save energy. Once he could see the objective, he skilfully manoeuvred the PLU within four metres of the vents. PLU's long telescopic grabber was designed to pluck samples from the seabed and to store the material in metal baskets that were positioned at the front of the craft. Smith had used the telescopic grabber many times before so had no problem separating two small rock samples and transporting them safely into the baskets.

'I can't wait to analyse these rocks,' said O'Farrell. 'But what interests me more is the composition of the gases and the emission rate. Can we get samples?'

'No bother.' smiled Smith who was eager to show off his skills as a submersible operator. 'We've a Fourier transform infrared spectrometer that I will place over the vent. This will identify the gases and measure the flow rate. Andy, please turn on the remote infrared analyser switch as we'll start to get readings as soon as I approach the vent.'

O'Farrell looked out the cockpit porthole as Smith moved the PLU nearer the orifice of the chimney. which was spewing hydrothermal fluid like a locomotive would at a temperature of 350 degrees Celsius: enough to melt PLU's Perspex glass if they got close enough.

This was a 'white smoker'.

'Wow, Maeve, look at the sulphide and carbon dioxide readings. They are very high. Too high for my liking,' exclaimed Andy. 'What do you think Maeve?'

The PLU crew could not hear the gasp of anxiety that came from the geologists on the RV *Celtic Explorer* who had quickly come to the same conclusion. In their experience strong emissions of carbon dioxide were a precursor and a valuable indicator of new episodes of magmatic unrest. What they also saw were defined fluxes of sulphur dioxide, also a proven indicator of imminent volcanic activity.

'Give us a minute,' said Gilmore taking charge. He switched off the comms link with the PLU. He sought views from his colleagues. The recommended course of action was unanimous.

He re-connected the comms. 'Andy, Maeve, the team suggests that you back off now. We've enough evidence to work with. We've shared the video footage and geochemical data with our British colleagues and American friends at the Hawaii Undersea Geological Observatory (HUGO) and Woods Hole. I know you have enough battery power for another hour's exploration, but the view here is that you should start the re-surfacing procedures. Besides there is a front coming in from the west and surface swells will increase within the hour.'

'Roger that, Gerdy,' said Smith. 'This first trip delivered more than we were expecting. I've no issues with a safe return to the mother ship. All right with you Maeve, Andy?'

Their silence was enough of a signal. He took the joystick and manoeuvred the PLU off to the left side of the vents and powered it up at a forty-five degree angle. Within ten seconds they saw a huge burst of lava from the vents that went ten metres high with small lava bombs scattering all around. Because they were in a confined space there was no audible sound. The seismometer needle on the front console started to shake as the characteristic zigzags filled the screen.

All that was audible within the cockpit was the soft noise of the PLU's electric motors as the manned submersible started to ascend to the surface. The PLU's crew had had enough excitement for one day.

CHAPTER 6

Reventon

'DAMIAN, WHERE ARE YOU?'

Simon tried to control his emotions. Tears were welling inside him.

'In the car park at La Cumbrecita. I'm dealing with an emergency. We lost four of our hikers who were on the Lomo de las Chozas viewing platform when it was hit by a sharp tremor. The outcrop fractured and they fell to their death.'

'Jesus, help us,' said Simon.

'And Margarida and I are now trying to calm down the survivors of the group. They want us to help them recover the bodies. That's easier said than done.'

'I've another situation that's an emergency.' Simon was aware that Damian was under pressure.

'Go on. Fill me in.' Damian feared the worst. He knew something had happened to his nieces.

'Maria and Claudine are missing,' said Simon, his voice trembling. 'We had arranged to meet them at the Reventon car park half an hour ago and they didn't turn up. There was another tremor close to the Cumbre Nueva trail and it may have hit them. Their mobile phone is not responding.'

'I could be with you in an hour,' said Damian, trying to be helpful. He was still trying to manage the aftereffects of a serious incident.

'Damian, we don't have an hour. Ros is going to stay at the car, and I'm making my way up the trail to try and find them.'

'It's time to put the MD into action.'

'The MD?'

'It's what I call my new camera drone: Margarida's Drone if you must know. It will take me five minutes to set up and we'll be flying thereafter. I'm on the opposite side of the Cumbre Nueva ridge. In fact, as the crow flies, I'm no more than five or six kilometres from the trail the girls were walking on. I reckon I could get the MD to the girls' expected position within ten minutes.'

'Get on with it then. I should be in that area around the same time.' Simon was too worried to be polite to Damian who made allowance for the abrupt end to the conservation given the circumstances.

There is nothing quite like controlling a flying piece of technology and having it respond at will with fingertip precision. Damian had already damaged two inexpensive smaller camera drones, but in doing that he had honed his skills. MD came with a first-person-view live-feed feature. He could see the landscape in front of and below the drone on his laptop.

He didn't dare tell Margarida, but her namesake MD was a top of the range machine. He had spent more than he could afford – two month's earnings – to get all the latest features, including night-time infrared vision, a thermal sensor and DSLR camera lenses. If it helped save their nieces, Margarida might forgive his latest extravagance.

He took a line of sight to the top of the Cumbre Nueva ridge, which was almost 1,200 metres higher than where he stood. He released MD. She shot off at eighty kilometres an hour.

Damian had walked the ridge dozens of times so was able to spot familiar signs and landmarks in the moonlight when the video feed appeared on his computer. He reckoned the drone arrived about a kilometre from where Ros believed the girls to be. He slowed MD over the trail and pressed the wide lens and thermal image function buttons. MD followed the trail, or what was left of it, downhill from two hundred metres above the ground. The well-worn ash-based walking path was cracked everywhere and had settled in a series of jagged random mounds. What the hell happened here? He said to himself.

His iPhone rang. Simon's name appeared.

'Damian, where are you?'

'Very close by, I guess. I've MD above the trail. I'll turn on her arc light.'

As soon as he did, the night sky lit up with the best that LED could provide.

'Wow,' said Simon. 'That's some lamp.'

Damian had never used the arc light before and had reason to be impressed.

'Damian, I can see the ground clearly. I'm about five hundred metres away down the trail to the right. Please guide the MD along towards me. I'll use my mobile's light so you can locate me.'

'What happened to the trail?' asked Damian.

'It was struck by a narrow shallow earthquake that didn't surface but caused the ground to disintegrate. Enough of that. We need to find the girls. Can you widen your lens and start searching on either side of the trail, I suspect they were thrown there by the force of the blast.'

'Will do.'

Simon sat down for a short rest to catch his breath. He was emotionally and physically exhausted. He would not live with himself if his decision that the girls should hike to the car park had cost them their lives. These mountains were dangerous under normal conditions, but this was anything but normal. He was all too familiar with the lingering smell of sulphur and was glad he had packed his oxygen mask in case it became uncomfortable and necessary.

Damian shouted over the phone. 'Simon, I found them. They are lying off the left side of the trail about a minute from where you are standing. They are prone, but the thermal sensor shows good body heat, so they are alive. I've a spotlight above them.'

'Yes, I can see it.' Simon sprinted like a cheetah towards the girls. The sharp contrast of the MD's LED gave him great visibility. Claudine was clearly concussed. Her breathing was shallow and slow. He decided to stabilise her first and did so by attaching his oxygen mask over her nose. Immediately she responded. She coughed violently. While covered in black dust, she didn't appear to have any injuries.

As she opened her eyes she said. 'I'm ok, look after Maria.'

Maria was in a much worse state. Apart from a deep gash across her forehead and multiple scratches to her arms and legs, she was struggling with her breath. He bent down towards her mouth to resuscitate her and was immediately met with a strong smell of sulphur. He knew that not only was she knocked out by the impact of the quake, but that the associated sulphur emissions could be poisoning her.

Claudine sat still, silent and stunned, and watched Simon give mouth-to-mouth resuscitation to Maria. After six blows of air into her lungs he quickly attached an oxygen mask and turned up the flow to full. The response was also immediate. Maria's eyes opened. She emitted a deep gurgling sound from the depths of her lungs. She coughed hard and spewed out. Once she cleared her air passage her breathing became less of a struggle. Simon held her close and smiled knowing she was on the mend. He got an even bigger smile back and a loving look from her blue-grey eyes. He took off the oxygen mask.

'Where are we?' said Maria.

'No longer on the dark side of the moon. Take it easy now. I'll look after you,' said Simon, lovingly.

She tried to laugh, but it hurt.

'Can you walk?'

'Let me see.'

Claudine helped her sister slowly to her feet. She wobbled at first, but her fitness and youth allowed her to stand straight up. Once she got her balance, she put one foot ahead of the other with Simon and Claudine supporting her on either side.

'I'll fly MD above you so you will have close to daylight visibility,' said Damian who had been watching the scene in silence on his laptop from the safety of the carpark.

'That's great. The last thing we need now are a few twisted ankles,' said Simon.

'It's a short walk to the Reventon car park,' lied Simon. Maria knew it was at least a kilometre. She knew he was trying to protect her.

'Thanks, Simon,' she whispered into his ear.

'Love you.'

'You too.'

She squeezed his hand.

By midnight, Maria and Claudine were tucked into their beds at the ORM. Sedated, sleepy but safe.

MD was also packed away. She had passed her first assignment with flying colours. Damian saw the potential of the MD assisting the Guardia Civil in mountain search and rescue work. He was eager to share his idea and Maria's recovery with Margarida over their evening Aperol.

At the same time what remained of the Malmesbury orienteering group were packing their bags. They would be on the first flight to Gatwick in the morning.

Twin Otter

Armed with a generous breakfast, the teams designated to cover sites ZX1 and ZX2 left the Summit Station in the two Bombardier Humvees. Seated beside the driver, two metres above ground level, Phil Teahon imagined he was a tank commander ready to go into battle. The route to site ZX1 was familiar as it was used frequently every summer. The Humvee, with its four narrow gauge tracks, could do ten kilometres an hour in perfect conditions. But in an environment of slush and uneven packed snow, it became necessary at times for two of the team to walk in front to find a path through what became very unstable ice conditions.

The radio phone crackled in the communication's room where Lars and Sean were having a coffee and a chat. Sean drank a filter coffee – a pale relation of the Turkish mud that kept Lars functional.

'Lars, this is Phil. I am with the driver of the ZX1 Humvee. We're making slower progress than planned. We've encountered conditions that are slushier than we experienced when we were here last month. This will delay our forecast site arrival time by a few hours. Visibility is good, though.'

'Roger, Phil. I'm not surprised given what we know. You take it easy and travel carefully. We're using the Humvee's satellite navigation beacon to keep an eye on your progress. As we'll not be starting ops until tomorrow you are under no time pressure.'

'OK, we'll proceed slowly. Roger and out.' Phil was glad common sense prevailed.

The following morning, the Twin Otter ski-plane was loaded with a drone and supporting equipment. As agreed, the estimated time of deployment at site ZX3, three hundred kilometres away, was around midday.

Alice, fully dressed in her survival gear, including an inflatable life jacket, packed her PC into her adventure rucksack and double checked her allocation of two hundred golf balls in the box at the base of her seat. She gave pride of place to the four camera golf balls that she placed in the pocket of her anorak. She zipped it closed.

Flying conditions were almost perfect with a light breeze from the west and some flecks of light snow. Within minutes they were airborne and soon reached cruising altitude at five thousand metres above sea level, or two thousand metres over the ice sheet.

The Summit Station teams went through their preparations for the local deployments. The equipment had been carefully loaded into containers on the ski-cat.

The huskies were made ready. They were harnessed to the sledge in a broad array fanned out in front of it. In this way the dogs had more freedom to move amongst themselves, to pull hard, to lay back and rest, or to sidle up to a friend. Once they were under way, the soft trotting of the dogs was therapeutic.

All was going according to plan.

There was much chit-chat over the radio communications as the deadline for the simultaneous launch of the golf balls approached.

'Lars, we're on site and should have ourselves set up within the hour.'

'Thanks, Phil. I will call you when Alice's team lands. The other Humvee team is also on target for a simultaneous midday deployment.'

Alice was seated behind the Twin Otter ski-plane's co-pilot enjoying a panoramic view of the designated landing area close to site ZX3. There was a strong reflection off the ice under the noon sun. Her designer polaroid sunglasses minimised the glare. The surface was like that of the moon. There were no discernible dominant features, just a landscape of small ridges of dirty ice as far as the eye could see with loose snow being driven by a light wind. At the end of the runway, identified by parallel lines of tall red poles, the Portakabin – the summer home for so many summer students over many years – seemed out of place.

The Canadian pilot spoke on the VHF radio.

'We might do a three-sixty over the landing area. It has been some time since we used this runway.'

'Roger that,' acknowledged Lars.

The plane banked slowly at one thousand metres and made a wide circle over the landing strip. The red flags that delimited the short landing strip fluttered lightly. The surface was flat. No significant snow had fallen in weeks.

'I can see the primary dropping zone to the far left of the Portakabin,' said Alice into the microphone on her headset.

In the distance, the darkened blue edges of a crevasse contrasted with the pure white of its surrounds.

'It is much wider and – goodness – so much deeper than I had expected. It must be melting fast up here,' remarked Alice.

'The landing zone looks OK to me,' said the pilot.

'Go for it,' said Lars.

The pilot told the support team members at the back of the plane to prepare for descent. He manoeuvred the ski-plane in a direct line to the landing strip.

They all had earphones on so they could hear Lars say, 'Good luck and talk soon.'

The Summit Station's communication's room was monitoring the cockpit conversations.

'Nine hundred metres and descending at 150 knots, clear skies, no obstructions visible, gentle breeze off our starboard. Seven hundred, six, five, four. Ready yourselves for landing, three, two, one.'

The ski-plane glided into the landing strip at the correct speed and made what appeared to be a perfect landing.

'Jesus, Oh Fuck,' shouted the pilot. 'The landing strip is not ice packed as it should be. We're landing on a lake of melted water. The snow was disguising thin surface ice that has now broken.'

The plane's skis were not designed to facilitate a landing on a watery surface. Instead of gliding straight along the ice the plane started to shudder abruptly as it tried to progress along the landing strip. It could not get traction on water.

Suddenly the plane veered sharply to the right off the designated landing strip. At over a hundred kilometres an hour it ploughed through the slush and meltwater cracking the thin veneer of surface ice that hid an all too different surface underneath. It careered past the Portakabin.

'Lars, we're in serious trouble.'

Lars looked at the images on his screen generated by the sky camera positioned in the nose cone of the Twin Otter. Without warning the plane halted suddenly on its side in what appeared at first to be a shallow pool of water. The left wing snapped off with the impact. The pilot cut of the engines to stop the propellers rotating. There was silence for a moment. Then, without any warning, the Twin Otter was moving again quite quickly.

The pilot was now in a state of blind panic. 'We've landed in a fast-flowing river of ice-melt and are being pushed forward. I can't control anything. We're like a bottle in the centre of a river current.'

What was a fast river torrent ended abruptly. The plane tumbled upside down some fifty metres into a deep precipice marked by sheer ice walls. It dropped down headfirst and hit a rock, or something solid, and jack knifed in the other direction in slow motion. The cockpit was sheared almost in half and the right wing split off with the rotors continuing to spin for several seconds.

'Oh my God,' said Alice, simultaneously in prayer and in amazement at what had happened in the past seconds.

'We're pointed face down about fifty metres into a precipice.'

What remained of the plane's left wing then broke under the pressure and the main fuselage dropped another twenty metres to rest precariously on a narrow ledge of a waterfall under the ice. The deep blue water thundered past them into the abyss showering everything with an icy spray.

'We'll never get out of this.' She knew her number was up. As if rehearsed, she unclipped her safety belt and searched for the box with the golf balls.

'Alice, what is happening?' Lars could barely hide his state of panic. He didn't know if the communications unit was still working. He was surprised when he got a response.

'Lars, good to hear your voice from seventy metres under the ice sheet. It may be my last act on earth, but I believe I can spill the golf balls into the chasm.'

'Alice, hang in there. We'll send help.'

'I'm sure you will, but I'm afraid all that will you retrieve will be frozen bodies. I'll complete the mission.'

Alice took off her headset and, to her amazement, easily opened the twisted passenger door of the plane. She sat on the base of the door of the shattered Twin Otter. The pilots were dead. The impact had smashed their heads. Blood flowed from ear to ear and was splattered over the cockpit. The drone support team had fared no better. Seated behind her, they had had their necks broken with the whiplash effect as a result of the fall into the precipice.

Heavily bruised, but with no broken bones, all she could see was a torrent of water flowing strongly about three metres away. The noise was deafening. She was, after all, on the inside of a waterfall. She stepped onto the base of the door with her precious cargo under her arm. She raised the box to shoulder height and started to throw the two hundred golf balls into the frozen subterranean river. They plunged out of the box like greyhounds chasing a rabbit, all eager to do their duty.

Within a short while the box was empty. The golf balls had left the first tee on their adventure into the depths of the Greenland Ice Sheet.

The computer screen monitoring the site at the Summit Station lit up as the software programme started to track the progress of the cargo.

She crawled back into what remained of the cockpit and put her headset back on. To her surprise it was still working.

'Lars, all the others are dead. It's only a matter of time before the plane is dragged further into the precipice. The flow rate of the ice-melt is ferocious.'

Lars knew that to be case as the monitor was showing a forty-kilometres an hour speed reading for most of the golf balls. A dozen or so were stationery, presumably isolated on ice ledges. He said nothing. He knew that Alice could not survive for too much longer.

'If I'm going to go, I may as well do it in style. I've the four camera golf balls in my hand. Can you see the images?'

Lars held back his tears, just about. 'They are crystal clear. The light on your safety vest is helping visibility.'

'Good. Bye then and give my love to all.'

Alice slid herself into the fast-flowing ice flow clutching her precious cameras. As soon as she exited the aircraft her head hit a jagged outcrop of ice. She lost consciousness. Even the shock of the frozen water into which she plunged didn't revive her. She died within minutes.

Her safety jacket gave her buoyancy, enough for her to stay above water. In her tumble into the ice-melt she inadvertently opened her hands and so released four camera golf balls. Three progressed independently and joined their two hundred or so fellow travellers as they made their way down and through the streams far below the Greenland Ice Sheet. The fourth became lodged in her safety belt.

Moments later the Twin Otter broke up. Its shattered fuselage was crushed to pieces in a wild descent to the base of the crevasse.

Eriador Seamount

The RV *Celtic Explorer*'s bridge was full to capacity ahead of a de-briefing about the day's activities.

'Before we schedule another dive by the PLU, perhaps as early as tomorrow morning, we need to find out if there was any seismic activity in the British sector north of our location. The scientists at HUGO will also have some observations, no doubt, about the analysis of the geo-chemical samples we gave them. Thanks to the on-board laboratory team that processed the data so quickly.'

Gilmore was conscious that the manned submersible launch team and all the supporting scientists were all equally surprised that volcanic activity, however small in scale, was evident from the time PLU went to the target location.

'What was the reading?' asked Gilmore.

Gallery had the facts at his fingertips. 'Just 2.1 on the Richter scale, so not much different from last week's earthquake. However, what is of more concern is the frequency between the readings.'

'Maeve, what should we make of this?'

She was expecting the question.

'We've every reason to be curious as the flanks of the mid-Atlantic rim have been dormant for as long as we've been tracking seismic activity. A minor tremor or two, or even three should not be of any concern provided this was an isolated sub-sea vent or cluster of small vents. We're here because seismic activity has been recorded along a line of some one hundred kilometres and we just viewed the southernmost location. I think …'

She didn't get to finish her sentence as the communications console panel lit up.

'RV *Celtic Explorer*, this is Áras 2 calling. Over'

The LÉ *Michael D. Higgins'* call sign was known to everyone.

'Hi, Captain. I assume you were monitoring our progress and the surprise package that we found?' said Gilmore.

'Yes, and I hope Maeve and Andy were not too shaken,' said Captain Brennan. 'I've no sympathy for young Smith of course! You will not be surprised to hear that the tremor was registered along the line we've been monitoring. The British submersible didn't launch today due to bad weather, but they also picked up a 2.1 reading and at a very shallow depth. The Global Seismographic Network got in touch with us through the US Geological Survey. They are getting early indications of a similar set of readings from La Palma.'

'La Palma?' asked Maeve.

'Yes, it appears there have been recent but recurring low levels of seismic activity in some of the Canary Islands,' said Captain Brennan.

'That is most unusual,' said Maeve.

She did not have time to consider the incident any further or to offer an opinion. The PLU's next dive was the priority.

Captain Brennan continued, 'As we've the most significant naval asset on site and are directly adjacent to the seismic line, we've patched the GSN into our comms network for PLU's future dives. It appears that this Operation Eriador is attracting a lot of attention. What are your plans?'

Gilmore replied. 'Oh, we'll be going back as soon as PLU's batteries are re-charged. In the morning, I guess. I've asked Captain Killen to take us to a new location about five kilometres to the north-east, directly above the edge of the Eriador Seamount. We've asked HUGO for an assessment of the geochemistry from yesterday's data, but we'll still proceed if we hear nothing.'

'That seems reasonable. We'll follow you.'

'Captain Brennan, this is Maeve O'Farrell here. Perhaps I might give you some insights as to why the US Geological Survey and indeed most other volcanic observatories will be taking a keen interest in what happens over the next while.'

'Go on Maeve. I'm all ears.'

'There is, unfortunately, a precedent and a recent one at that. In 2004, seabed earthquakes appeared along a hundred kilometre stretch of the Sunda Trench that's located off the northern tip of Sumatra. Within days the intensity of seismic activity rose surely and steadily but gave no cause for alarm. However, it was followed by what became known as the St Stephen's Day Tsunami, caused by a 9.1 megathrust earthquake at a depth of just twenty kilometres below the seabed. With the available technology at the time, it wasn't possible to predict such a massive upheaval. We know much more now, thanks to advanced satellite, submersible technologies and a variety of sophisticated seabed sensors. What I'm saying is the glitch we saw this morning could be just that, an isolated series of small vents. But we should be alert to a scenario that this could be a pre-cursor to wider and more extensive volcanic activity.'

'That's very cheerful, Maeve! We should be prepared to anticipate a more aggressive environment in future dives.'

There was silence in the room, a deep air of reflection, as everyone digested what they had heard.

Captain Brennan sensed the mood despite being on another ship a kilometre astern. He tried to open up a new line of conversation.

'By the way how did the other research team get on?'

'Tony, what's the story?' asked Gilmore.

'No whales, no lava bombs, and no evidence of a fully working column. There was very poor salinity at depth. We can only confirm that at this location the satellite observations of a partial but significant collapse can be confirmed. The specially designed electrically conductive devices and the water canisters captured all the data we needed from the location. I'm glad we're moving north-east. We can conduct another ROV dive while the PLU is being prepared.'

Doherty took a long sup of coffee. He took comfort in the fact that his experiments, and the careful preparation that was done in the past months, had paid an instant dividend.

He wasn't allowed to muse for too long.

'Tony, I've an idea – even an inspired idea'.

O'Farrell stood up as if to make a speech. She caught Doherty's eye and talked directly to him, but loud enough for all to hear.

'Rather than PLU spending unnecessary time searching

the seabed for signs of volcanic activity, could the *Holland 2* join the party by carrying out an advanced video mapping exercise of potential vents. In that way, we can drive to a more precise location if you find anything of interest.'

'Yes, that's very doable. On the basis of today's experience, we should be finished our salinity testing within four hours, well before most of you get up for breakfast, and can easily maintain the ROV at the seabed until the PLU arrives. We also have 4K video HD so can transmit pictures to the control room and onwards to your screens. Our lamps are not as powerful as PLU's, but I can guarantee you they are good enough to illuminate an area ten metres square.'

Gilmore nodded. 'That makes a lot of sense. Given the time difference and the slight delay in setting up the PLU's second dive, we might manage to get some insights from HUGO about their findings and some guidance about what more we should be looking for.'

Captain Killen had the final word.

'Let's wrap up now and set the tables for dinner. Its movie night later and will be showing the mariner's all-time favourite: *Jaws 2*.'

'Prophetic,' muttered someone.

CHAPTER 7

Observatorio Roque de los Muchachos

THE DEEP THROB OF the rotors could be heard in the clear mountain air long before the military Sikorsky appeared above the thick nimbus clouds that were below the mountain peaks. As the helicopter got nearer to the landing area beside the ORM car park it hovered overhead for what sounded like an eternity before it settled effortlessly onto the helipad.

'Simon, what's going on. What's that racket?'

Ros rubbed his sleepy eyes. He wasn't a morning person. He was certainly not a six o'clock in the morning person. His customary habit of using Twitter and Facebook into the small hours of the morning was a contributing factor to his tiredness.'

'That's a helicopter,' said Simon. 'I believe we're getting an official visit of some sort. As it might be Mark, we better get dressed I suppose.'

Minutes later, as they approach the helicopter, they saw a group of six men who were in the process of taking off their emergency gear. ORM staff were busying themselves unloading several huge crates.

Antonio Farillo, the ORM Director, was talking over the noise to a tall, tanned, bearded man in his mid-fifties who wore a New York Yankees baseball cap . They instantly recognised Mark Doyle who walked over to them.

'The brothers Rodriquez, I assume?'

'Yes, Mr Doyle,' said Ros, somewhat in awe.

He was after all meeting his hero for the first time.

'No need for the 'Mr', Ros. Call me Mark. I have little time for formalities, I'm afraid.'

'Sure,' said Ros.

'I would murder a double espresso. Let's go inside so that I can introduce my team.' Mark walked into the ORM with a brisk step.

Ros and Simon had never started work at such an early hour. They took their place at the end of the boardroom table and nursed their first coffee of the day. It was so early that the kitchen staff had not even baked the daily supply of croissants and fresh bread.

'It's not yet 7 a.m. and this guy has a bundle of energy, having flown from Hawaii and across the Atlantic overnight. How are we going to survive this pace?' said Ros.

'The jet lag will get him sooner rather than later,' replied Simon.

'No, it won't,' smiled Mark, who had overheard what the brothers thought was a whispered conversation. 'Let's get started. We've identified several potential target areas from the seismic data to date. This mountain area along the entire length of the Caldera de Taburiente from Roque Palermo to Pico de la Nieve is at most risk as are the volcanoes along the rim of the *Ruta*. There have also been worrying readings at the base of the National Park. I'm less concerned about the southernmost area of the island, but we'll need to monitor it. We've a great base camp here at the ORM that has all the support facilities, communication links and logistics that befit an emergency coordination centre.

He paused and took another sup of his coffee.

Mark, who had thirty years' experience of volcano watching across the globe – most of it at very close quarters, didn't show his intense sense of foreboding. The series of seismic readings from across the Canaries to the Mid-Atlantic Ridge was now a cause of deep concern to all the Governments on the Atlantic Rim. While the intensity of the earthquakes wasn't too severe, the fact that so many locations were showing readings wasn't a good sign. Getting a handle on the significance of the collective readings was his priority.

He started his introductions.

'This is Franco Bradelle, a colleague of mine at the Global Seismographic Network, when he's not abseiling down the rim of an active volcano. I'll let him explain what we've got in mind.'

One would never have guessed that Franco was Portuguese. He spoke English with a mid-Atlantic drawl with a trace of an English university accent. He dressed and behaved like a US Marine and his tone of voice was that of a leader. Judging by his tailored head-to-toe work fatigues, his favourite colour was desert khaki . He dressed to impress.

'Thanks Mark. To cut to the chase, we need to set up two core monitoring teams, one for each of the priority zones we've identified. We've a lot of recent experience from our visits to Iceland that we hope to put to good use here. Two military sized drones with supporting computers are being unpacked as we speak. We've adapted the drones to enable them to measure gases from newly formed vents as well as taking high resolution photo images. Importantly, these gadgets can also take thermal infrared heat seeking images that will allow us identify vents before they hit the surface. We'll deploy one drone along the Caldera de Taburiente and the second lower down in the National Park.'

'Where do we fit in?' whispered Ros to Simon.

He didn't have to wait long to get an answer to his question.

'Mark and I will take charge of the monitoring teams for the two target areas. Our expert drone operators and data technicians will be shared out. Given your local knowledge, Simon and Maria will work with me and Ros and Claudine will help Mark. What we're looking for above anything else are thermal signatures that may be pre-cursors to a vent developing. Given our recent experiences in Iceland, if we manage to locate an area displaying a rise in surface temperature, we can try to predict subsequent levels of potential activity. The ORM Director and his staff will manage the communications from here and will deal with the Guardia Civil. I expect that Carmen and her team will arrive sometime tomorrow, so we'll have enough bandwidth to cover most circumstances.'

'Sounds like a plan,' said Ros aloud.

The drones were assembled and ready to fly within two hours. Ros, who helped unpack the boxes, was fascinated. He had seen small camera drones before but nothing as big as the industrial sized flying instruments that were constructed before his eyes. Damian would be so jealous. These machines dwarfed his toys.

The technicians had their consoles and PCs set up on the ORM's boardroom table. From there, now that the clouds had burned away, they had a panoramic view across the entire Caldera de Taburiente and down to the base of the National Park. The GPS systems were calibrated and synchronised with a NASA satellite that had been made available. Mark's influence clearly went way beyond procuring military helicopters.

Later on, Mark assembled his team at the window that probably offered one of the best views of mountain scenery in the world.

'Listen up. Based on the data we have to hand I'm expecting a significant increase in low level seismic activity at shallow depths. We need to know what to look for. A magnitude 4 earthquake could rupture about a square kilometre of the fault surface area. If we experience a Richter 6 event, I would expect the entire central part of the island to be affected. If there is a magnitude 8 quake we don't want to be here as this place will vanish: the mountain will slide towards the northern coast at great speed and with catastrophic impact. The network of seismic and sulphur dioxide monitors across the island will give us one layer of data, however crude. These drones should help us get more comprehensive data and a lot faster. As Franco told you, our top priority is to get an initial thermal ground image map of the target zones.

'What sort of timescale are we talking about?' enquired Ros as he paused from taking notes – ever the eager student.

'Good question, but one where I can't give an answer at this stage. We'll know much more when we get the first set of thermal images from the drones. Normally, seismic activity would increase gradually and spread. But I fear this is not a normal situation. We'll introduce a rising colour code alert. I will call in military support if we get to amber. The Sikorsky will stay on station. It will provide us with secure communications to the air force base on the island of Tenerife.'

'I suggest we start at the location where Maria and Claudine had their off-the-ground experience,' said Simon.

'Good idea. Talk to the drone team and set up the coordinates. You and Maria should try and spot any unusual features as the drone flies over the area in a grid format.'

They wasted no time getting to the drone teams.

Simon approached the drone operator he was to work with.

'What do you call it?'

'PD1'

'PD1?'

I got the naming rights on this magnificent piece of equipment – my name is Pedro Dunato. My influence is such that the call sign for the other drone is 'PD2'. In our line of business there are few perks other than having the right to give our toys an identifier.'

'Where have you used your drones before?' asked Simon.

'Iceland, or Eyjafjallajokull to be more precise. This was the volcano that closed most of Europe's air space in April 2010 with 95,000 flights cancelled. We were able to track and anticipate lava flows using the thermal image cameras and to test the composition of the ash clouds. It was far too dangerous for volcanologists or helicopters to get close to the action. An early version of PD1 did the business. The poor thing got singed a bit but that's part of the job. We have also deployed more recently at Nyiragongo in DR Congo and Rincon de la Vieja in Costa Rica. We learned an awful lot from these major events. Let's hope the adjustments and additions we made to the kit will be put to good use here.'

Half an hour later PD1 was ready to start its first run along a line of ten kilometres across the northern rim of the Caldera de Taburiente and down the centre of the *Ruta* to the first target area close to Refugio El Pilar.

Qooqqup Kuua River

While Lars was trying to cope with the loss of the Twin Otter and all on board, the other teams were unaware of the disaster. He had restricted the two-way communications with the plane to the small team at the Summit Station. As a result, they got on with their appointed tasks.

The team at site ZX1 successfully deployed two hundred golf balls and four camera golf balls as planned. The drone hovered overhead and relayed images back to the Summit Station control room of a landscape that appeared to be solid on the surface apart from two distinct lines of zigzag fracture. As the Norwegians wanted their machines returned undamaged, the operator guided the drone to return to the Summit Station, which it did without incident. Phil Teahon felt he had done something worthwhile and important.

The second Humvee team at site ZX2 had a similar positive experience jettisoning two hundred golf balls, along with four camera companions, into a vast crater-shaped structure. It was supplied with ice-melt from several nearby lakes. It was a good call not to require the ski-cat to travel the full distance as the images sent back showed regular but shallow depressions – most filled with slushy ice-water – over the entire terrain. Everywhere was wet. The ZX2 team didn't dawdle at the site. As soon as they got the signal from Lars they plotted their return journey to the Summit Station.

The site ZX4 team had visited their chosen location several times over the past three months and their drop and delivery was routine by comparison. While there were some slushy sections, these were not a problem.

As the teams started to report on their experiences they were told by Lars over their radios of the fate of Alice and her colleagues. They were all visibly shocked and upset. Phil sobbed as his chest tensed up. He had grown quite fond of Alice and enjoyed her sparkling company and her perennial inquisitiveness. Now she was gone. Nobody had imagined that there were serious risks attached to dropping golf balls into crevasses. Were these deaths worth it? he asked himself.

Lars brought the teams together after they all returned to the Summit Camp. He knew they were grieving for lost friends and colleagues.

'There is nothing we can do. Even if I judged there was a prospect of retrieving the bodies from under the ice sheet, it is far too risky. The surface at the crash site is, in effect, a large ice pool. We should pay our respects to our friends.'

He said a few prayers and once finished Sean concluded with an old Irish lament sung in a low baritone voice.

Lars gave everyone time to reflect. As they were scientists, they knew they had to finish the task at hand. Like the companions of soldiers who fell in the trenches, those who survived continued to follow orders and get the job done. They reconvened later that evening to review progress.

'How are my golf balls progressing at the other locations?' asked Sean.

Everyone's attention turned to the bank of computers that was tracking the golf balls at the different sites.

'What's the data telling us?' said Benny.

'We deployed all the golf balls more-or-less at the same time, as planned. Their progress is quite astonishing. See here,' replied Lars.

An operator pointed to the screen and to the small red dots that represented each golf ball. Quite a few were stationery, suggesting they had been grounded as they progressed beneath the ice sheet. While the tracks of the vast majority moved slowly on the screen in the meltwater, the pace of quite a number was quite different.

'It seems, as I suspected would happen, that a few golf balls got stranded in isolated pools. But all appear to be sending back signals.'

'They sure are. Look at the feedback from the other sites.'

Over the coming hours the teams saw hundreds of tracks descend down hitherto undiscovered underground rivers, moulins and channels. In most locations the ice-melt flow rate was higher than had been previously measured. While many golf balls got lodged in cracks or ice hollows, most were moving. The slow track of some golf balls suggested they were floating on sub-glacial lakes, moving towards the next descending channel. These lakes had never been mapped before. The existence of so many deep sinkholes, drove the golf balls deep into the bowels of the ice sheet. As the dropping zones were spaced quite a bit apart there didn't appear to be any interconnections, at least so far, between the rivers, rivulets and sub-glacial lakes.

'Have the cameras worked?' Sean asked.

'They sure have. All are transmitting. Look at the cameras dropped at site ZX2. One has just tumbled down a sinkhole and the infrared picture shows the ceiling of a large cavern as it has slowed down. This must be a big lake. How big, we can only guess. This is the first evidence that the ice sheet has hollowed out.

Another operator tried to get everyone's attention.

'I've produced a preliminary 3D map of the five sites we're looking at.'

Despite the fatal incident, Lars had instructed everyone to actively monitor the location where Alice and her colleagues had died.

'You can see the track of ice-melt flow twisting and turning as the golf balls continued their descent through the glacier. At site ZX3, the golf balls descended almost two thousand metres in little under six hours,' said the operator.

'Amazing,' acknowledged Lars.

'At site ZX1, the golf balls are moving at an average speed of between twenty-five and thirty kilometres an hour in an east-north-east direction. More interesting, is the slope of the underground rivers. As the gradient falls the water speed increases. See the cluster that Alice deployed? They have just veered off down another almost perpendicular vent: a drop of over two hundred metres. While some were dispersed and are stationary, the majority are moving to an exit at the coast that will soon be revealed,' said the operator.

'What does this mean?' asked Benny.

'My guess is that the aquifers beneath the glacier are deeper and longer than we thought, and certainly interconnected in some way. The ice-melt is certainly carving away the innards of the ice sheet. It appears there are sub-glacial lakes feeding into lower channels. It is too soon to say for definite, but I would not be surprised if this load didn't make an appearance at the source of the Qooqqup Kuua River.'

The operator switched to the PC monitoring the other sites. The trend was the same. On entry into the crevasses the vast majority of the golf balls had plunged into the Greenland Ice Sheet through a series of deep drops as they moved across pools where fast currents seemed persistent.

'The group of golf balls dropped at site ZX2 are now almost stationary having reached a level of three hundred metres below the surface in under two hours. They are all drifting at two kilometres an hour in a north-westerly direction. Perhaps they are resting on a sub-glacial lake awaiting a further plunge into the bedrock that lies below?'

Sean watched in astonishment. Never in his wildest imagination could he have seen such remarkable readings. He had honestly believed that the chances of success were no better than fifty-fifty. Even the renowned Irish book-maker Paddy Power would not have given odds on this pilot project being a partial success.

The operator continued his running commentary.

'There are so many golf balls – I reckon at least six hundred – generating live data that we'll be able to generate a detailed 3D map of their progress through the ice sheet. Can you believe how important and impactful this will be for our future research?'

'Anymore images from the cameras?' asked Lars.

The operator switched on the PC showing one of the camera golf balls deployed by Alice.

Lars knew what was going to be shown and approved the viewing despite the tragic circumstances.

'Is that an underground cavern?' exclaimed Benny.

The team all looked at the image that one of the golf balls was showing, having descended nearly a thousand metres in under six hours. They all reacted simultaneously with shock when they realised that the camera golf ball was attached to Alice's battered body at her final resting place. She had obviously ended up in a seated posture judging by the camera image display of a panoramic view from water level to ceiling of a cavern of some hundred metres in height and nearly half a kilometre long. While it was dark, they were able to see the general contours of the cavern because Alice's safety lamp was turned on. This allowed the camera to capture the vastness of the sub-glacial lake. The camera didn't have a zoom feature but that didn't matter. This was the eighth wonder of the world. A vision that nobody had ever seen before. Simultaneously one of beauty and one of sadness. Here was the evidence they needed of the hollowing out of the ice sheet.

The other camera balls showed consistent images of fast flowing water through interconnected tunnels, but none as vivid as the footage from Alice's camera.

'This data confirms what we've suspected for quite some time,' said Lars.

'This is the first clear evidence that the ice-melt is fracturing the interior of the ice sheet to a much greater extent than we could have imagined. I had surmised that most caverns were quite narrow – maybe a height of five metres or so. And there are so many! The sinkholes of water are carving deeply into the core of the glacier. It's early days yet, but I imagine within twenty-four hours some of our golf balls will be out in the North Atlantic.'

The Gulf Stream

Tony Doherty and his team felt a bit redundant. The ROV had indeed completed its research mission in under four hours. The column they were asked to observe had more or less the same characteristics as the one they tested the day before. Salinity at depth was very poor. The column had narrowed to such an extent that it was barely functioning.

As would be confirmed over the coming weeks, the research vessels on location from four other Atlantic nations recorded similar findings. Thirty of the central columns in the mid-Atlantic driving the Gulf Stream had stopped functioning or were at a point of near collapse. The phenomenon was significantly worse in the seas immediately south of Greenland and Iceland where the flow of meltwater from the Greenland Ice Sheet was at record levels.

The collective findings of the four research nations would be coordinated, critically assessed, attributed and presented. The plan was to have all the evidence ready for the annual meeting of the United Nations Climate Change Panel. The findings were potentially devastating, not least because the rapid deterioration of the moderating effects of the Gulf Stream could not be reversed. This was one of the climate change tipping points campaigners had been warning about for decades. The only point of debate was timing, with some scientists predicting extended sea ice formation starting almost immediately in the North Atlantic.

An early occurrence of this phenomenon would, ironically, prevent the otherwise total demise of the Greenland Ice Sheet.

Doherty and his team were assembled at the bridge. Their consolation prize was that they had something practical to contribute to Project Big Bang, as they had privately renamed Project Eriador.

'Please re-direct the ROV to the target location. It should be there in about an hour. Paul could you take charge please,' instructed Gilmore.

McCrossan manoeuvred the joystick that controlled the ROV's thrusters and the *Holland 2* set off to the pre-designated target area. At the same time the PLU's dive crew prepared the manned submersible for its second launch. The standard operating safety procedures for the launch were adhered to in detail.

O'Farrell and Gallery listened patiently to Mike Smith as he went through all the pre-dive protocols with McCrossan and the deck hands. They were a bit more at ease. The first dive had been quite an experience, not one they would have wished to partake in unless for strictly professional reasons. Soon, the PLU was winched off the deck, positioned into the water and started its slow descent. In line with protocol, their diver escort saluted them with a tap on the cockpit window.

The sunlight disappeared and, as before, Smith turned around to start up a conversation to distract his passengers from dwelling on the potential challenges that lay ahead. He didn't succeed as both had donned earphones and clearly preferred music over his dulcet tones. He had enough sense not to interrupt.

O'Farrell was preoccupied with Andre Rieu's Maastricht summer concert. She removed her earphones as they approached the seabed. 'Did I miss anything Mike?'

'Well no. Any thoughts about what conditions we might expect to encounter?'

'As low seismic readings have been recorded, I expect we may see other small vents along the edge of the Eriador Seamount,' said O'Farrell. 'What I'll be looking for is evidence of recent lava flows and gas bubbles that are a signal of sulphur gas emissions.'

Gallery chipped in. He too had concluded his musical interlude. It was back to business. 'We'll have the advantage of getting advanced visuals from the *Holland 2*. This will forewarn us of heightened activity. How soon can we access the live camera feed?'

'Let's ask McCrossan.' Smith clicked the microphone switch on the console. 'Paul, Mike here. Any visuals yet from the *Holland 2*. I reckon we're about forty minutes above the ROV.'

'Timely call, Mike. I'm driving the ROV in a north-north-west direction about four hundred metres short of our first target zone. Hold on while I turn on the main arc lamp.'

'We've all the time in the world, Mike. Should I turn on our computer screen?'

'Sure. Just give me a second.'

The images of the sea floor from the *Holland 2* lit up the PLU's monitor.

'That's very clear,' said O'Farrell.

'Good to know that Maeve,' said McCrossan.

'I reckon the *Holland 2* is about ten metres above the seabed. The black grey surfaces are basalt but nothing of recent origin.'

As the *Holland 2* glided along with its headlights on full, they saw a myriad of small fish and other creatures that eked out an existence in pitch black at fifteen hundred metres below sea level. None seemed too perturbed by the intense light penetrating their environment. It wasn't as if they had frequent visitors.

The ROV moved along the seabed at three kilometres an hour, a slow pace, with her tether system expertly managed by McCrossan. The progress of both the ROV and the PLU were monitored constantly by McCrossan and the PLU support team. The main screen in front of him showed both vehicles as throbbing green dots. The one risk they were all aware of was the possibility of the PLU becoming entangled in the power and communication tether lines attached to the ROV. To avoid such a situation the respective plots of both vehicles had been pre-programmed to keep them at least five hundred metres apart.

'Looks like we've some new visuals,' said McCrossan.

'Wow!' exclaimed O'Farrell.

The screen showed a thin crimson line of lava oozing slowly from a four-metre high vent. Some gas bubbles filled the area around the fissure.

'Paul, please zoom into the top of the vent but stay at least ten metres away.'

'Roger.'

The ROV's zoom lens focused on the head of the vent.

'See the fluidity of the magma. It is flowing out at a steady pace like melting wax.'

'What does this mean, Maeve?' asked Smith.

'This suggests that the eruption started perhaps several days ago. Its fluidity means there is a chamber close to the surface of the seabed. Though it is strange we didn't pick up any seismic readings from this location. Perhaps this is a secondary lower vent. Mike, please drive us to where the ROV is positioned so we can have a closer look and take samples.'

McCrossan spoke. 'Mike, I will move the ROV away along the right side of the Eriador Seamount so allow ten minutes before you move forward. At all times you must avoid the ROV's tethering system.'

'Roger that.'

Within half an hour the PLU arrived at the location of the vent. It was still spewing its crimson flow. Expertly, Smith took chemical and rock samples with the PLU's mechanical arms. The sulphur dioxide sensor lit up immediately showing an above average reading. This was the marker that they all focused on. The scientists at HUGO wanted to gather data from as many sites as possible as these emissions, in particular their intensity, were a possible precursor of more troublesome volcanic activity.

The ROV and the PLU conducted two back-to-back surveys in short order at adjacent vents with similar results.

'Where next, Gerdy?' asked Smith.

The Chief Scientist and other scientists across the globe had been monitoring the emerging data from the three sites at the base of the Eriador Seamount. They were all aware that volcanic vents at sea level were a commonplace occurrence but not at this location.

'What do you think, Maeve?' asked Gilmore.

'What strikes me as strange is the intense fluidity of the magma flow and the absence of any explosive activity. This is not unusual at surface level as you know. Perhaps we could take a look up the higher levels of the Seamount?'

'How is your battery level, Mike?'

'Five hours at least.'

'Then let us take advantage of the ROV being with us and proceed up the slope that defines the western flank of the Seamount.'

'All OK with that?'

'Let me re-set the *Holland 2*'s plot before I drive it up the slope,' said McCrossan.

No sooner had he begun to manoeuvre the ROV than the red warning light on the seismograph screen lit up. The signal was picked up not only on the RV *Celtic Explorer* and on the LÉ *Michael D. Higgins*, but by all the agencies who were involved with Project Eriador.

'It's a 3.1.'

The PLU Shack was stunned into silence as the seismograph jumped again.

'There are three sources about fifty kilometres apart,' said Gilmore with a strange sense of calmness.

'Mike, all OK?

'Yes, Paul. There was a small eddy of displaced water that has just buffeted us about a bit but there is no movement now. Let's just say we were shaken but not stirred. I reckon we are about two klicks from the first seismic reading. It will take us thirty minutes to get to that location. Before you remind me, we'll proceed with caution.'

'This is a unique opportunity to witness and record the after-effects, so let's get going,' added O'Farrell.

'I'll pull back the ROV and hold her in reserve,' said McCrossan.

The PLU moved upwards slowly and in silence as its passengers tried to absorb the impact of the Richter scale readings. At a distance Smith noticed a small red light that grew into a deepening pulse.

'Maeve, check out what is ahead.'

'Slow down Mike. Put the Lumen arc lights on maximum. Hold back until I review the vent with the zoom lens.'

The vent they were observing was quite different from the previous fissures. The slow oozing crimson emission was replaced by a larger cone with small molten rocks being showered across a wide area. At a safe distance of a hundred metres, the PLU's passengers were agog as the vent's activity intensified. The vista, against a background of deep black, was of intermittent bursts of red, yellow and crimson lava bursting at high speed from the vent. The PLU's cameras sent images to a wide body of observers.

After a short while, Mike spoke into his microphone. 'Paul, I think it's too precarious to take rock or gas samples.'

'Agreed, Mike. Best you start to prepare to ascend back to the mothership.'

'Roger that.'

Three things happened simultaneously.

A new seismic shock, this time 3.4 on the Richter scale, was registered on the PLU's dashboard. This shook the PLU vigorously.

A plume of deep red lava shot into the air lighting up the PLU's cabin as if it were daylight.

The PLU lunged violently as it was hit by rocks blasted from a new vent located close to the craft.

'We're hit,' roared Smith as he put the PLU into immediate reverse while switching on the Lumen arc lights to full capacity.

'Jesus Almighty,' cried O'Farrell as her head hit PLU's ceiling.

'Fuck,' added Gallery as he was thrown from his seat.

The PLU's cameras showed the external environment to the horror of those on the surface.

It was evident that the PLU was almost directly above a large vent that had blown its way through the side of the Seamount. The initial explosion would have been fatal to any craft on land in such proximity. The surrounding water had reduced the impact and severity of the blast.

The damage became obvious almost immediately. Smith tried to move the PLU forward, but it barely responded. 'Paul, I think we've a problem. As the propellers and thrusters are at the base of the PLU, I suspect they've been struck by volcanic debris.'

Smith tried hard to control his emotions, but he realised immediately that his craft was in trouble. He didn't have much time to think as a secondary blast struck the PLU. Judging by the sounds at his feet a barrage of rocks clattered against the PLU's base.

The worst possible thing happened. A barely audible hiss could be heard. Simultaneously, an alarm bell rang signalling that the fabric of the PLU had been compromised.

'Oxygen!' roared Smith. Another alarm attached to the monitor detecting a drop in internal pressure levels rang loudly. Very soon the PLU's crew were all attached to their respective emergency oxygen bottles.

After a few minutes Smith knew the level of oxygen supply wasn't fully compromised. The gauge measuring internal oxygen levels had fallen but was stabilised. Smith turned around and told O'Farrell and Gallery to disconnect their oxygen emergency supplies, which had enough capacity for three hours.

'Paul, we're in trouble.' Smith spoke the truth. He could not be sensitive to O'Farrell and Gallery's growing sense of apprehension knowing they all shared the same communications channel.

'What's your assessment?' said McCrossan in a calm voice. Above all else, he needed to remain calm.

'We're almost immobile in the midst of an active vent. There is the first sign of an airlock leak.' Smith struggled to maintain his composure. He knew from experience that his blood pressure was rising.

McCrossan took the initiative. 'I will drive the ROV towards you and it should be there within five minutes. It has a heavy-duty mechanical arm that I will try to connect to the PLU. If that works, we should be able to pull you away from the vent to the surface using the ROV's engines and the tethers. In the meantime, use whatever power you have to get out of the direct line of fire of the volcano.'

'Be quick, Paul,' pleaded Smith.

O'Farrell and Gallery were so scared they did what they were told without any questions. The current carried the PLU slowly away from the vent. The five minutes it took to drive the ROV to the PLU felt like five hours.

The respective cameras of both vehicles captured the scene in slow motion.

'Mike, I'll drive the ROV under the PLU to see how bad the damage is.'

Smith's prognosis was confirmed. The PLU's aluminium chassis was severely shattered, and the two main thrusters were fractured beyond repair. The base was pock-marked with scars from the lava rock hits.

'Let me position the ROV astern, then I'll deploy the mechanical arm. I'll try to grab the base of the chassis at the rear of the bracket of the remaining thruster. If I get a good connection, we can start the process of using the ROV's power to bring you to the surface.'

The mechanical arm locked on the chassis on the second attempt. The PLU crew heard the noise of the arm as it locked on the rail surrounding the main thruster. However, in trying to get the best possible grip, McCrossan unintentionally snapped the fibre optical cable that provided communications from the PLU Shack to the PLU. The line went dead. He assumed, incorrectly, that all communications had been severed. In fact, as the inward comms line was unaffected. The PLU's passengers could hear what was being said aboard the RV *Celtic Explorer* but could not transmit to the PLU Shack.

'Damn.' McCrossan was annoyed with himself for making such a stupid basic mistake. He needed to re-focus.

He moved the joystick and the ROV pulled the PLU away from the danger zone on a slow trajectory towards the surface.

Smith knew the return voyage to the safety of the surface could take more than six hours. It would require great skill and a fair amount of luck for a ten tonne ROV to drag a thirty tonne PLU from the sea floor to the surface.

O'Farrell and Gallery shared his sense of impending doom as the PLU ascended slowly, very slowly, through the darkness of the abyss.

They all sat in silence.

CHAPTER 8

Pico Bejenado

THE ORM BOARDROOM WAS full to capacity. A sense of anticipation was in the air. While everyone had worked all hours of the day and night on their assigned tasks, they only had a preliminary assessment across all the target zones.

Mark stood up to address his team with his coffee cup, as ever, in his hand. He looked strained – as well he might. He had had little sleep since his arrival on La Palma. 'Let's recap the data we've gathered over the past week. I'm keen to get a clear picture of the current situation so that we can start planning for all eventualities.'

'Franco, let's start with you and your team.'

Franco Bradelle shuffled to the front. 'As agreed, we focused on two areas where there had been a noticeable increase in activity. All the seismometers have been working as programmed and have been monitored on a 24/7 basis. We started with relatively mild tremors at uneven intervals, but in the past twenty-four hours we've had two 3.1 Richter scale events within twenty minutes of each other. What is causing us some concern is that not only are both shallow, but it now appears there are at least two epicentres, and they may be linked.'

'Two?' Mark asked.

'Yes, one is located some three thousand metres to the right of where we are, in the centre of the National Park near Pico Bejenado. The second is offshore, some five kilometres north of the island.'

'Talk to me about the offshore readings,' Mark said casually, not wishing to exacerbate stress in an already fraught group. He knew the emerging situation was anything but routine.

'The NASA satellite and our instruments have tri-located the epicentre at a depth of ten kilometres, some five kilometres off the northern coastline in a line from the town of Barlovento,' said Franco. 'There are no records of previous earthquake activity in this area offshore. We therefore can't explain the phenomenon.'

'What makes you suggest that they may be linked?' said Mark.

'It now appears that the magma chamber that's under the Pico Bejenado was the reason for the recent volcanic activity along the *Ruta*. The onshore eruptions may have caused a fracture and allowed a deeper chamber to emerge. If that's the case the parameters of a significant volcanic eruption could be as wide as twenty square kilometres. This may mean that the entire northern part of the island, including a zone five kilometres offshore is at risk.'

'Anyone got some good news?' asked Mark, instinctively knowing the answer would be negative.

'I'm afraid not,' said Franco. 'The drones have mapped

the Pico Bejenado target areas in detail with infrared thermal sensors and chemical sensors. While there have been no vents apart from the secondary fissure Maria and Claudine saw some days ago, there are five significant hotspots all growing in intensity that are sub-surface for the time being.'

Mark knew everyone was expecting him to call it given the growing evidence.

'I was expecting these results from around Cumbre Vieja as we're getting similar readings from La Gomera. But the prospect of an offshore epicentre has me totally puzzled. Antonio, you should alert Marco Lesle and the Guardia Civil. Tell them to start evacuating the villages on the northern shores. The emergency centre in Santa Cruz de la Palma should be able to manage as the area is not heavily populated. I'm glad hill walking and mountain trekking were suspended a few days ago. Many of the tourists have left the island. This make matters a bit less complicated.'

Having spoken to the head of the island's Guardia Civil, Simon and Ros had no confidence there was the slightest chance Marco Lesle would be bothered. He always seemed to have other priorities than his principal job.

As the brothers suspected, Antonio Farillo's urgings to the head of the Guardia Civil fell on deaf ears.

Mark knew the pattern. It was inevitable that there would be at least one major eruption. What was known was that a volcanic eruption close to the National Park was practically a certainty. The known unknowns were its intensity, the likelihood of multiple vents, and the impact that a major earthquake could have on the stability of the entire length of the Caldera de Taburiente.

'We're scientists in the first instance, so let's do our job. The largest hotspot that PD1 has identified in the National Park is close to Pico Bejenado. We need a physical inspection of the terrain. We also need to get rock and gas samples. Would anyone like to volunteer to join me in undertaking this task?'

The Rodriquez brothers, Claudine and Maria raised their hands simultaneously.

'Youthful enthusiasm. I trust the girls will not take offence, but it's perhaps best if the boys joined me on this occasion.'

Maria could see that Claudine was about to object. She touched her on her arm with a warning look. While she shared her sister's frustration, she knew now wasn't the time to get into gender politics.

'We'll need to get you fitted out in the heat suits,' Mark addressed the brothers. 'Have you worn one before?'

'No,' replied Ros.

'I had a dozen shipped here on the Sikorsky. They are the latest design and can withstand temperatures as high as 1,650 degrees Celsius. They have built in radio communications headsets so we can all talk to each other and to the control room here. We tested the suits last year in Iceland. I'm confident, provided we stay at a safe distance, and they are not penetrated, that they will protect us.'

Mark spoke to Pedro Dunato. 'The two drones should be deployed at the perimeters of the area we're going to investigate. There's not much else you can do other than to be on hand should an emergency rescue be necessary. The Sikorsky team have been briefed and know what to do if called upon. By my reckoning we could witness a significant volcanic eruption within twenty-four hours. Let's get kitted out and be on site before the fireworks start.'

They headed to the changing rooms in the basement of the ORM complex. They got into the protective suits but didn't seal them. Within minutes they were equipped and ready to go.

Mark drove the ORM's Range Rover down the mountain and into the middle of the National Park. Despite the earlier incident, the car park at La Cumbrecita was selected as the most suitable site because there was a direct line of vision to the ORM over one thousand metres above.

While Mark and the brothers were en route – it would take them ninety minutes to arrive at the car park – the drone operators got to work. Pedro knew how to get the best from his toys. He set the drones on autopilot in a circular pattern at either end of a diameter, around a kilometre apart. In that way the cameras were able to get a full panoramic perspective of the base of the National Park. Once in a holding pattern he turned on the infrared thermal detectors and waited for the results. The shade of red indicated on his monitors had deepened compared to the previous day. The alert on the monitors started to shrill. In the control room it jarred everyone's senses.

Without hesitation he called Mark on his mobile phone in the Range Rover.

'Mark, this is Pedro.'

'Yes, Pedro. Trouble?'

'I think we're even closer to an eruption than we expected. Where are you now?'

'Just short of the car park.'

'I suggest you stay there. The infrared sensors show a growing area of thermal activity on the left flank of Pico Bejenado. That's no more than a kilometre from your location.'

'Pedro, we'll wait a while as you suggest. Time to be cautious. We have to respect Mother Nature. Keep your mobile on and give us a running commentary. We'll switch to radio communications once we're sealed into our protective suits.'

Pedro moved towards the computer screen that displayed the camera feed from PD1. Maria and Claudine looked over his shoulder. Soon a large deep red semi-circle formed in the middle of the screen. He had seen this phenomenon before in Iceland. He was watching one of nature's most unique features: the birth of a volcano.

'I better fly PD1 higher. I suspect we're about to witness an explosion.'

He turned off the autopilot. No sooner had the drone withdrawn from the immediate vicinity than lava started to ooze slowly from one vent at first and within minutes an area of three hundred square metres was alight. The lava was just below the surface and rising.

'Wait for it.'

The sound was deafening. The drone's acoustic capability did the business in relaying the blast in stereophonic sound. Seconds later the sound wave hit the ORM and the Range Rover's passengers almost simultaneously.

From a height of over a kilometre, PD1 had a grandstand view of the main vent of the emerging volcano that started to spew lava bombs over a wide area. Some rocks were thrown almost two hundred metres into the air. The slow trickle of lava suddenly changed as the flow increased. There was a further loud explosion that blew open what was by now a large cavity. Lava bombs flew in all directions like arrows from a bow. As if in slow motion, the top of the mountain fractured and collapsed inside the volcano's growing crater. A dense brown ash cloud grew, like a small nuclear mushroom cloud, and rose higher and higher into the otherwise clear blue morning sky. As particles of ash rubbed together, they created an electrostatic charge that soon turned into a flow of electricity. This current exploded the air around it, creating multiple lightning flashes.

It could have been a scene from Dante's *Inferno*. PD2 was the first casualty. Although located at what should have been a relatively safe distance, a cluster of lava bombs struck the drone and it melted and disintegrated. Its monitors went blank.

This was not a good sign.

'Pedro, pull back PD1 for goodness sake,' shouted Mark from the relative safety of the front seat of the Range Rover, when he heard what had happened.

The drone operator manoeuvred the gear stick and PD1 flew out of immediate danger.

'Mark, check out the seismic readings on your laptop.'

Mark turned to the laptop that was on the front passenger seat to see the amplitude graph zigzag at speed. The reading lines darkened the page they were so close together.

'Don't tell me that's offshore, oh please don't!'

His worst fears were confirmed. A Richter 4 earthquake reading pinpointed the Pico Bejenado episode at a depth of five kilometres. An almost identical reading was recorded at a similar depth and at the same time due north of the island.

The initial tremors lasted thirty minutes. Mark and the Rodriquez brothers remained in safety in the Range Rover. They knew there would be aftershocks. After an hour, Mark decided it was time to move. He was, as ever, impatient.

'Boys, let's get going.'

'Back to the ORM?'

'Hell no. I will drive the Range Rover to a safe distance from the Pico Bejenado. I want to get samples and to see what type of volcano we're dealing with.'

'You can't be serious,' said Simon. He was surprised at Mark's reaction.

'I am,' replied Mark. 'In my experience, after the initial volcanic blast, there may be a period of relative calm before the eruptions start again. We need to take rock and chemical samples if we are to make any sense of what is happening.'

The brothers trusted Mark Doyle. After all, he was the doyen of the volcanic scientific community. They did not demur further or question his intentions.

As the tarmac road wasn't badly damaged, they got to the car park without any trouble. They got out of the Range Rover. It didn't take long to seal the heavy survival suits.

They observed the scene a kilometre away. The distinctive peak of the Pico Bejenado that had stood at some 1,800 metres for many millennia was shattered. The initial lava explosion had resulted in the top edges falling into a wide volcanic crater that was bubbling with small bursts of liquid magma.

'Holy Shit,' said Mark.

'What's happening?'

'Simon, once an eruption of this type breaks the surface, we can expect it to expand and the lava flows to move by gravity down the most direct route. The initial blast has opened up a crater about a hundred metres in diameter. With a bit of luck there will be a pause before another episode. We can expect some minor aftershocks though, so be alert.'

The brothers were scared. They had every reason to be. They knew that forming volcanoes were notoriously unpredictable. The theory of volcano formation, which they had been studying for years, was suddenly starkly real in front of them. Only three weeks ago they hadn't a care in the world. If only the clock could be turned back!

'We should try to take some samples from the edge of the lava activity. If the lava is slow moving and dense then the development of this crater may be slow. If the magma is highly liquid that would suggest a deep chamber is feeding the volcano. If that's the scenario we'll get out of here as fast as we can.'

Mark adjusted his protective suit and tested the radio communications. 'Pedro, I'm with Simon and Ros. We're going to walk to the edge of the formation to take some samples. The lava bombs have stopped. For as long as it is safe, we'll proceed.'

'Roger that. PD1 is unscathed and back at the ORM. We'll insert a new lithium battery and have it overhead within the hour.'

'Good. It'll take us that long to walk the trail to Pico Bejenado in these suits.'

Mark took the lead on the uphill climb. This was one of the island's more testing walks in normal circumstances.

In protective suits it was a serious challenge. They passed along a forestry track through sparse pine with Canary citrus undergrowth. They could see that the trees at a higher altitude were on fire. They zigzagged along fire breaks. They stopped at the sheer wall of the Punta de los Roques cliff face to take stock.

'Are you alright?' Mark spoke softly on his radio microphone.

'I guess so.'

The reception was so poor that Mark could not ascertain which of the boys had spoken. He knew they were well out of their comfort zone. They needed to hear a calm and confident voice.

'Good. Stay alert.'

'Simon, look after yourself.' Maria's voice could be heard over the radio from the ORM.

Simon sensed the nervousness in her trembling voice.

'Maria. Don't worry. We're in safe hands with Mark.'

He hoped that were true.

Without notice, a severe earthquake shook the ground. The rocks at the top of the cliffs they were using for shelter hurtled toward them. Worse still, lava bombs – some the size of dustbins – started to fall from the sky and exploded on impact. They knew it was only a matter of time before the tinder dry Canary pine needles would be alight.

'Mark, get back to the car park now.'

Pedro's instruction fell on deaf ears. Mark's head and shoulder took a glancing blow from a lava bomb. It split his suit between his lower neck and shoulder. He collapsed. Oxygen whistled out of his suit.

'Mark's down,' screamed Ros.

They were beside him in a moment. He and Simon assessed that he was alive. The rock had concussed him badly, but he was breathing. They got him into a prone position and moved him under the edge of the cliff face. The lava bombs fell around them. Being so close to the cliff face protected them from another direct hit.

'What are we going to do?' Simon spoke his thoughts aloud and got an instant response from Claudine.

'You and Ros need to get Mark back to the Range Rover pronto. It will take you ages if you try to do so in your protective suits. Leave Mark's on but take off yours. It's a gamble I know but the situation around the Pico Bejenado is deteriorating.

'It sure is,' said Pedro.

He continued. 'PD1's thermal image detector is showing rising levels of subterranean volcanic activity. The footprint of the Pico Bejenado volcano is expanding. Get moving boys.'

The suits were stripped off within seconds. The smell of sulphur was immediately evident. They knew from experience it wasn't yet at a toxic level. They lifted a still-unconscious Mark and propped him between their shoulders.

'On my call: one, two, off we go.' Ros took charge.

While they struggled for the first hundred metres, as soon as they got into a rhythm their pace accelerated. The path back to the car park was downhill and this also helped.

All the while they talked to each other. Pedro and the girls had enough sense not to interrupt. Besides, Pedro had other matters to address. He couldn't tell the boys, but the thermal readings showed rapidly rising levels of underground magma covering a much greater area. He knew immediately that the initial eruption at the Pico Bejenado was only a foretaste of a larger event. If only the boys and Mark could get to the Range Rover, they had a chance of avoiding what could be a catastrophic increase in volcanic activity.

Ignorant of what was happening many metres underneath them, the boys arrived at the entrance gate that was on the edge of the car park. The Range Rover was only thirty paces ahead. They paused, took a deep breath and with care got Mark to the door of the car.

He started to gain consciousness.

'What's going on?' he mumbled. 'My head aches.'

The boys ignored him. Ros opened the rear passenger door and manhandled him onto the seat. They then swiftly got into the front seats. No time for safety belts.

'I'll drive,' said Mark.

'Not on this occasion I'm afraid.' Simon took the wheel and started the engine.

The ground shook violently.

The tremor rocked the Range Rover.

The boys looked in absolute terror into each other's eyes.

Despite its weight the Range Rover was catapulted into the air like a soft toy and thrown upside down over the side of the cliff on which the car park was situated. As it dropped over the vertical edge, a blast of lava from what was to become known as the Pico Bejenado eruption incinerated it in an instant. Only bits of the steel frame remained in mid-air before striking the forest far below in a firebomb. The occupants died instantly – cindered in a second.

High above, PD1 captured the entire episode on camera. The graphic video of the scene was relayed on the ORM's monitors.

'Oh my God. My Simon is gone.' Maria fell sobbing into her sister's arms.

Neither she, nor the crew at the ORM, had any time to grieve.

Events moved rapidly.

They didn't need the drone's video to show them what was happening beneath them in the National Park. Within an hour, a huge and rapidly expanding plume of ash and poisonous gases rose skywards and soon blotted out the sun.

What had been a small almost dormant crater was transformed. The cauldron of Pico Bejenado widened, deepened and emitted streams of molten lava that flowed into the rivulets and streams of the National Park. Red hot lava bombs were jettisoned into the sky like grape-shot from a large shotgun. The scale and violence of the eruption intensified. The forest and undergrowth at the base of the National Park was on fire.

The earthquakes also became more frequent and more severe by the hour. They shook the ORM and the entire northern part of the island to its core. In the face of a rapidly deteriorating situation, the federal police finally instructed the Guardia Civil to mobilise and assist the population of the most exposed towns and villages along the northern shoreline. They were told to evacuate every-one down the coastline to relative safety south of La Palma.

Marco Lesle could not be contacted.

And all the while the volcanic explosions at Pico Bejenado went live on global television. The footage from PD1 was streamed around the world. Social media channels were full of comments about the possible implications of the event. The death of Mark Doyle and the Rodriquez brothers got barely a mention.

Black Bush

The following evening, Lars reviewed the events at the Summit Station with Benny and Sean over dinner. Sean had had the good sense to bring a bottle of Black Bush Irish whiskey. He poured a large measure into the teacups that served as whiskey glasses. The three men sipped and gasped as the fiery liquid hit the target. Sean was old school and didn't believe in adding water to whiskey.

Lars broke their long contemplative silence. 'I feel so guilty that we didn't do a proper ground site surveillance at site ZX3. It's my fault that the Twin Otter and everyone on board was lost.'

'We all feel horrible,' said Benny. 'Wasn't this landing area used a few weeks ago without any problems?'

'It was, but we should have done a quick drone site survey when we got feedback from all the teams of the increasingly slushy texture of the surface snow.'

'That was Alice's call. ZX3 was her responsibility. She wouldn't deny it, if she were here.' Benny took no pleasure in stating the obvious.

Perhaps understandably, Lars was full of remorse and anguish. He was clearly in a black mood and detached from the conversation.

'On a positive note,' chipped in Sean, 'the data you're getting is transformative. When this experiment ends – when all the surviving golf balls enter the Greenland Sea – it will be possible to provide a far more accurate estimate about the annual loss of water from the Greenland Ice

Sheet and the locations at most risk. For example, at site ZX1 to the west the golf balls didn't descend any further than four hundred metres. On the other hand, all the golf balls heading toward the east coast of Greenland are expected to reach the edge of the glaciers and in some cases may reach the sea. From what we've seen, the current forecasts and perceived wisdom about the extent of the melting are off the mark to a considerable degree.'

'Yes, Sean, we need to look at the overall outcome of Project Masters,' Benny agreed. 'Early days I know, but as Sean's golf ball technology has worked it might be worth placing an order for a much wider deployment over the entire surface of the Greenland Ice Sheet in time for next season's weather window.'

'Yeh, that should be doable,' confirmed Sean. He had already alerted the Galway office. The team were more than willing to do the business. They didn't need any persuasion as they were well aware of the attention they were receiving because of increasing world-wide coverage of Project Masters. Sean's interview from the Summit Station with CNN and BBC World had gone global. Because the Norwegian Government didn't wish to be at the centre of the publicity Sean was asked to lead with the media. His only condition was that he could wear his Galway County jersey. Local Irish media had done interviews in the Galway office. The staff felt like stars, not least because Sean credited the team's effort in all his appearances. There was an immediate and positive side effect as online orders for the trackable 'traditional' golf balls rose sharply. It was win-win-win for Sean and his business.

Lars took another large sip of the whiskey. Alice's death lay heavy on his shoulders. He struggled to join the conversation, but he did.

'I agree in principle that we should start planning for next year. But we'll need to produce a summary of our findings before a decision of that magnitude can be taken. If the Greenland ice-melt is pouring into the seas all around the eastern and western shores of Greenland, it is only a matter of time before this will impact on the Gulf Stream. The prospect of sea ice extending as far south as the British Isles will catch a lot of attention.'

'The word is out among the climate science community according to my well-informed sources,' said Benny.

'What the story?' asked Lars.

'Social media is full of the events at the Summit Station over the past few days. There is a lot of "I-told-you-so" from some of the more opinionated commentators.'

'I've no time for armchair climate commentators.' Lars was getting more agitated as his grief deepened.

'Whatever our experiences, we are not the only community affected by natural events,' said Benny.

'What do you mean?' asked Lars.

'Have you not been watching TV?' replied Benny.

'No. I've had other matters on my mind, in case you haven't noticed.' Lars was in no mood for small talk.

'There has been a huge volcanic eruption on the island of La Palma. Early reports suggest there have been many fatalities,' said Benny.

'Mother Nature must be really angry with us,' said Lars. Alice's death had put him in an uncharacteristically philosophical frame of mind.

Benny, while sensitive to his friend's feelings, continued on a different line of conversation.

'There have been abnormally warm weather conditions with higher than average air pressure over the summer months across the Baffin Sea. The number of melt days is at a record high as a consequence, increasing the impact of summer melt across Greenland beyond all previous readings. The fact that a zone of high pressure has been positioned much further south in the mid-Atlantic during most of the summer has raised awareness about the difference between weather and climate. What is most important is the awareness we've raised about the potential collapse of the Gulf Stream. Governments are being asked for explanations from their concerned citizens.'

Lars snapped momentarily out of his stasis.

'I was told by one of our American researchers over a morning coffee that the outlet glaciers we saw last week at Jacobshavn Glacier are flowing at a rate of over fifty metres a day. This is a record. It's as remarkable as it is scary. They are actively monitoring one iceberg that's ten thousand square metres in surface area that contains gigatons of ice. If it splits …. It's so large that it will float into the North Atlantic shipping channels west of Labrador within two months. Titanics beware! How this giant chunk of ice and snow, and hundreds like it across the North and South Poles, will disappear is the overwhelming uncertainty of the world of climate science.'

Lars walked around the room slowly. He needed to be on the move. His mood was getting better as he began to accept that he was not to blame for what was truly an accident, not of his making.

'Earlier I was contacted by my contacts in NASA who are more than impressed with the preliminary results. We've been promised satellite support next summer. In the meantime, we'll try and integrate our tracking results with their Operation IceBridge programme, which is using highly sensitive ice penetrating radar sounding, gravimeter and laser profiling software to map the base of the entire Greenland Ice Sheet. Our data has increased their concerns that the ice-melt is affecting the stability of parts of the base of the ice sheet close to the east coast.'

'I assume the satellite we had use of is back monitoring Russian and North Korean missiles?' asked Sean.

'Of course. Aren't we lucky there was no attack last week! Can you imagine the embarrassment of the Pentagon if they had to tell their President their military assets were checking golf balls and not inter-continental ballistic missiles,' said Sean.

Benny's phone rang. It was an unknown number. Normally he never took a call from a 'User ID Unknown'. He made an exception given the situation.

'Who is that please?'

'Hi.'

Lars and Sean watched as Benny frowned and smiled. Obviously, his caller was making an impression.

'Yes.'

'Yes.'

'We will be on hand to join the conference call tomorrow with the other prime ministers.'

The call continued for a few more minutes. Benny was in listening mode.

'Thank you, Prime Minister.'

Lars looked at Sean with a sense of pride once he realised who was on the line.

'Sure, I will brief you personally on my return.'

'I should be in Oslo next week. I will pass your appreciation to the entire team. It was after all a team effort. Goodnight Prime Minister.'

Benny placed his iPhone on the table. 'You would never guess who that was?'

'The woman who gave you all the resources we needed?' said Sean cheekily.

'And a promise to provide on-going funding. The penny, cent, krona whatever has finally dropped in political circles.'

At the mention of funding Sean decided to pick his moment. He had avoided any discussion of the dirty subject of money until now. 'Would it be timely for me to give you my invoice?'

'Sean, we should not put a price on your contribution, but of course all your costs will be met, said Lars. 'I expect you to add a good mark-up when you quote us for next year's supply. The Norwegians can afford it.'

'Given the huge reaction to Sean's interviews, the Prime Minister told me she is going to convene a summit of the leaders of the North Atlantic nations next month. She wants a more coordinated approach to resourcing the climate scientists, meteorologists and geologists working across Greenland on dozens of independent research programmes. She wants the Polar Space Task Group to up their game. Norway, for one, wants to know not if but when the Greenland ice-melt will cause critical disruption to the warming influence of the Gulf Stream. The key challenge in the light of Project Masters is to get a full understanding of the pace of the ice melt across the entirety of the Greenland Ice Sheet.'

There was a condition.

'Sean, she wants you to be the keynote presenter.'

'You can't be serious?'

'It is a jacket and tie event. No Galway supporter jerseys will be allowed on the podium.'

'I'll drink to that. *Sláinte* lads. It was a pleasure doing business with you.'

'Sean, I hope your country recognises the massive difference your interest in golf has played in the world of climate science. You are a real golf professional!'

'Judging by our government's track record in reducing carbon emissions, I very much doubt it. No matter. What's important is that you guys continue the good work.'

'What are your plans Sean?' asked Lars.

'I'm going to bed. I'm on a flight in the morning back to Ireland via Reykjavik. By the way, when you're on the call to Dublin in the morning say 'hello' to the Taoiseach for me! I'll call you next week for a catch-up. Goodnight.'

Sean left Lars and Benny to reflect in silence. The bottle of Black Bush whiskey was empty. It had served a medicinal purpose. They had to cope with the shock of the loss of lives, while at the same time cope with the natural elation at their unexpected success.

'We also need a good night's sleep after what has been a momentous few days,' said Lars. 'Let's gather after breakfast to find out if any of Sean's circular friends were retrieved from the salty sea.'

They were. While many were never recovered, the golf balls provided unprecedented data about the innards of the ice sheet.

Merrion Street

Unnoticed, the Mercedes EQ 350 glided through the open gate at Government Buildings on Merrion Street in Dublin. No outriders. No pennants flying. The only tell-tale sign was the CD plates. The limousine parked at the side entrance opposite the four-column Edwardian portico, as had three others in the preceding twenty minutes.

The driver moved to open the door for his passenger, the Norwegian Prime Minister. The Irish Prime Minister walked over to greet her visitor.

There was no media present. This meeting was a 'below the radar' deniable event planned with great secrecy in less than twenty-four hours. The fact that the meeting was taking place early on a Saturday morning allowed the participants to access the complex in small groups without drawing attention to themselves.

'Taoiseach, thank you for making the arrangements at such short notice. It is always a pleasure to visit Ireland, but I wish it were under better circumstances.'

She had the phonetic pronunciation of Ireland's Prime Minister, the 'Teeshock', well- rehearsed.

'Prime Minister, you are most welcome. The others have arrived so we can start soon.'

The two women walked purposefully up the ceremonial staircase. They moved along the carpeted corridor to the left with their advisors in close proximity.

'We're here,' said the Taoiseach's Chief of Staff as he opened the door of the Sycamore Room. The two politicians entered. The room was full, despite the fact that only those who had a need to know, or a necessary contribution, were in attendance. The dress was casual: after all it was a Saturday.

'Ah, Michelle, nice to see you again.' The Norwegian Prime Minister greeted her Danish counterpart with three carefully placed kisses to her cheeks.

At the same time, the Taoiseach motioned the British Prime Minister to his seat after the customary greetings were complete.

'Shall we get started?'

It had been agreed in advance she would chair the discussions. She was eager, as they all were, to get the briefing underway. 'This is where I normally meet and greet our State visitors but today, as you can see, the Sycamore Room has been transformed into an incident centre. If I may, I will ask my Chief of Staff to explain what we hope to do over the next few hours.'

He didn't need to add too many explanations as the four wide screen monitors said it all and the various prime ministers had been well briefed by their teams.

The monitors were labelled 'Summit Station', 'ORM', 'Woods Hole' and 'RV *Celtic Explorer*'.

'We all know why we're here. There have been a series of apparently disconnected natural events that could, in a worse-case scenario, have serious implications for our peoples. At the outset I want to thank the Norwegian Government for funding some essential research in Greenland.'

'Delighted to assist,' replied the Norwegian Prime Minister.

'I suggest we start with the Summit Station.'

The conference call got underway. The assembled leaders, along with observers from the US and Spain, were linked live by way of secure satellite communications to the four research centres.

'Professor Brun, can you please brief us about your work? Before you start, on behalf of all of us here we would like to express our condolences to all at the Summit Station for the loss of your colleagues. Very sad.'

All eyes turned to the screen designated 'Summit Station'.

'Thank you. Losing colleagues and close friends in such circumstances has us all numb. But we need to finish our work. I can give you a heads up on the presentation I'm working on for delivery at the Polar Space Task Force summit that the Norwegian Prime Minister will chair a few weeks hence. All thanks to the foresight of my home country I should add.'

Like the other non-political participants, Lars Brun had been given less than a day's notice to join what he was told was going to be a de-briefing session with the aim of the mutual sharing of intelligence across a number of areas of research. Just before he joined the conference call, he was told its true nature: a group of very concerned Prime Ministers needed guidance about the inherent risks of rapidly emerging findings in what appeared, at first sight, to be quite separate natural phenomena.

'The Greenland Ice Sheet is at an advanced stage of collapse at its maritime fringes, even those high within the Arctic Circle. We've known that for a year or two but what Project Masters has revealed is that the core of the Greenland Ice Sheet is hollowing out at a much faster pace than anyone had anticipated. Some areas have already imploded exposing vast lakes below the surface. The movement of large sections of the glaciers has caused serious structural vibrations, not unlike an earthquake. If this continues, I anticipate a domino effect leading to a major structural disintegration of significant parts the Greenland Ice Sheet. If that happens a tipping point could be reached.'

'Could I stop you Professor, please,' the British Prime Minister interrupted. 'What are you saying? We need a better appreciation of the likely timelines.'

He was clearly agitated, judging by his fidgeting. He had a habit of combing his thick curly blond hair with both his hands when he was getting stressed. Billy van Os whispered into his ear.

'And if I could ask a supplementary question,' said the Prime Minister. 'What are the consequences for the British Isles, if I could be forgiven for including Ireland in that strictly geographical description?'

Lars Brun didn't hesitate before he replied. 'All scenarios present a risk to our populations. The best-case scenario is that the collapse will be gradual and could take decades to have a material impact on the Gulf Stream. While next year's research will be of a scale to give us more definitive answers, what I'm witnessing here tells me you should anticipate a worse-case situation.'

'Meaning?' The British Prime Minister wanted a clear answer.

'To be blunt, if large parts of the Greenland Ice Sheet collapse and cause a deluge of meltwater to enter the

Atlantic Ocean it is only a matter of a couple of years – possibly only months – before the climate-moderating effects of the Gulf Stream stop. In such an event, winter ice will start appearing almost at once in the North Atlantic. The sea ice will be thin at first but as it thickens it will disrupt shipping. Over a period, maybe within a decade, Arctic conditions will become a regular occurrence perhaps as far south as the southern coast of England, just as happened 20,000 years ago. Sub-zero temperatures over the winter months will become the norm. There will also be a commensurate rise of at least four metres in sea levels.'

'Shit!' The British Prime Minister's reputation for the use of profanities was justified on this occasion. His briefing papers had come to the same conclusion. In fact, unknown to him, a briefing paper prepared by M16 a decade earlier had reached exactly the same forecast.

'I must stress this is mere speculation at this stage,' added Lars.

His job, like that of all scientists, was to collect reliable and verifiable data and to draw conclusions based on this evidence. However, he decided to take a different approach. Until then, he had never spoken to a Prime Minister before, never mind four, so he decided not to miss his opportunity.

'We're long past the point of no return. That's for certain. Even if all the governments in the northern hemisphere did all that was expected of them to reduce carbon emissions, it's far too late to reverse the Arctic melting process. Nature will take her course. Let's pray she does not spring too many surprises.'

At this stage the political temperature in the Sycamore Room was clearly rising as Lars Brun's pithy assessment was digested. Each delegation was speaking in low tones to their respective leaders. The Taoiseach intervened thanking Professor Brun for his contribution. 'Professor Gilmore, can you please up-date us on the two projects under your charge.'

All eyes focused on the screen 'RV *Celtic Explorer*.'

'Will do, Taoiseach. I will be brief. I can confirm what you have just been told about the Gulf Stream. As you are aware, there are four research vessels testing the strength of the columns of water that move the Gulf Stream. We've just shared our preliminary findings after the initial phase of our work. I'm afraid the news is not good.'

He looked into the Taoiseach's eyes on the camera and detected a deep sense of sadness and foreboding. And that was before he delivered the main punch line.

'What was expected has happened. All the columns tested are almost non-functional. If the Greenland Ice Sheet starts to disintegrate, I dare not imagine the consequences.'

'And what about Project Eriador?' asked the Taoiseach.

'We have recorded multiple seismic events along the flanks of the Eriador Seamount. It seems the situation is getting worse. I'm sorry to tell you that within the last hour the crew of the manned submersible witnessed a massive underwater volcanic explosion, accompanied by a quake that measured 3.1 on the Richter scale. The craft was disabled. It was too close to the magma explosion. We're trying desperately to pull the submersible to the surface.'

'Shit!' Now it was the Taoiseach's turn.

'If the PLU is successfully salvaged, our unmanned submersible will be prepared for a close visual inspection of the site where the last eruption took place. We hope to know more within the hour.'

Billy van Os spoke. 'We are also receiving reports from our sources of increasing seismic activity with at least three epicentres along the length of the Eriador Seamount. A massive imminent eruption seems inevitable. What we can't predict is the direction and force of the tsunamis.'

'Tsunamis!' said several voices simultaneously.

'Yes. A significant sea floor rupture at several locations is anticipated.'

That opinion silenced the room.

Franco Bradelle didn't wait to be called in to speak. 'Franco Bradelle here from the ORM on La Palma. Nothing to do with climate change, but we too are experiencing a potentially serious situation as seismic activity has re-appeared on La Palma. What's happening in the mid-Atlantic is being replicated here. The main difference is that pyroclastic explosions have quite different impacts above ground to sea floor events. We've survey teams out doing their best to test a series of volcanic incidents across the island, but I fear the worst as we've lost communication with one of the teams that was near the main source of volcanic activity.'

The Norwegian Prime Minister had heard enough. 'Three separate events? Or three linked events? Can anyone make sense of this?'

'If I may Prime Minister?' All eyes switched to the screen from Woods Hole. Three grim faces appeared. 'We're coordinating the deployment of NASA and NORA satellites that are now monitoring the three locations. The news is bad. The Mid-Atlantic Ridge is volcanically active along its full length. We also anticipate imminent seismic activity under the Greenland Ice Sheet. Even a small event, whenever it might occur, could have devastating impacts on a hollowed out ice sheet. The La Palma and Eriador Seamount incidents are part of a common emerging volcanic phenomenon along the extremities of the Mid-Atlantic Ridge. I'm afraid sooner or later a calamity may be upon us.'

'Next steps?' The Taoiseach addressed an open question to the room.

The British PM spoke. 'This situation is most unnerving. We're clearly on the cusp of potential devastation on a scale not witnessed for generations. If we tell our citizens to expect massive flooding, there will be widespread panic. There is really nothing we can do. Am I right or am I wrong?

The Taoiseach responded. 'The scientists have given us advice based on the best available evidence. We're getting unequivocal advice of imminent events, but the scale of these events is as yet unknown and, more importantly, we haven't got a clear indication in relation to the timing. I'm inclined to allow our eminent scientists a little while longer to monitor the danger sites. If nothing else this will give us a few days to reflect on what we've heard and to plan our respective – and hopefully coordinated – responses.'

'I think that makes sense,' said the Norwegian Prime Minister. 'We might ask our senior officials to keep in daily contact and to escalate matters if deemed necessary. Under no circumstances should we brief the press about this meeting never mind about the content. This meeting didn't happen. Clear?'

'I'll go along with that,' added the British Prime Minister. The Danish PM and the Taoiseach nodded simultaneously.

The Merrion Street Summit concluded.

CHAPTER 9

Barlovento

FRANCO BRADELLE WAS NOW in charge. He knew from his experience in Iceland that the Pico Bejenado volcanic eruption was a precursor to a cataclysmic event. When it would occur, he wasn't sure. What was certain was the entire length of the Caldera was at severe risk. PD1 was showing the footprint of volcanic activity wasn't stopping or slowing. On the contrary, there were grave signs that it could be only a matter of time before La Palma recorded the biggest volcanic explosion since Krakatoa in 1883.

The loss of Mark, Ros and Simon hung over everyone. It was a struggle to cope with their deaths. But struggle on they did.

Carmen Ortiz and her experienced team, who had flown in from Madrid, provided additional resources as Bradelle tried his best to get a handle on the rapidly moving events. The ORM was covered in a thick layer of black ash. The sky was obscured by deep grey clouds of dust, ash and gasses from within Pico Bejenado.

They met for a quiet coffee away from the younger scientists. The growing volcano rumbled in the background.

'What's your assessment Carmen?' said Bradelle.

'The main vent we were observing at Pico Bejenado clearly hid a secondary enormous magma chamber that arrived at the surface with such force that it disintegrated the immediate area. We could not have known the volcano could have been so powerful.'

'It appears to have subsided quite a bit.' Bradelle was looking for comfort.

'We've had a period of relative calm for the past few hours, but my guess is that the next eruption could happen at any time. We may get little or no notice.' She supped her coffee.

'The pyroclastic flows that we can expect will contain a much higher proportion of gas to rock and will be able to travel at speeds of seven hundred kilometres an hour or more. In 1902, such an event wiped out the population of Saint-Pierre on the Caribbean island of Martinique – some thirty thousand people.'

'Should we evacuate the ORM?' asked Bradelle. A Sikorsky sat outside fully fuelled and ready for action.

'We have a decision to make: stay and observe or take flight,' Carmen said in a calm manner. 'We should be cautious. I suggest in the circumstances that just a handful of us should remain. You might sound the alarm and get everyone else, especially the young scientists, off the mountain.'

'OK,' said Bradelle.

After he phoned the pilot, who was seated in the cockpit, he walked into the ORM's large boardroom. There was no need to ring the alarm as everyone was there.

'You are being evacuated. No questions. No luggage. Just get to the helicopter without delay. It takes off in five minutes.'

'Maria, let's go,' said Claudine. She pulled her sister to the exit door. Others followed. No questions. No luggage. Just a group of very scared people.

The noise of the helicopter blades was deafening and obliterated all other sounds. They ran to the open door at the back. Half the group had boarded when an almighty booming sound drowned out the sound of the swishing blades. Eardrums were shattered. The shock waves took two seconds to hit the area. Facial features were scorched. Immediately afterwards a blast of pyroclastic materials enveloped the ORM and the entire mountain top. Bodies were vaporised.

The second volcanic explosion at Pico Bejenado shattered and collapsed half of the Caldera de Taburiente that formed the northern part of La Palma. The remnants of the ORM fell into the valley below.

PD1 was the sole survivor. At a height of two thousand metres and safely off to the right of the Caldera, the drone continued to send pictures of the event to NASA, HUGO and to many other research centres that were linked into direct video feeds. All watched in awe as the centre part of La Palma was blown apart within an hour. Soon all the global TV stations were showing pictures from PD1, unedited as before.

What had started as a classic volcanic eruption soon turned into an unprecedented occurrence. The Caldera de Taburiente pyroclastic event sent a mixture of large coarse boulders, pumice, light coloured igneous rock blown into the air in a semi-liquid state, and lava fragments flowing at ground level, while the kinetic energy of the hot ash plume above this rubble flattened everything in its path. It had the same destructive impact as a meteor hitting the earth.

Earlier, the day had been going well in the village of Barlovento on the north end of the island. The entire population of four hundred had turned out to watch the tri-annual re-enactment of the Battle of Lepanto. Minor tremors and volcanic eruptions were not going to deter the holding of this ceremonial event as the centrepiece of the village's summer festival. The ash filled clouds drifting over the fields were a minor distraction.

As with most festivals in Spain, the re-enactment was based on deep-seated tradition.

On 7 October 1571, the sea galleys of the Holy League (comprising the Knights of Malta, the Papal States, the Duchy of Savoy and others) defeated the navy of the Ottoman Empire in a fierce battle off the coast of Greece. Over five hundred galleys and some 80,000 soldiers were involved in the largest naval battle in Western history. Over two hundred of the ships were sunk, burned or captured. The Holy League credited their victory to the Virgin Mary, the town's patron saint: La Virgen del Rosario.

In the small fields around the village square a hundred able men, dressed in period naval costumes, manipulated ten mock galleys on wheels in a fierce fight that resulted – as in all previous years – in a decisive victory for the Christian forces. The battle was reaching its crescendo: the capture of the galley of the Ottoman commander, Lal Kara Mustafa Pasha, who was played by Marco Lesle, resplendent in a flowing bright red kaftan.

Lesle believed this was a real job. One that was appreciated. Far better than evacuating coastal villages with his colleagues from the Guardia Civil.

Over the loudspeaker system Lal Kara Mustafa Pasha could be heard urging his troops, or trying to, as the entire pageant was based on an agreed written script.

'To the flag, to the flag, defend the Ottoman Empire with your lives.'

He didn't sound very convincing.

The leader of the Christian forces replied loudly.

'For the Pope, for the Pope, down with the infidels.'

The firecrackers were lit to mimic the galleys' cannons and in the din that followed Holy League soldiers rushed on deck to capture the commander, as the story demanded.

The spectators cheered. They knew the battle would be over as soon as Marco Lesle surrendered. Once that happened the bars would open, the food tents would start serving and the flamenco guitarists would weave their magic: the party could begin. They didn't get that far. Most of the crowd in the main stand didn't even get to their feet. Ten seconds after the Pico Bejanado volcano at the base of the Caldera de Taburiente exploded, the sound waves from the blast hit the field of battle in Barlovento. The participants stopped in their tracks and all eyes turned to the source of the noise. Was this an Ottoman counterattack that wasn't in the script?

The deep shuddering effects of the accompanying earthquake took a bit longer to reach the battlefield. As the surge moved away from the centre of the blast the explosion gathered rocks, water, air, vegetation, trees, animals, people and anything else that was in its path. It fused them all into a three hundred metres high wall of scalding hot ash and vapour.

The mayor and other town dignitaries had the best view. They sat high on the reviewing stand that faced outwards to the top of the Caldera some ten kilometres to the south of the village.

The mayor rose from his seat. He noticed a surge of heat on his cheek. The sunny sky had turned black and was full of electricity. Before he realized what was rushing towards him, he and everyone else was incinerated by volcanic gases at a temperature of five hundred degrees Celsius. Seconds later, they were entombed in mud-like debris travelling at a speed of over five hundred kilometres an hour down the width of the mountain towards the coast. They died as the heated gas tore their lungs apart. Their skin and body tissue melted at the same time. All that was left was dust. It was so hot that no skeletons were ever found.

Two seconds later the bathers at the picturesque baths and rock pools at Fajana, just below the village, met the same fate. One swimmer ducked under the water on seeing the avalanche of muck and debris swarming down the cliff face. It made no difference as the water evaporated instantly in the heat.

The debris crashed into the sea along a twenty-kilometres wide stretch of the northern coast. The resulting tsunamis rose slowly. Off the shoreline their intensity and height grew.

The explosion of materials didn't relent for nearly an hour, after which time the Pico Bejanado eruption paused, briefly.

Damian and Margarida sat silently on their veranda watching the local TV's coverage of the events further north of the island. They knew it was only a matter of time before they met their fate.

'Aperol Cherie?' said Damian.

'Of course,' smiled Margarida.

They toasted each other.

'Adiós,' he said.

leant sideways to kiss his wife goodbye as hot molten ash fell in thick lumps on their roof and in the garden. Their house was engulfed in seconds.

PD1 continued to show everything live. The world watched as La Palma disappeared.

Mark was right. But he never got the chance to tell anyone. The epicentres were linked.

Almost simultaneously to the Caldera eruption, an 8.5 Richter earthquake was recorded five kilometres off-shore. What did the damage was its linear reach. While the Caldera's seismometers had pin-pointed the shallow epicentre, it had not identified that a fifty-kilometre fault line was at risk. It displaced the seabed by three metres: more than the rupture of the Sunda Trench fault that gave rise to the devastating St Stephen's Day tsunami in December 2004.

The tsunamis generated by the Caldera blast moved offshore within minutes of the main eruption. A second tsunami triggered by the offshore earthquakes followed north in the general direction of the British Isles, increasing in speed and height over the four thousand kilometre journey.

The combined effect was a catastrophe of epic proportion, not just for La Palma but for all of the British Isles. On reaching landfall at the southern shores of England, Wales and Ireland four hours later, it wreaked havoc of biblical proportions as the surge poured into the Irish Sea at a height of over forty metres. Secondary tsunamis of somewhat reduced strength followed behind and continued to flood the coastlines for several hours.

They finished off a job of total destruction.

Cobh

The Harbour Master jumped down onto the deck of the ocean tug, the *Santa Maria*, the proud possession of the Port of Cobh Harbour Company. Despite his mature age he managed the distance and different heights between the two swiftly moving vessels with agility. He had just assisted the captain of the *Queen Mary* navigate its exit from one of the largest natural harbours in the world. The *QM2*, as she was called, had spent the day moored to the cruise berth in Cobh in southern Ireland. The *QM2* was an annual visitor keeping up the Cunard Company's connections with a town made famous as the last port of call before the *Titanic* set sail for New York in April 1912.

He returned to the safety of the Harbour Company's Control Centre located on an elevation to the west of the town. It commanded uninterrupted views across the wide expanse of the harbour. He signed off and in checking his roster noted he needed to be at the mouth of the harbour at 6 a.m. the following morning to assist with the navigation of the next luxury cruise ship to the quayside. He drove a short distance to the coastal town of Ballycotton, where he and his wife lived in a converted lighthouse. Time for a bit of gardening: his roses needed his attention.

All part of the daily routine of a Harbour Master.

The priorities of the 2,560 passengers aboard the *QM2* were somewhat different. They had just spent the day visiting the many tourist highlights within easy distance of Cobh. A fleet of busses had taken them to the Irish whiskey distillery and visitor centre in Midleton, to the adjacent university city of Cork, with its famous 'English Market', and to Blarney Castle, where managing an upside-down kiss of the Blarney Stone gave one the gift of eloquence (allegedly). There was much animated chatter about the day's outings and experiences over pre-dinner drinks, in the Grill and in the ship's many bars and lounges. There was a high degree of expectation as the guests queued for their tables at the *QM2*'s traditional black-tie dinner. One of the UK's top comedians was the star of the show in the ship's theatre. They were guaranteed a good laugh, so they thought.

Being on a ship they paid little attention to world news. TV coverage of volcanoes was less important than the coverage of the latest soccer news. In any event, La Palma was so far away it could have been on another planet.

On the bridge, the *QM2*'s captain calmly reviewed the proposed line of navigation to Reykjavik with his officers, a two-day sail in moderate to high seas. That task completed he left to host a dinner table in the Queen's Grill for a small group of Cunard's special guests. The largest ocean liner in the world picked up speed and moved ahead at a steady twenty knots with its stabilisers on. The officers were not paying attention to the events in La Palma. As they were over four thousand kilometres away, it did not matter to the safety of the ship.

Another routine day on the *QM2* was drawing to a close.

As day turned to night, four hundred kilometres to the north-north-west, the mood was very different aboard the RV *Celtic Explorer*.

Routine it wasn't.

The immediate and obvious priority was to get the PLU to the surface. This burden fell on the shoulders of McCrossan as the ROV operator, and Captain Killen and his officers who had to sail the ship in a manner and direction that best assisted the planned slow ascent. Operating without communications with the PLU made the task more stressful.

While they did their best to cope with the circumstances, the crew of the PLU faced a different challenge. They were resigned to the worst. One of the PLU's cockpit seals that was struck by a lava rock continued to weaken. Water started slowly to fill the bottom of the PLU's compartment. Wet and cold feet and a diminishing supply of oxygen wasn't a great mixture. Their day was anything but routine.

Mike Smith knew his number was up. The maths didn't work. There wasn't enough time as the ROV could not pull the PLU to the surface any faster. If they survived drowning, they would probably suffocate. What a choice. He reckoned they might meet their demise within an hour or two. Ever the professional he didn't share his fears with the two passengers that he had grown fond of. In reality, they were press ganged into service at short notice to undertake this expedition, and for what purpose. There was no time for survival training.

The conservations between them were intermittent as each person contemplated their predicament and weighed up the meaning of their lives. There were so many other things that could and should be done. If only they got to the surface.

The scientists on board the RV *Celtic Explorer* were also pre-occupied, greatly pre-occupied in fact, given the data sets they were reviewing. The volcanic eruption that damaged the PLU, while small was powerful, with the resulting earthquake registering 3.1 on the Richter scale. It was but one of several incidents registered on the flanks of the Eriador Seamount.

The Chief Scientist gathered his colleagues and Captain Killen around him on the bridge and linked Vice-Commodore Brennan in on the communications network.

'Captain, we've a developing situation that may prove to be a bit of a problem.'

Gilmore summarised the events of the past hours.

'Best I connect you to our British neighbours and the team at HUGO. I believe they too have had their fair share of unexpected observations,' said Vice-Commodore Brennan.

Soon all channels of communication were open. Unknown to the speakers, the three members of the PLU heard everything that was said but could not communicate back as their outwards communications cable had been severed.

Smith, O'Farrell and Gallery with one eye on their dwindling oxygen levels knew they were on their way to the surface. The ROV's power to pull the much heavier PLU was an obvious problem. McCrossan was doing his best. He had to be careful lest the mechanical arm snapped under pressure. They wanted to be saved. They cared little about wider implications. They faced death unless they got to the surface without any further delay.

Gilmore started.

'On the basis of the seismic readings and recent visual observations, there is a high risk that a large magma chamber is developing underneath most of the western flank of the Eriador Seamount. We're talking about a zone that may be some thirty kilometres in length.'

'We agree.' The HUGO team confirmed. A bit too quickly it was observed.

Their lead scientist continued. 'It has been seven weeks since the first signs of initial seismic activity were recorded. The trend, if it continues, suggests we may be heading for a major eruption or a series of connected eruptions. The sulphide samples that the PLU managed to take at many locations show markers of increased sub-surface activity. But what is most disturbing was the sight of metre wide gas bubbles from the event that damaged the PLU. We witnessed similar signs offshore Iceland when the Eldfell volcano was being formed.'

Gilmore was getting more and more agitated. He was hugely sceptical ever since Billy van Os disturbed his night out at the British Embassy. He now suspected, quite correctly, that the British knew much more than they were revealing.

'What about the seabed sonar devices that the British and US have scattered across the floor of the approaches to the Western Atlantic?'

There was silence.

'Gerdy, Johnny Drew here.'

Drew spoke from the safety of the LÉ *Michael D. Higgins*. Gilmore knew at once that he was going to get bad news. 'The sonar devices have picked up all the seismic activity over the past two months. Their data is no different to what we've seen in the past few days. The main difference is that the seismic activity you believe is concentrated in and around the Eriador Seamount is on a line almost five hundred kilometres long. The Eriador Seamount may be the epicentre of much wider sub-surface volcanic activity.'

'What does that mean in practical terms?' Gilmore asked the obvious question. His Jesuit education came to the fore.

'Gerdy, HUGO here again. In a benign situation, we believe initial volcanic activity across such a wide area has peaked or will soon moderate.'

'Or?' Gilmore was getting impatient.

'Or, in a worse-case scenario, we may witness an intensification leading perhaps to a cataclysmic eruption.'

Gilmore roared. I've just come off a conference call with several Prime Ministers. They have demanded we provide verifiable evidence. I need more than a prediction please. We were tasked to sail to the Eriador Seamount at the express request of the British Government. Do we have any hard evidence that what was suspected weeks ago is becoming a reality? And, if so, when? Guys, what is the worst possible scenario?'

'Gerdy, this is a potential Sunda Trench situation, but arguably worse if the magma chamber that lies within the depths of the Eriador Seamount erupts in a series of episodes.'

'Christ, will someone tell me in plain English what is happening!' Gilmore was rapidly losing his patience.

Johnny Drew spoke, clearly, calmly and without emotion.

'If the Eriador Seamount explodes, it will cause massive tsunamis. We're just four hundred kilometres due west of the west coast of Ireland. We've calculated that a seismic event of 8 or greater on the Richer Scale will generate a series of three-hundred-metre high waves that will hit Ireland on a line almost one hundred kilometres long within thirty minutes and the wider British Isles within the hour.'

Gilmore was now more than livid. The mood among the scientists darkened as his anger boiled over. Luckily for Drew, he was on the LÉ *Michael D. Higgins*.

'How long have you known this might happen – and for a change be honest?'

'Long enough,' Drew said in a nonchalant manner.

'Well fuck you,' spat Gilmore.

Gilmore knew he had to bring the meeting to a close.

'There is no point in us all waiting for an event that may or may not happen. I suggest five of us stay on watch until dawn. Vinnie will you do the night shift? Sound the ship's siren if we've to muster. In the meantime, getting the PLU to the surface must be the priority. Captain, you and I can take over at dawn.'

Captain Killen took the opportunity to get a short rest. His officers manned the bridge and were on hand to support the PLU Shack and the ROV operations centre. He retired to his cabin and sat on his bunk and looked across at the photograph of his lovely Orlaith. Her brown eyes looked back at him.

'I told you so, didn't I?' he said to her.

Her eyes told him he was right. He struggled initially but soon fell into a deep sleep.

The first people to witness what was later called the Eriador Eruption were the crew of the PLU. They were all on high alert. They were just two hundred metres from the surface. The cockpit was now over half-full with cold water. They shivered in their jumpsuits. If they continued to breath slowly with little movement, they had enough oxygen for the remaining minutes it would take to get to the surface.

Miracles happen, thought Smith to himself. A sentiment shared by his passengers.

The PLU Shack monitored the progress of the ROV as it continued to pull the PLU to the safety of the surface. On McCrossan's orders, two divers slid into the waters ready to open the PLU's hatch at the earliest possible opportunity. Captain Killen sailed the RV *Celtic Explorer* into the wind to maintain a degree of stability in the rough seas.

There was a traumatic jolt as further simultaneous seismic eruptions shattered the sea floor. The strong seismic sound waves travelled to the surface in seconds. The PLU crew had a few seconds to realise their fate as the first hints of sunlight could be discerned above them. They had no time to prepare for meeting their Maker. It was as if the beacons of bright sunlight were calling them to Him.

'Maeve!' exclaimed Gallery. He caught her eye, briefly. It held a sad expression. They acknowledged each other visually. The final glance. There was no time to speak.

They transitioned from the surrounds of deep darkness to sheer brilliant light. The erupting magma chamber propelled from the sea floor with exceptional force gave no notice. No sound. No movement. No chance of survival. No remains. Just deep red deadly molten lava.

The PLU and the ROV were dissolved by a blast of red-hot magma. The crafts' micro remnants were scattered into the waters around the RV *Celtic Explorer*. The bodies were obliterated beyond recognition. Death was instantaneous and painless.

It was confirmed later, by NASA satellites, that a 9.2 Richter scale quake coincided with the eruption that burst through three deep fissures along the western slopes of the Eriador Seamount almost simultaneously. The outer core of the Eriador Seamount collapsed into a growing series of fractures along a length of thirty kilometres. The sea water meeting exposed molten lava at great temperature caused further explosions.

The second set of people to bear witness to the Eriador Eruption got a few more seconds notice.

The crew on the bridge of the RV *Celtic Explorer* were admiring the rising dawn. A deep red skyline filled with low clouds lit up the horizon: a signal of good weather. They were tired after the night's shift. Soon their replacements would be on duty.

The first sign of something unusual was a wide mass of gas bubbles that struck the ship, which shuddered on impact.

Crowley didn't hesitate in pressing the alarm siren three times. All mariners knew the import of such a klaxon call. The crew and scientists rushed out on deck to be met by a sharp odour of sulphur dioxide, the smell of rotten eggs was overpowering.

Boggle eyed and with only a few hours' sleep, the crew and passengers of the RV *Celtic Explorer* felt the sea rising slowly at first like they were being raised onto someone's shoulders. Then up another layer and then another, all in slow motion at first. The RV *Celtic Explorer*, and the LÉ *Michael D. Higgins* astern at a 'safe' distance, were soon like corks on the crest of the wave, over two hundred metres above what had been sea level. The crest rose slowly but higher as the dynamic impacts of the earthquakes below triggered a series of massive landslides that displaced huge volumes of water before propelling them forward to the surface like heavy calibre projectiles. The RV *Celtic Explorer*, inexplicably still upright, was positioned just under the crest of the highest wave.

Clutching onto handrails, everyone just watched and waited in silence and in awe. Then several narrow arrows of red lava shot into the air through the crest of the rising wave having travelled from the depths of the volcano's many openings. The red dawn sky met its colourful match.

But the crew were still alive. Not for long. Like a surfboard, and without any forewarning, the RV *Celtic Explorer* was propelled out of control under the crest of the line of the peak wave. Bodies were soon swept off the deck like flies in the wind. The ship gathered speed reaching two hundred kilometres an hour within twenty seconds. Suddenly, the RV *Celtic Explorer* exited the wave and was expelled like a bullet into the open air.

Captain Killen decided to spend his last minutes in bed saying farewell his wife. He clutched his duvet and looked out the porthole at the blue sky in his final moments.

'Orlaith, pray for me.'

Fifty kilometres due east early breakfast was being served at a leisurely pace in the *QM2*'s famous Queen's Grill on deck seven. It was a relaxed atmosphere as the early joggers and gym enthusiasts settled into their green teas, rye bread and natural yoghurts. The breakfasters got a few seconds warning – really no warning at all – as a wall of water four times the height of the ocean liner hit the ship broadside. The impact was like a head on car crash. But nobody was wearing seat belts.

The crew on the bridge didn't get a chance to sound the ship's alarm never mind send an SOS. They were monitoring a news alert of a possible tsunami off the Canary Islands. The First Officer was viewing the beauty of the skyline with his Swarovski Optik binoculars when the skyline disappeared to be replaced by a wall of water. He didn't have time to absorb what he was seeing. It all happened so fast. He just closed his eyes in resignation as the hyper-powered wave, crashing into the bridge shattered the control centre of the world's largest ocean cruise ship.

Half an hour later, as the Port of Cobh Harbour Master watered his roses, an early morning ritual, he heard an enormous roar like several jet planes taking off at the same time. He looked over the wall at the back of his garden to the broad expanse of sea off the entrance to the Cobh Harbour only to see that the sky to the west as far as the horizon was filled with water. A huge wave the height of a multi-story building was approaching him at great speed. His last memory was a thought that the object in the middle of the surge looked like the *QM2*, upside down, spinning slowly under the crest of the leading tsunami wave. He recognised her classic red funnel.

His roses got a watering of an epic proportion. And as for the unprepared people of the island of Ireland … Later that morning the La Palma tsunamis arrived.

Tasiilaq

'There is a saying: "our future is written in ice."' The tour guide looked at his clients and got blank stares in response. 'Scientists agree with this philosophy. There is compelling evidence to hand that the Greenland Ice Sheet is a tipping element in the earth's ecosystem.' He was speaking to a group of Norwegian tourists at the reception area of the Hotel Angmagssalik in Tasiilaq. They had just arrived, fresh out of Oslo.

Tasiilaq, located in a sheltered bay, is the biggest town in the vast eastern region of Greenland known to the locals as 'Tunu', meaning 'backside' – the other side from West Greenland. The hills around the settlement are lined with two hundred prim Danish-style houses painted in all the colours of the rainbow.

As the hotel was located on a hill above the settlement, it commanded sweeping views across the bay to the Qoqqartiuaa Mountains. The town was constructed around its hills and its multi-coloured houses fanned out from the newly constructed all-weather AstroTurf soccer pitch, the town's pride and joy. The calm waters off Oskar Point at the entrance to Tasiilaq were full of small icebergs. The much larger icebergs, some the size of football pitches, calved off the nearby Helheim and Johan Petersen Glaciers down the adjacent Sermilik fjord into the open sea.

This had become an exclusive resort. Access was provided by an eight-seater Bell helicopter commuter service operated by Greenland Air. The nearby airport at Kulusuk, where the helicopters collected their passengers, had been modernised to cope with additional tourist traffic. The hotel, a comfortable three-star operation, was at capacity – as it had been for the past few tourist seasons. Everyone wanted to see the glaciers before they disappeared.

Tasiilaq, a picture postcard village, was Trip Advisor's most highly recommended destination for iceberg and glacier tours but had a troubled community.

Since reports of the threat of Greenland's melting glacier became world news, with 'Project Masters' topping the list of most Googled phrases for many months, Greenland's population of 57,000 were inundated with tourists. While direct flights from Europe and North America were a boon for the local economy, they also caused significant problems. The country's transport infrastructure could not cope with the invasion of well-heeled visitors and their expectations. Tasiilaq was a typical settlement where investment in tourism facilities couldn't keep ahead of demand.

The guide fancied himself as an expert in climate science, despite the fact he was a third-year law student in the University of Aarhus. After all, he had studied the literature. Expert or not, he didn't lack confidence. He had the patter off by heart.

'Ice is melting for a simple reason. The Arctic is warming faster than anywhere on the planet. As the ice vanishes its reflectivity changes. As you may know, snow is the most reflective substance known in nature. Clean fresh snow reflects away about ninety per cent of the sunlight that hits it. But as the ice softens its structure changes, lowering the reflectivity and absorbing more heat. As it melts away, more water and land are exposed, both of which are darker, and both of which absorb still more heat. This, in turn, melts more ice, creating a feedback loop that has been accelerating in Greenland. Just look at the astonishing vista outside. You may be glad to experience a fine sunny day, but this is not good news for the planet.'

'When is the trip starting?' Interjected one of the tourists.

She was a glamorous twenty-something dressed head-to-toe in designer clothing. The guide knew she would freeze as thin silks and cottons, and slip-on Prada shoes were totally inappropriate for the six-hour trip that lay ahead. 'I must remind them to wear proper equipment before they set off,' he said to himself.

She had little interest in science – or the climate for that matter. Like many others, she came to Tasiilaq to take the much advertised and highly rated skimobile ride to the top of the glacier. She didn't need windy explana-tions. She wanted to get going. She wanted the promised 'adventure'.

The tour guide was impressed by her multi-tasking. As she was speaking to him with direct eye contact, she was also typing a message on her iPhone.

'Patience! We'll be off soon enough. You'll enjoy the experience on the glacier better if you have a good grasp of how things have changed here since thirty years ago. Back then, winter temperatures of minus twenty degrees Celsius froze the sea ice out in front of you. One could drive a car from this hotel to the airport at Kulusak some thirty kilometres away over the ice. The city council even marked out a road. No need for helicopters then! It is important to understand the pace of change. When you stand atop the three-kilometre-wide Johan Petersen Glacier later today and look around, it is possible that there will be nothing there a couple of decades hence. Witness the environment and respect it.'

The tour guide concluded his standard briefing quite pleased with himself. Most – but not all – of his group had done their homework and didn't need convincing. A small majority really didn't care and just wanted to get value for the adventure holiday they had been promised. Fair enough.

Within the hour, the tour guide and twenty of his charges, all suitably kitted out, were at the dock of the small harbour in the centre of Tasiilaq. They were transported in two small open boats across the fjord to a camp at the base of the glacier managed by the tour company. There they were allocated their two-person Yamaha skimobiles. Following a safety briefing, the ski bikers with local guides – all Danes – set off on the twenty kilometre journey to the top of the Johan Petersen Glacier. As this was early in the season there was good snow cover along the marked track to the top.

Also at the dock, another group of older tourists and families with children were embarking on a cruise up the Sermilik fjord, into which the Johan Petersen Glacier calved icebergs at a record rate. The *Sama* was an old iron-hulled ice-certified boat with a thirty-person capacity that could navigate its way safely through brace ice. It had clearly seen better times. The captain, a native Inuit from the village, swarthy and compact, had been doing this tour every day during the tourist season for the past decade. He was experienced. He knew the waters and the ice. Unlike

the adventure tours offered to the young tourists this was a far more leisurely option. A routine voyage.

In his culture clocks and calendars were irrelevant. Time was dictated by the ice. In his Inuit dialect the word for 'winter' also means a 'year'. Hence, he took a leisurely approach to getting the boat ready. The guide from the local tourism office shepherded her paying guests onto the boat. As soon as she completed the safety briefing, he put *Sama* into gear. Soon she was moving northwards in the strong current off the dock.

It took both tour groups around three hours to reach their respective destinations.

As promised, the view on the top edge of the Johan Petersen Glacier, looking towards the Sermilik fjord, at nine hundred metres above sea level, was breath-taking. Even the most cynical in the group could not control their emotions at the sheer beauty and rawness of the scene. It was unique, so vast, so white, so pure that it bankrupted the vocabulary of description.

The cameras on their iPhones were dispatching photos and WhatsApp messages to their friends across the globe. The most striking colour was the deep sapphire blue of the waters captured in dozens of small lakes to the rear of the glacier that peppered the icescape as far as the eye could see. As with all glaciers, there was a constant deep groaning and growling as the ice moved, twisted and re-shaped. Future icebergs calved off the front face of the glacier, usually preceded by a loud gunshot sound, and toppled into the Sermilik fjord far below, where the *Sama* was moored at a safe distance.

The boat's passengers also had an astonishing view, but from a different perspective. They were situated four hundred metres opposite the glacier. The mountains of earth and rock that framed the glacier reached for the heavens where a few lazy cirrostratus clouds contrasted with the cold blue arctic sky. In the fjord, and in their midst, massive white and pale blue icebergs baring a thousand frozen teeth brooded among the smaller chunks and floes creeping in from wider waters. The late morning sun produced differing reflective colour effects on the face of the glacier.

They too were impressed with the raw beauty. Fewer WhatsApp messages were sent.

The previous week there had been two level 3.3 Richter scale earthquakes recorded twenty kilometres further east, with the epicentre under the vast expanse of the Johan Petersen Glacier. Significant jolts were caused as ice moved and collapsed within the glaciers and as millions of litres of water were displaced. Such was the sheer physical impact that these movements registered on the Richter scale themselves. These incidents had been commonplace in the few months since Project Masters' findings had highlighted the hollowing out process of the Greenland Ice Sheet and the consequent accelerated collapse of maritime glaciers.

Of course, the Norwegian group's guides and the *Sama*'s captain didn't mention this in their safety briefings. While the tourist office had been alerted to anticipate small aftershocks, nobody was expecting a 6.5 Richter scale earthquake from deep within the glacier.

The shock waves generated at the epicentre of the earthquake cascaded violently through the length and breadth of the glacier. The bikers and their guides stood motionless in awe as the landscape changed in front of their eyes. The growing vibrations rumbled noisily as they approached the top of the Glacier at speed. In a matter of seconds, a wide and widening fracture line appeared. Simultaneously, the blue sapphire waters from the lakes were tossed high in the air. The shock waves accelerated their way forward. A wave of meltwater and ice shards about a kilometre wide flew into the air.

A catastrophic collapse of the world-famous Johan Petersen Glacier was moments away.

The first hint the ski bikers had that they were in serious trouble was when a small fracture line appeared under their feet. In a split second the ground where they stood opened up to reveal a sheer ice cliff descending into the dark. The ground vibrated violently throwing everyone off their skimobiles. The rumbling noises intensified in a matter of seconds. An ice-cold wind kicked in. Cheeks prickled in the cold air that escaped from the abyss. The ski bikers didn't have time to get to their feet, never mind plan an escape. The ground they were on collapsed into a steep ice crevasse far below. They were unceremoniously thrown into the ice abyss. Had there been anyone in a position to heed their screams for help, they could not be heard over the roar of the meltwater gushing through the fissures created by the earthquake's secondary shocks.

At the inevitable inquest, it became a matter of debate whether they died first from drowning or from traumatic internal injuries as sharp ice fragments travelling at great speed cut them apart. One way or the other their departure was instantaneous. The bodies were never found so the cause of death could not be determined. The coroner concluded death was due to 'misadventure'.

The *Sama*'s passengers could not see the deadly transformation that was happening behind the top of the glacier. They were not even aware they were in the path of an earthquake. The noise was deafening and disturbing, but its source was still a matter of conjecture. The din became over-powering: like being close to the thrust engines of an Apollo spacecraft. There was nowhere to hide from the noise.

They realised instinctively they had problems to cope with as soon as the seismic vibrations started to create large rippled waves, which tossed the boat like a cork in the ocean. The captain's instinct was to raise the anchor and pull the reverse lever, which he did. He knew he had positioned his boat far too close to the sheer front face of the glacier for comfort.

Unlike the ski bikers, whose demise was almost instant, the *Sama*'s passengers witnessed the collapse of the Johan Petersen Glacier in slow motion. The initial shocks dislodged huge bus-sized ice blocks along the width of the glacier that cascaded like confetti into the waters below, creating hundred-metre-tall splashes that drenched the boat with muddy ice water. All the time the *Sama* reversed away. But it was too late.

The first visible cracks in the glacier appeared at the left edge, about half-way up near a craggy outcrop of soot coloured ice. What looked like liquid ice moved slowly down the surface of the glacier's face. This displaced looser fragments, which, in turn, spliced the lower sections in a blitz of powdered snow and ice. The noise was unbearable. A high-pitched thunderous growl signalled something more dramatic was about to happen.

From an elevation of nearly a kilometre, meltwater was projected over the *Sama*, from a widening fissure, with an impact like a giant power-hose. The growing pressure of the water expanded the size of the fissure, which in turn caused more meltwater and chunks of dark grey ice to exit the glacier's face with the speed of a jet propulsion engine. Similar cracks appeared at four other locations with the same phenomenon. The domino effect was instantaneous. No sooner did the entire front of the glacier collapse than the next ridge of ice burst apart with even more devastating effects shattering everything in its way.

The explosive effect of the systemic collapse of the Johan Petersen Glacier was the equivalent to two atomic bombs. Soon the entire area at the base and immediate surrounds of the glacier, along a line of three kilometres was showered with the avalanche debris of the glacier. A chunk of ice the size of Manhattan had cascaded into the sea.

The *Sama*'s passengers' sense of impending doom was coloured by the sight of vivid twin rainbows that formed elegant crescents over the vast expanse of what remained of the glacier's face.

This wonder of nature was their last living memory.

As more fissures appeared it was only a matter of time before the central part of the glacier cracked open from top to bottom. The impact was worse than a major dam implosion. The multiple tsunamis created by icebergs the size of football stadia being driven into the Sermilik fjord picked up the *Sama* and carried it down the water-filled fjord at elevation and at speed.

The boat capsized, righted itself and capsized again before it was thrown upside down the length of the fjord for twenty kilometres. Given the remote location of the Johan Petersen Glacier the only casualties there were the thirty souls on the *Sama*. Nobody was wearing a life jacket – not that it would have made any difference.

It took less than two hours for the entire Johan Petersen Glacier to fully disintegrate, with ice ten kilometres long and to a height of nine hundred metres displaced. This was the largest ever collapse of a maritime glacier.

The shattered shell of the boat was found days later by search and rescue parties thirty metres above sea level in a bay to the side of the fjord. The tsunamis – some reckoned the waves must have been over one hundred metres high at the start – had propelled it at over two hundred kilometres an hour until it came to its place of final rest. The thrust of the ice water removed any remaining vegetation on the shoreline. The fjord was stripped of all green shoots. What remained was polished undulating brown rock.

The torn bodies of half the passengers were found at many locations along the length of the fjord. They too died of 'misadventure'.

As part of the detailed search and rescue effort, the volunteers also found dozens of golf balls embossed with the Norwegian flag. Two still functioning camera balls were retrieved.

While the death toll resulting from this major natural disaster was relatively low, the impact of this incident and at many other comparable glaciers was irreversible.

As soon as the news broke, Lars arranged to meet with Benny for a coffee in the Lysebu Hotel in Oslo to discuss developments.

'Another tipping point has passed,' said Lars.

'Of that there's no doubt,' said Benny. 'It's only a matter of time before further glaciers collapse and disintegrate.'

'True,' said Lars. 'We will continue our work next year at the Summit Station with an added degree of urgency and motivation. Much more research needs to be done.'

'How's Sean by the way?'

'We have been in regular contact since the Atlantic tsunami hit Ireland,' said Lars. 'His production unit is at an elevation of over one hundred metres, so it was not damaged. And when the waves struck everyone was at work. Sean and his team are alive and well. But the countryside in Galway is badly flooded.'

'What makes me so sad is the inevitability of what happened,' said Benny.

'What do you mean?' asked Lars.

'It has taken one high profile incident to prove what scientists have been saying for years.'

'Governments do not respond until catastrophe face them. They don't like dealing with inconvenient truths,' said Lars.

Epilogue

THE ATLANTIC TSUNAMI HIT the west and south-west coast of Ireland without warning. Electricity generation installations and communication sites were rendered useless within minutes. With all national communications silenced, and with no forewarning, the waves washed over the countryside, eventually petering out just short of Dublin.

The tsunamis generated by the offshore earthquake at La Palma were deadlier than their Atlantic counterparts. They travelled at a speed of seven hundred kilometres per hour across the deep ocean towards the British Isles. While the original height was three hundred metres, the crest was only thirty metres when it struck the south east coast of Ireland after six hours. It hit the Dublin Bay region twenty minutes later. The landslide displacement into the Atlantic Ocean of the Caldera de Taburiente and the entire mountain range of northern La Palma resulted in even more devastating secondary tsunamis arriving an hour afterwards.

The low-lying City of Dublin was washed away in the space of two hours. Only the iconic twin chimneys of the City's power station remained fully intact. The La Palma waves, much higher, faster and stronger than the Atlantic tsunami, penetrated nearly fifty kilometres inland around the southern and eastern coasts of Ireland.

The triple-hit tsunami episode rendered huge parts of the country uninhabitable. By the time the flood waters had receded, all critical infrastructure, ports, roads, railways, airports, commercial centres, schools, the energy grid, telephone masts and hospitals, were shattered beyond repair as was all low-lying housing. Millions died.

Slowly, surely and noticeably over a number of subsequent years the collapse of the Greenland Ice Sheet, compounded by the rapid disappearance of the warming effects of the Gulf Stream, resulted in sea ice forming as far south as Dublin Bay initially. Soon the whole Irish Sea was frozen over.

The Iceapelago that was once Ireland began to form. The Arctic foxes were among the first of the new immigrants. They were comfortable in this environment. Ice was their home. Their hardship was mirrored by the humans they did everything to avoid. The humans of their nature adapted, adjusted and argued. They had no option. They survived, they built, they recovered. So did the Arctic foxes as they settled into familiar tundra conditions.

It began with ice and ended with ice.

The tale of the inhabitants of the Iceapelago has yet to be told.

Acknowledgements

MY WIFE MARGARET HAS been a great support during the time I researched and wrote this novel over the past two years. She travelled with me to La Palma where we explored all the locations mentioned in the book. In Greenland, I visited most of the key sites – apart from the Summit Station – and met many guides and locals who were so proud of their wonderful nation. The Marine Institute was generous in allowing me to visit the RV *Celtic Explorer* and Oisín McManus gave me many insights about the operations of the research vessel. Many thanks to Kevin Treacy, Jim Kinsella, Sean O'Keeffe, Adrian White and Peter O'Neill who reviewed the draft manuscript. Ferdia Mac Anna gave me great insights about turning what at the time was a rough draft into a readable book. Vanessa Fox O'Loughlin (www.writing.ie) has been a stalwart providing me with valuable advice and contacts. Andrew and Rebecca Brown of Ardel Media were a great help in getting the book over the line and in the setting up of www.iceapelago.com. I owe a particular debt of gratitude to Niamh Hatton who in a very professional manner copy-edited the book and proofed the final manuscript.

Printed in Poland
by Amazon Fulfillment
Poland Sp. z o.o., Wrocław

58560451R00195